Born in Paris in 1947, Christian Jacq first visited Egypt when he was seventeen, went on to study Egyptology and archaeology at the Sorbonne, and is now one of the world's leading Egyptologists. He is the author of the internationally bestselling RAMSES and THE MYSTERIES OF OSIRIS series, and several other novels on Ancient Egypt. Christian Jacq lives in Switzerland.

Christian JACQ
the beloved of Isis

The Mozart Series

Translated by Tamsin Black

SIMON &
SCHUSTER

London · New York · Sydney · Toronto · New Delhi

A CBS COMPANY

First published in France by XO Editions under the title
L'Aimé d'Isis, 2006
First published in Great Britain by Simon & Schuster UK Ltd, 2011
A CBS Company

This paperback edition first published, 2012

1 3 5 7 9 10 8 6 4 2

Simon & Schuster UK Ltd
1st Floor
222 Gray's Inn Road
London WC1X 8HB

www.simonandschuster.co.uk

Simon & Schuster Australia
Sydney

Simon & Schuster India
New Delhi

A CIP catalogue record for this book is available
from the British Library

Paperback ISBN: 978-1-41652-664-3

Typeset by Hewer Text UK Ltd, Edinburgh
Printed and bound in Great Britain by CPI Group (UK) Ltd,
Croydon, CR0 4YY

If Virtue and Justice strew glory on the broad path, then the earth is a heavenly kingdom and mortals are like gods.

The Magic Flute, Act I, Scene 19.

We wander through the power of sound, happily through the dark night of death.

The Magic Flute, Act II, Scene 28.

1

Impervious to the bitter chill that had gripped Vienna, Geytrand himself was on the lookout. As the right-hand man of Joseph Anton, Count of Pergen and chief of the secret police responsible for spying on the Freemasons, he might have stayed in the warm and given the ungrateful task to one of his henchmen. A big fellow, heavy-jowled, dull-eyed and generally ill-favoured, Geytrand had left the Order when it refused to make him head of his lodge. Out of spite, he now hounded his former Brothers and dreamed of destroying initiation. So he served his boss with total devotion, convinced the secret society was a threat to the current regime.

Although the lodges had been summarily restructured and their numbers reduced to two with fewer than four hundred Brethren, the Freemasons were battling on, and some were still very active, like the composer

Wolfgang Mozart. Today, Geytrand was watching him move house.

Returning to the city centre after a spell in the suburbs, Mozart was now going to live in 'Mother of God' house on the Judenplatz. The move brought him closer to his lodge, where he was an influential Master Mason and possibly an undeclared Venerable.

The partial success of *The Marriage of Figaro* and the failure of *Don Giovanni*, together with money troubles and well-managed slander campaigns, had taken their toll, and Mozart was going through a difficult time. Yet that had not stopped him spreading Masonic ideas through his music and becoming, as a result, a dangerous agitator.

Just then, his family appeared.

Mozart did not cut a particularly striking figure. Of slight build and medium height, with fine fair hair, a long nose and rather prominent eyes, he might have gone unnoticed had it not been for a piercing gaze that suggested a forceful personality.

His wife, Constance, was a pretty woman. Dark hair framed a delicate face set with a small mouth, a pointy noise and bright eyes. Her narrow waist and elegant clothes won admiring glances from the men. She was holding the hand of her little boy, Karl Thomas, born on 21 September 1784; their dog, Gaukerl, trotted along beside them. Three other children, a girl and two boys had not survived. Rumours about Mozart's dissolute habits were excellent material which Geytrand fully intended to exploit, but he knew that the composer had a high regard for keeping his word and that he was a loving, loyal husband. He and Constance were a united couple and had already gone through plenty of ordeals without drifting apart.

The Mozarts explored their new home. It was a modest dwelling compared with the sumptuous apartment they had occupied in the days when Wolfgang was composing *The Marriage of Figaro,* performing night after night and earning good money. Now, the Turkish war being waged by the sick and ageing Emperor Josef II had overshadowed Viennese cultural life. In any case, Mozart was no longer in vogue and he had had to settle for an official position at court that required him to write dance music for the grand balls at La Redoute, the imperial palace. His remuneration was no more and no less than the job was worth.

According to Joseph Anton, Mozart was attending secret meetings and working on a new ritual opera that would inspire vocations and strengthen Freemasonry, so opposed to authoritarian regimes and devoted to freedom of thought.

Many Freemasons were just manipulated followers; Mozart, however, was a creator. He had withstood assaults and woundings and appeared to be indestructible.

Geytrand scratched his head thoughtfully, and withdrew. The family scene looked so calm and ordinary. Maybe Mozart had already given up a losing battle and was resigned to becoming an ordinary musician.

The Count of Pergen's evil assistant had not realised that he was himself being watched by a curious character dressed as a coachman concealed behind the horses.

Thamos the Egyptian had long suspected that a secret service was spying on the Freemasons. By questioning a dull-witted agent, he had obtained a description of his boss. It matched exactly the podgy individual before him now, who was observing the Mozarts moving house.

He was probably not the mastermind but he might be a second-in-command with instructions to carry out orders and make sure the dirty work got done.

Thamos, the rich and respected Count of Thebes, was the disciple of an Egyptian sage, the Abbot Hermes. Before fanatical Muslims had destroyed his monastery, he had been tasked with the arduous mission of coming to the West to look for the Great Magician, who alone could revive initiation and pass it on to future generations.

Having found Mozart, Thamos had to prepare him for the discovery of the mysteries by gradually revealing to him the *Book of Thoth*. But what brotherhood would be worthy of receiving him? Thamos had travelled the length and breadth of Europe to assess the various Masonic systems, which saw him as the 'Unknown Superior'. Eventually, he had lighted on the three basic symbolic degrees of Freemasonry: Entered Apprentice, Fellow Craft and Master Mason all had their roots in Egyptian esotericism.

With the help of Ignaz von Born, he had deepened

4

and modified the rituals. When Mozart had experienced them, he had become aware of the immense responsibilities of being a Master Mason.

Success or failure did not really matter. In *The Marriage of Figaro*, the composer depicted the passage from the Entered Apprentice to Fellow Craft, the struggle between the two degrees, and the crucial role of Wisdom, one of the Three Great Pillars of the Lodge. In *Don Giovanni*, he described the Fellow Craft's betrayal, the assassination of the Master of Work, death through initiation and the ordeal of the secret fire that led, for some candidates, to the degree of Master Mason.

The road had not ended there. How would Mozart evoke the mysteries of the Middle Chamber and the alchemical furnace? How would he formulate the initiation of the future, beyond his own era and lifetime?

Thamos the Egyptian was ready to lay down his life to protect the Great Magician and help him accomplish his work, although few people, including the Freemasons, would understand its true significance.

As though life's routine trials were not enough, politics and power had got involved. Freemasonry was barely tolerated and its survival uncertain. Serious unrest was starting to unsettle Louis XVI, King of France, presaging devastating upheavals that would put freedom and initiation at risk of obliteration.

Thamos followed the man with the flabby face in the hope of discovering who he was.

Long familiarity with clandestinity had given the

Egyptian a heightened awareness of danger. His vigilance saved him, for two policemen were looking after their boss and checking that he was not being followed.

Like a casual passer-by, therefore, Thamos changed direction.

2

As a result of an imperial decree, only two Masonic lodges remained in Vienna: Truth, and Crowned Hope* to which Mozart belonged.

In 1785, a thousand Freemasons were active in several workshops, but the expansion of the Order had worried the authorities. Forgetful of his liberalism, Josef II had hearkened to the Count of Pergen's warnings and had intervened with a heavy hand, causing a number of Brothers to resign, among them the Order's spiritual master, the mineralogist and alchemist, Ignaz von Born, who was powerless to retaliate. Before he left, he had asked Mozart, his disciple, not to abandon his lodge and to propagate a genuine philosophy of initiation.

---

* Its full name was New Crowned Hope (thanks to Josef II), but the 'New' was soon omitted. Truth Lodge was dormant.

Thanks to the hospitality of their Sister, Countess Thun, whose husband was a member of their lodge, Ignaz von Born, Mozart and the clarinettist and Wolfgang's childhood friend Anton Stadler, together with Thamos and a few Master Masons, continued to hold secret meetings where they pursued their research into the rites and symbols of the Egyptian tradition.

Not content with the watered-down version of initiation Freemasonry permitted to women, the countess was working with Mozart, Thamos and von Born to develop a ritual appropriate to the genius of women. Since adolescence, the composer had been obsessed by the subject of the play *Thamos, King of Egypt* by his Brother Tobias von Gebler about priests and priestesses to the sun. Thamos was the name of his initiator, the messenger from the Orient, who had been watching over him since his birth.

Depressed and exhausted, von Gebler had resigned from his position as Venerable and had left the Freemasons before he died.

'Your new home is being watched,' Thamos warned Wolfgang. 'The anti-Masonic secret service is on your trail. You must be on your guard at all times.'

'What about von Born?'

'Since he abandoned his Masonic duties, he has been left in peace.'

Vienna, 27 January 1789

Wolfgang had no opera in view and no more concerts. His Masonic Brother, the publisher Artaria, was selling six contredanses* and he had his annual salary of eight hundred florins. Vienna was no longer interested in him as either a pianist or a composer. Sometimes he thought back with nostalgia to glorious evenings when he had been applauded by a packed audience. What pathetic vanity! His destiny was taking him along other paths. During this melancholy winter of war against the Turks when no one knew what would happen, he composed next to nothing†, working instead for his official lodge and his secret lodge. He was also reading extensively: Moses Mendelssohn's *Phaedon or the Immortality of the Soul*; novels about initiation by the Latin authors Heliodorus and Apuleius; books on alchemy and numerology; Rosicrucian texts, and Egyptian esoteric teachings. His readings provided him with armour and informed his future compositions.

His little boy, Karl Thomas, came into his office.

'Do you know what day it is, Papa?'

'I can't remember.'

'The 27th of January: it's your birthday!'

---

* K462/2 and 534–535a, arranged for piano. K is the abbreviation for Köchel (1800–1877), who produced the first catalogue of Mozart's works.

† In January, he composed just one aria, K569, a work that has been lost.

Dimpling with smiles, the little boy jumped on to his father's knee.

'How old are you?'

'Thirty-three.'

'That's old!'

'Not as old as all that.'

'Anyway, you're going to live forever!'

Constance had not forgotten the date and had prepared a special meal for the occasion. On the menu that night were smoked trout from the Alps, a capon, a cake, and an excellent Champagne.

Wolfgang adored his wife. She never complained, she kept an admirable house and she faced all their hardships with indomitable courage. In addition, she knew her husband's operas by heart, and she supported his creative endeavours and helped him to work in whatever way suited him best. About his Masonic allegiance, there was never a word of criticism or reproach. Her influence provided him with the stable background he could not do without and sheltered him from the passion and excitement that militated against true creation by placing an individual at the mercy of his instincts.

Vienna, 10 February 1789

New tax legislation that reformed the old feudal system and made it fairer had just been introduced, to prove the generosity and intelligence of the regime. Meanwhile,

Wolfgang was composing a Piano Sonata in three movements* depicting a harmonious Masonic meeting.

Majestic and serene, the first Allegro reflected the opening of the temple where the Brothers held a joyful meeting to experience another ritual. The Adagio celebrated their recognition of one another through the signs and numbers they had learned. Finally, a short Allegretto extolled the delights of the banquet and celebrated spiritual and earthly nourishment.

Although operating on a restricted basis, Crowned Hope Lodge continued to hold its ceremonies. Its members took care never to criticize the regime and to emphasize the necessity of Virtue, which, for Freemasons, went far beyond ordinary morality in its demand for righteousness in every aspect of an initiate's life. As an ideal, it was barely attainable, of course, but without it, Freemasonry would have been nothing but masquerade.

Vienna, 28 February 1789

On the initiative of Abbé Lorenzo Da Ponte, the official librettist of *The Marriage of Figaro* and *Don Giovanni* – the Masonic significance of which escaped him completely – musical medleys that included some of Mozart's arias were being performed in Vienna.

In the small ballroom of La Redoute, the imperial

---

* K570, in B flat major.

palace, hundreds of party-goers in fancy dress ate and drank and listened distractedly to Mozart's latest German Dances* as they twirled about to the music.

Wolfgang worked hard on the orchestration of these pieces and did not take lightly work that had become his livelihood. With no concerts planned and no subject for his next grand opera, he needed to prove that he knew his business.

Friends like Anton Stadler, who was saddled with many mouths to feed and who was always in debt, were sorry to see Mozart reduced to this, but the current trend for mediocrity, which played into the hands of insipid composers like Salieri, was creating a difficult artistic climate.

Constance tenderly leaned her head against her husband's shoulder.

'I have excellent news, my darling.'

'You . . . are you sure?'

'Sure as sure. Karl Thomas is going to have a little brother or sister.'

Perhaps, after taking away three of their children in infancy, Heaven would smile on them this time.

* K571.

3

Vienna, 6 March 1789

Mozart was warmly welcomed by his Brother, Count Johann Nepomuk Esterházy, and he joyfully conducted Handel's *Mass**, which he had rescored at the request of Baron Gottfried van Swieten. Not content with a superficial reworking, he had treated the monumental and powerful work as though it had been his own, adding wind instruments and recitatives and abridging arias. The job was badly paid, but he overlooked this slight to produce a piece that had all the resonance of music by Johann Sebastian Bach.

Dutch-born Baron van Swieten was the son of the private doctor to the deceased Empress Maria-Theresa and he had enjoyed a brilliant diplomatic career before being appointed Prefect of the Imperial and Royal

* K572.

Library, President of the Commission for the Study of Education and Culture, and head of censorship charged with overseeing publications.

No one could prove that he had been initiated as a Freemason during a visit to Berlin between 1770 and 1777, and not even the emperor realised that he was acting as the Freemasons' protector by making sure they did not step out of line. Whenever he found himself in the company of influential luminaries eager for malicious gossip, the Baron took care to declare himself hostile to Masonic ideas and deeply suspicious of a society that was still too secret.

Mozart was eternally grateful to him for introducing him to the genius of Johann Sebastian Bach, whose music had been all but forgotten. He had worked hard to assimilate the Master's message and his own music had been influenced by it.

'Reports from France are extremely worrying,' the Baron confided to Mozart. 'The people's animosity towards Louis XVI and his wife, Marie-Antoinette, continues to grow, and the government is having enormous difficulty dowsing the fire. Which is why Josef II is thinking of reforming his policy and hardening his attitude towards subversive ideas and protest movements.'

'Does Freemasonry fall into that category?'

'I am afraid so, respectful though it is of the regime. Please be extremely careful, Mozart.'

Vienna, 10 March 1789

Joseph Anton, Count of Pergen, President of the Government of Lower Austria and an impeccable administrator, had devoted several years to a task he deemed essential: that of directing the secret service charged with the surveillance of the Freemasons.

Time and again, he had feared that the emperor would terminate his mission and dismantle the organisation he had so patiently established. But Josef II, acknowledging Anton's efforts and fearful of the expansion of uncontrollable and non-conformist Freemasonry, gave the Count of Pergen free rein, provided he did not cause a scandal. Consequently, since the mineralogist, Ignaz von Born, the Order's erstwhile spiritual leader, had stepped down, it was impossible to spy on him. The former Freemason now limited his activities to academic research and the emperor refused to persecute him.

However, Anton believed that von Born was still a danger and the initiator of secret meetings attended by his favourite disciple, Wolfgang Mozart. With von Born on the outside and Mozart on the inside, the two Brothers toiled in perfect harmony. On the sly, the mineralogist was building up a formidable network for the composer to use in the future.

Thanks to well-paid renegades, Joseph Anton had an insider's knowledge of the Masonic rites and he could see just what the musician was up to. Mozart was now the secret head of Viennese Freemasonry.

He was a leader who might need obliterating if his influence grew too dangerous. So, the Count of Pergen had abused his administrative position and initiated financial legal proceedings against Mozart to give him serious worries and quite possibly ruin him. Moreover, the musician would be bound to suspect that the unknown plaintiff was one of his Brothers!

Brandishing a massive report, Geytrand was looking smug.

'We are at last making progress on the difficult territory of Prague,' he rasped. 'Two Brothers have managed to unblock our investigations: Count Canal, who is tremendously well connected, and Father Unger, who has the support of the Church. They are now under surveillance and I am preparing a case against them to prove to the emperor what trouble-makers they are. But Prague is a complex city where it is difficult to move and our agents keep coming up against obstacles. If we rush things, we are doomed to failure. So I have come to ask you for more time.'

'Agreed, my friend.'

'Brother Leopold-Aloys Hoffmann is informing on the goings-on in Mozart's lodge. On the face of it, there is nothing untoward: steadfast support for the emperor, respect for moral values and charitable practices. A harmless purring.'

'Hoffmann is a gullible fool!' growled Joseph Anton. 'Hard to believe he was a member of the Illuminati before he denounced them . . . It makes you wonder if he ever received so much as a flicker of light! Try to wise him up a bit and show him how to look and listen better.'

Vienna, 25 March 1789

Just as his Brother Artaria was preparing the German Dances and Minuets for publication, Wolfgang was struck another administrative and financial blow. It was lucky that Constance put his salary to such good use, and the little family never went without. Nevertheless, Wolfgang was forced to look for another loan.

He thought of Franz Hofdemel who had recently applied to enter Crowned Hope Lodge. The thirty-four-year-old lawyer and chancery clerk at the court of Vienna was keen on music and had a fine piano and three excellent violins. He prided himself on his elegant life-style and hosted concerts in his magnificent apartment on Grünangergasse, and his young wife of twenty-three, Maria Magdalena, a gifted pianist, had just become Mozart's pupil.

In a letter, Wolfgang assured Franz Hofdemel that he would soon be able to call him 'by a finer name' (the name of 'Brother') and asked him for a hundred florins.

The future Freemason agreed, and on 2 April, Mozart wrote a draft in his favour: 'I agree to pay within four months this sum to Herr von Hofdemel or in his favour; I have received the exchange value in money; I agree to reimburse him by the due date and am subject to the

Imperial and Royal Commercial and Exchange Court of Lower Austria.'

The following day, the document was sent to Joseph Anton, who seized on the new debt with glee. A hundred florins was already a sizeable sum, but he decided to put it about that the loan was for a thousand, and emphasize the irresponsible behaviour of the Freemason Mozart, who could not manage his budget.

4

Vienna, 3 April 1789

At the end of a well-lubricated evening at the Mozarts', Wolfgang sat down at the piano and composed an impromptu comic Quartet* for Constance, Gottfried von Jacquin, Anton Stadler and himself to sing. The words were hilarious and would hardly have been suitable for the general public: 'My dear, push and scoff, lean and swallow, squeeze and gulp!' Helping themselves liberally to snuff, the riotous company roared with laughter as they sang this saucy song.

Constance, who was delighted to be pregnant again, was as merry as any of them.

When the guests had gone, Wolfgang kissed her tenderly.

'I have to go to Prague,' he told her, 'and I'm going to

---

* K571a.

stop off in several German towns to try to win commissions. We need more than my eight hundred florins' annual salary.'

'The Freemasons of Prague have asked to see you, haven't they?'

'That's right, and I must keep my word. But I'm hoping to sign a major contract in Berlin to secure our future.'

'You look anxious.'

'High society is more interested in war than in music, especially mine. If Vienna has got the sulks, I must seek my fortune elsewhere. This time, unfortunately, I can't take you with me. So I have written you a poem.'

Wolfgang shyly handed Constance the text:

Before the planned journey, because I'm leaving for Berlin, I'm certainly hoping for honour and glory, but if I turn a deaf ear to praise, you, my wife, stay dumb before flattery! When we see each other again, we will hug and cover each other in kisses and taste sublime bliss. Till then, tears of sorrow will flow and break our hearts.

Vienna, 8 April 1789

On the advice of Thamos and Ignaz von Born, Mozart was about to set out for Prague to contribute to the progress of research into initiation and strengthen connections with the Viennese lodges. In these troubled times, the mission was crucial, and the renown of a composer, who was little short of worshipped by many Freemasons in the city that had taken *The Marriage of Figaro* and *Don Giovanni* to its heart, made his task easier.

As a novice going through the degrees of Entered Apprentice and Fellow Craft, he had listened to the Master Masons and done their bidding. Now, it was up to him to shoulder the heavy responsibilities associated with his degree.

Travelling without Constance and Gaukerl, who looked crestfallen at being left out of the expedition, was a trial for him. Wolfgang felt lost and abandoned to all manner of duties.

'Do you like my carriage?'

The arrogant, pleasure-loving face of Prince Karl von Lichnowksy appeared.

'The height of luxury!'

'Then, let's get going!'

Countess Thun, a Masonic Sister who hosted secret meetings at her house, had suggested Wolfgang travel with his Brother Lichnowsky. The prince was also the composer's pupil, and although he showed little aptitude for music, he had useful contacts.

Constance and Karl Thomas, now aged four and a half, went to stay with Brother Michael Puchberg, the family's financial protector.

'The atmosphere in Vienna is dreadful!' Lichnowsky declared. 'There's this interminable war, cultural life is degenerate, that rat Salieri is ubiquitous and everyone is suspicious of our beloved Freemasonry! You are right to be going away, Wolfgang. Berlin holds delightful surprises in store for you.'

'Business prospects are important, of course, but they were really only an excuse.'

'Has the lodge sent you on a mission?'

'I must re-forge the links in our chain.'

Lichnowsky raised an eyebrow.

'I hear rumours that, as Ignaz von Born's favourite disciple, you are the closet Venerable of the Viennese Freemasons. Is that true?'

'Titles and honours are unimportant, my Brother. Effective action is all that matters. These are perilous times for our Order and we must boost the structure's coherence.'

'So you're the ambassador of initiation! You are taking big risks.'

'Do we ever take enough to realize our ideals?'

Following them at a judicious distance was Thamos's carriage. The Egyptian would escort the musician throughout the journey.

Budwitz, 8 April 1789

When they stopped on the first evening, Wolfgang felt terribly depressed and wrote to Constance to tell her how much he missed her. *Darling little wife*, he wrote, while Lichnowsky chatted about horses,

*are you thinking about me as much as I am about
you? I keep looking at your portrait and crying
half for joy, half for sorrow. Don't worry about me,
because there is nothing wrong, except that you
aren't here. I shall write something more readable
from Prague where I'll have more time.*

Time was exactly what Geytrand's henchman
appeared to have. Posing as a postman, he had questioned the prince's coachman and discovered where
Mozart was going. He would write a report to send to
his boss and get a local officer to take over from him.
The Masonic musician would be under surveillance at
all times.

The fake postman had already tailed everyone the
authorities had marked out as needing to have their
every move recorded.

Now he was starving and went to find lunch.

'May I join you?' a coachman in fine livery asked him.

'If you want.'

'I've just received a bonus, so the wine's on me!'

'I won't say no. Where are you going?'

'Prague. I'm driving a musician.'

'Not Mozart, by any chance?'

The coachman thought for a moment.

'A name like that. Funny chap, though.'

'What makes you say that?'

'Because he hid a trunk in the barn next door to the
inn. Odd, isn't it? Still, it's nothing to do with me.'

23

Before the meal was over, the pretend postman excused himself for a call of nature and left the table.

Hardly had he entered the barn in question, when the powerful fist of Thamos, the perfect coachman, descended on his head.

The link with the policeman's employees was now broken and Mozart could go on his way in peace.

5

Prague, 10 April 1789

When he arrived at half-past one that afternoon, Mozart put up at the Unicorn Hotel in the city centre. After going to see a barber, where he was groomed and shaved, Mozart dressed and took a carriage to visit his Brother, the Count Canal.

Thamos was already there.

'The house is being watched,' he told Wolfgang. You should go to your friends the Duscheks and come back at the end of the evening. I shall have found out more by then.'

The Duscheks were out. Josepha was on tour in Dresden and her husband was dining with the Leliborns.

The two friends were glad to see each other again and break bread together. Afterwards the composer went back to Count Canal's.

The moment the carriage drew up, Thamos jumped in and ordered the coachman to drive off.

'The main dignitaries at Truth and Union Lodge are under surveillance,' the Egyptian announced. 'We are not staying long enough in Prague for me to organize a high-security meeting. Things will be different on our next visit.'

Back at the hotel, Lichnowsky was kicking his heels.

'Where have you been all this time, Mozart?'

'I went to see some friends.'

'Brothers?'

'No, the Duscheks, musicians who gave me a splendid welcome last time I stayed in Prague.'

'People have been asking for you. I warn you, I have no intention of hanging around here. I have urgent business to attend to elsewhere. We are leaving tomorrow.'

Mozart met Domenico Guardasoni, the vivacious impresario at the Prague National Theatre. Although nearly sixty, he still had grand projects afoot.

'I should like you to read a libretto by the poet Metastasio, *La Clemenza di Tito*. The grandeur of an emperor who pardons his enemies: don't you think that's a fine subject?'

It was hardly what Mozart had in mind for his third ritual opera.

'I can give you two hundred and fifty ducats for the piece and fifty for travel expenses. As I have to travel to Vienna myself, I don't have time to draw up a proper contract, but you may consider this a formal commission.'

'Very well. I shall work on it.'

The promise of decent wages made the offer worthy of his attention. Although he had not been able to see his Prague Brothers, Mozart felt the journey was not going too badly.

Dresden, 12 April 1789

Because of the state of the roads, it took Lichnowsky and Mozart till six in the evening on Sunday to get to Dresden. Leaving the prince at the Poland Hotel, the musician went to the house of his friend Neumann, the Dresden Kapellmeister and a Mason at Golden Apple Lodge, on the pretext of passing on a letter to Neumann's guest, Josepha Duschek.

The singer was delighted to see Mozart. He gave her the letter from her husband then withdrew with his Brother and Thamos.

'Is your lodge being watched by the police?' asked the Egyptian.

'Of course,' answered Neumann. 'We have to declare our names and specify the nature of our works if we want to enjoy some sort of peace. The regime is afraid of the underground influence of the Illuminati, despite their official disappearance from the scene. One or two Brothers still believe Strict Observance has a future, but their number is dwindling every day.'

'Can we organize a secret meeting and let you know the results of our research?' suggested Thamos.

'Alas, no! Dresden is a small inward-looking community. That kind of initiative would be denounced and we would have serious trouble. I shall do what I can to obtain an audience at court, although I can't make promises. Music is not high on the agenda here, and strangers are unwelcome. On the other hand, there are several salons, including the Ambassador of Russia's, that would be delighted to listen to Mozart.'

Dresden, 13 April 1789

At seven o'clock, Mozart wrote a letter to Constance and poured out his ardent love and desire for her, then he walked to the court chapel. There, he met the 'director of pleasures', who, much to his surprise, told him that he was requested to give a concert next day at half-past five.

The musician toasted the good news by dining at the Poland Hotel with his Brother Lichnowsky, Josepha Duschek and Neumann. When he got back to the chapel, Mozart played the organ and accompanied a trio he had written for Puchberg. Josepha sang arias from *The Marriage of Figaro* and *Don Giovanni*.

After this moment of relaxation, Thamos took Mozart to a street of elegant town houses. They passed under a porch discreetly engraved with the Masonic square and compass and gave the ritual knock at the door of a first-floor apartment.

There were only five Freemasons. The youngest was twenty-eight, the oldest fifty.

'Welcome, my Brothers. What news from Vienna?'

Mozart narrated the vicissitudes that had led to Ignaz von Born's resignation and described the sorry state of Freemasonry.

'That is no reason to despair,' he added. 'The Brothers who weathered the storm are more determined than ever. We make a show of submission to the emperor but we are celebrating our rites and continuing our research on the tradition of initiation in Ancient Egypt.'

'Aren't you afraid the Church will interfere?'

'The Archbishop of Vienna hates Freemasonry and has posted spies in the lodges. We don't confront Christianity head-on, not like the Illuminati who paid dearly for it. We are only interested in the Great Mysteries, not in criticizing religion and the current government.'

'What is it you want from us, my Brother?'

'We should like you to set up a research lodge based on materials and rituals that we will pass on to you.'

The dean bowed his head.

'The task would be too onerous. As you can see, there are only a handful of Brothers here who are interested in getting back to the roots of initiation, and Dresden is not the best place. But there may be one last chance . . .'

'What is that?'

'You should go and see our Brother, Christian Gottlieb Körner, counsellor to the court of appeal. If he decides to try his luck, we will follow suit.'

6

Dresden, 15 April 1789

At his concert at court on the previous evening, Wolfgang had played his Concerto in D major. The audience had not been very appreciative, but he had nevertheless been given a purse containing four hundred and fifty florins. The interview with Körner was fixed for the 17th, and in the meantime, the musician went to see the Russian ambassador, Beloselsky. There, he played several pieces to the great delight of the assembled company.

'Do you know Hässler, Dresden's leading light?' the ambassador asked him. 'He is a pupil of a pupil of Johann Sebastian Bach, a composer whose genius is underestimated today.'

'The name is vaguely familiar to me.'

'I know him very well,' Lichnowsky put in.

'He wants to challenge Mozart to an organ competition,'

the diplomat added. 'According to him, no one from Vienna knows how to play it properly.'

'He should watch out!' the prince declared. 'He could be making a bad mistake. Still, if he insists . . .'

At four o'clock, Mozart sat down at the organ and made the instrument sing.

When he stood up, Hässler was ashen.

'Your turn,' said Lichnowsky, tapping him on the shoulder.

'I don't think . . .'

'Ah no, my good man, you can't get out of it like that! The challenge was yours!'

Having merely learnt Bach's harmonies and key changes by heart, Hässler could not develop a fugue with the brilliance Mozart had just displayed.

'Give him a second chance,' Prince von Lichnowsky called out, sportingly. 'Let's go back to the ambassador's house and give the two champions a tie-break on the fortepiano.'

There was no competition. Mozart gave a dazzling performance and Hässler threw in the towel and slipped away.

'I am thinking of organizing a grand tour of Poland and Russia for you,' the ambassador told Wolfgang. 'They would give you a hero's welcome and you would earn a lot of money.'

'Impossible at the moment, but in the future, why not?'

'As soon as you're ready to go ahead with the project, get in touch with me.'

Lichnowsky and Mozart spent the evening at the opera, a miserable affair, where the composer greeted a few second-rate singers, among them, his Sandrina from *La Finta Giardiniera* of 1775.

Tired and anxious, Wolfgang was preparing to pass a difficult night, when he received a wonderful gift: a letter from Constance! He shut himself in his room and kissed it a hundred times before he had even opened it. He read it hungrily.

At half-past eight, he wrote back:

Darling little wife, I have all sorts of things to ask of you.

1. Please don't be sad.

2. Look after your health and don't trust the spring air.

3. Don't go out on foot alone and, better still, don't go out on foot at all.

4. Have total confidence in my love. I have never written to you without putting your dear portrait in front of me.

5. Take care in your conduct not only of your honour and of mine, but also of appearances. Don't be annoyed that I ask this. Indeed, you should love me all the more because of the importance I attach to honour.

6. And finally, please give me more details in your letters.

Every night, before I go to sleep, I talk to your

portrait for at least half an hour, and I do the same on waking.

In future, always write to Berlin, poste restante.

I hug and kiss you 1,095,060,437,082 times. You can practise saying that out loud!

Dresden, 17 April 1789

In 1786, Schiller had written an *Ode to Joy* for the Freemason, Christian Gottlieb Körner, and the poem had been used in several German lodges.

'Officially,' the counsellor to the court of appeal said to Mozart, 'you have come to sit for my sister-in-law, Doris Stock, who draws with lead pencil.* When she has finished your portrait, you can improvise at the piano. Then we will talk.'

There was nothing Mozart liked more than to give free rein to his imagination, put his fingers on the keys and draw from them a melody that he would develop in infinite variations. Eventually, however, he had to stop.

'My Brothers told me of your proposition,' Körner told him. 'I do not think it would be possible to establish a secret lodge in Dresden, firstly because it would

---

* This was the last portrait produced of Mozart. 'He has bulging eyes', observed Hocquard (*La pensée de Mozart*, p. 24), 'but they shine with a lively inner flame.' And, concerning the authentic portraits, he noted: 'everywhere, the same absent but haunting gaze.'

soon be found out by spies and informants, and secondly because there are not enough Freemasons here to undertake genuine research into initiation. You will have to forget about Dresden, Brother Mozart.'

Vienna, 18 April 1789

Joseph Anton brought his fist down on the desk.

'Disappeared?' he thundered. 'What do you mean, Geytrand?'

'That is a strong word, my lord. We have temporarily lost sight of Mozart, it is true, but we will soon catch up with him again.'

'I strongly advise it for the sake of your future career! Tell me what happened.'

'One of our agents, who was posing as a postman, thought Mozart was hiding a trunk in a barn. He had barely got through the door when he was struck a blow from behind and lost consciousness.'

'Who was his aggressor?'

'Our agent didn't see. When he came to, Mozart's carriage had been gone several hours.'

'Did anyone set eyes on him in Prague?'

'Unfortunately not.'

'If he is hiding there, we will have a devil of a job to lay hands on him.'

'He is bound to turn up somewhere or other, my lord. Apart from his Masonic mission, Mozart has to earn money and that means giving concerts and signing contracts. I am sure my informants will come across him in some princely court or other before long.'

'Is Prague well patrolled?'

'Not yet, but our structure enables us to keep tabs on the most active Masonic personalities, like Count Canal and Father Unger.'

'Have you bribed a Brother at Truth and Union Lodge?'

'Only a Servant Brother, but he is not allowed in to third degree meetings and is not party to Masonic decisions. He has not yet come up with any information of interest. The hermetic nature of this lodge seems very significant to me. The Brothers are very much on their guard, and they are obviously involved in secret works of a subversive nature.'

'At least,' judged Joseph Anton, 'we are aware of the danger. Maybe one day the Emperor will give me the means to eradicate it.'

'This deplorable incident is the proof that Mozart is being protected,' added Geytrand. 'Given the importance of this journey, a guardian angel must be watching over him. He must have identified my agent and got rid of him.'

'Unless I am wrong, Ignaz von Born already enjoyed that kind of privilege.'

'Indeed, my lord.'

'We must find out who this protector is, Geytrand, and stop him queering our pitch!'

'He is as discreet as he is skilled. We have no leads whatsoever.'

'Everyone makes mistakes. For the time being, find Mozart for me!'

7

Mozart ought to have hastened on his way to his ostensible destination, the court of Potsdam, where he hoped to attract the attention of Frederick Wilhelm II. But he could not resist stopping in Leipzig, the homeland of that first among musical genii, Johann Sebastian Bach.

Prince Karl von Lichnowsky could have done without the interruption to their journey, but Mozart's determination won him over. On the evening they arrived, he played at the house of Platner, the university rector, and he spent the following day poring over Bach's scores. Thamos was quick to point out the subtle numerological references to Cabbalistic, and therefore Egyptian, thought. Although he had been a Lutheran and a believer, Bach had been initiated into parallel sciences and he had used them in his

37

compositions. Wolfgang was fascinated and benefited from this instruction.

On the 22nd, Mozart improvised at the organ of St Thomas's, while the Cantor Doles, who had been Bach's pupil, and Görner, the instrument's owner, worked the stops. Wolfgang laid his fingers on the keys with a feeling of awe at the thought that his musical idol had played them before him, and he let his soul speak. He felt as though he was communing with his spiritual father.

Then a kind of miracle occurred.

When Wolfgang finished improvising, Cantor Doles, who was deeply moved, murmured: 'Johann Sebastian Bach has arisen.' And they sang a motet for two choirs by the Master of Leipzig whose every note was a joy to Mozart.

'There will never be an end to what we can learn from him,' he told his hosts.

Potsdam, 26 April 1789

Mozart asked to be announced to King Frederick Wilhelm II, who had succeeded his illustrious uncle, the Freemason Frederick II, on 17 August 1786. Frederick Wilhelm was interested in secret societies and had been very close to the leaders of the former Golden Rose-Cross before the Order was dissolved.

So Mozart would not be addressing a profane monarch, and he was hopeful that Thamos would make serious contacts in Potsdam and Berlin with lodges eager for initiation.

He was greeted by the cellist, the Frenchman Jean-Pierre Duport, His Majesty's teacher and the director of royal chamber music. Duport was a wizened little man with a crumpled face and all the children he taught were afraid of him.

'You want to see the king, I am told?'

'Indeed, Monsieur,' Wolfgang answered in French.

'Ah, you speak my language?'

'A little. I lived in Paris when I was a boy.'

Duport softened.

'What exactly do you want?'

'I wish to offer my services to His Majesty?'

'The king is very busy and . . .'

'Might I perhaps present him with a brief improvisation based on one of your minuets?'

The Frenchman hesitated.

'That is a splendid idea. How about the 29th, after dinner?'

Potsdam, 29 April 1789

As arranged, the king listened while Mozart played him six variations on a minuet by Duport*.

* K 573. Mozart turned his improvisations into a structured work while staying in Berlin, and the Artaria edition of 1792 included 29 variations.

Frederick Wilhelm's pleasure was obvious, and he congratulated the excellent pianist on his elegant playing and stylistic refinement.

'It would be a great honour to compose for your court, Your Majesty.'

'I shall think about it, Mozart, and we will talk it over in due course.'

Duport was no longer hostile and this first contact seemed promising.

'You are no longer being followed,' Thamos told Wolfgang. 'Your spies had lost track of you, but after this public appearance, the Viennese police will be back on your trail. We must meet as many Brothers as we can, before they do.'

Potsdam, 2 May 1789

Prince Karl von Lichnowsky was sulking. Why was Mozart not including him more in his activities?

'Had a good evening, last night?' he asked, sourly.

'It is not easy to make an impression here,' the musician answered.

'Aren't we Brothers?'

'Yes, of course!'

'Then why are you hiding so much from me?'

'Brotherhood is not about gossip and ordinary friendly relations. It involves the duties of initiation and I am doing what I can to fulfil them.'

So, Mozart would not talk! Although convinced he was attending local lodges, Lichnowsky would not find out any more.

'I am hurt by your want of trust in me,' he grumbled.

'It's not that, my Brother. I don't doubt you at all. I'm simply accomplishing my mission. If I behaved otherwise, what credit would you give me?'

'I'm bored with Potsdam!' the prince pouted. 'I need to go to Berlin then on to Leipzig for business. Come and find me there.'

'I didn't intend to go back there.'

'I shall organize a grand concert and you will be the star. It will bring you money and prestige. I'll wait for you in Leipzig.'

Potsdam, 3 May 1789

'We are on dangerous ground,' Thamos told Mozart. 'As far as I can see, Potsdam is swarming with the emperor's spies. Meeting Brothers who enjoy a certain amount of liberty means travelling to Berlin.'

'I'm expecting the king's decision later this afternoon. And Lichnowsky wants to arrange a concert in Leipzig.'

'I don't like the prince's attitude.'

'He is not an easy character, but he is a friend of our Sister Thun and about to marry one of her daughters.'

'You should be careful of Lichnowsky. His aristocratic

title and Masonic allegiance are no guarantee of his honesty.'

Still shaken by this unexpected warning, Mozart went to the royal palace where he was granted an audience with Frederick Wilhelm II.

'I appreciate your talents as a composer and performer. Your reputation as a man of honour is in your favour. I am therefore commissioning six sonatas and six quartets for an advance of seven hundred florins. And if you stay in Berlin, you may work for the court.'

'I am most honoured, Your Majesty, and I promise to think it over.'

Duport was waiting for Mozart after his audience.

'You could be earning 3700 florins,' he whispered.

A small fortune in prospect! But all the money in the world would not separate him from his Vienna lodge.

8

As soon as he arrived, Mozart went to find Prince von Lichnowsky. The prince beamed his satisfaction.

'There you are, at last!'

'I always keep my word, but I have to leave immediately for Berlin.'

'Nonsense! A grand concert awaits you on the 12th.'

I'm so sorry, I won't be able to take part.'

'Don't turn your back on Leipzig. You seem to have a good reputation here, but you will ruin it if you are discourteous. Do be reasonable.'

'I didn't know you cared so much for the city.'

'I'm just thinking of your fame, my Brother.'

Leipzig, 12 May 1789

Why did Lichnowsky want to detain Mozart in Leipzig? Thamos wondered. He was obviously doing what he could to delay his departure for Berlin, as though keen to prevent the composer from making contact with lodges in that city. Hedonistic and prone to anger and jealousy about his Brother's Masonic standing, the prince displeased him more and more.

Irritated by this setback, Wolfgang nevertheless treated Leipzig to a huge concert. In rehearsal, he protested at the orchestra's carelessness and stamped his foot so violently that a buckle flew off his shoe, but at least it shook the lazy musicians out of their inertia.

On 12 May, they played two Symphonies* and two Concerti† at the Leipzig Gewandhaus and accompanied Josepha Duschek in two arias; Mozart concluded the concert with improvisations at the piano.

It was a pity that the hall was half empty and the reception decidedly cool.

Leipzig, 14 May 1789

'What was all that about a resounding success?' Wolfgang demanded of Prince Karl von Lichnowsky.

---

* K 504 and 550.
† K 456 and 503.

'Are you cross?'

'You have made me waste my time to no avail. Aside from the pleasure of making music, the evening was a flop.'

'Let's forget about it and go home to Vienna.'

'You go back to Vienna. I have to go on to Berlin.'

'You will just have more disappointments there, believe me.'

'We'll see about that.'

'I am the one with the carriage,' the prince reminded him. 'Of course, I am staying with it, so from here on, you will have to pay your own way.'

'I shall manage.'

'Don't be so stubborn and come back with me.'

'Sorry, our roads diverge here.'

'In that case, give me a hundred florins.'

'Have you run out of money?'

'It is a kind of legitimate pay-off for the favours I've done you. And I'm sure you won't refuse to help a Brother in difficulty. My business has not exactly been booming and this journey has ruined me. I need those florins urgently.'

Disconcerted, Mozart did as the Prince asked. At least he was about to be rid of him.

Leipzig, 16 May 1789

Thamos had managed to gather together a few Master Masons for a welcome meeting in Mozart's honour at the house of the organist Karl Emmanuel Engel. In his lodge, Engel directed the choir in Schiller's *Ode to Joy* and was delighted to meet the composer of so many pieces that captured the spirit of Freemasonry.

When the works were over, the organist asked Mozart to write a few words in his album. Mozart wrote a funny little thirty-eight bar Fugue* that was both a tribute to Bach and an exploration of new harmonies. Its originality took Engel's breath away.

'What a relief to be shot of Lichnowsky,' Wolfgang announced to Thamos, who had hired another carriage, after checking that no policeman was trailing them.

'Did he try to find out what you are doing in Berlin?'

'No, he wanted to go back to Vienna and take me with him.'

'It is lucky that Lichnowsky knows nothing about the secret meetings. Whatever you do, don't take him into your confidence.'

Before leaving Leipzig, Wolfgang wrote to Constance to tell her that he was well and to ask her to send a last reply to the Duscheks in Prague. In that way, she would escape censorship. He told her that he would be spending at least a week in Berlin and would not be back in

* K 574.

Vienna before early June. Finally, he begged her to love him as much as he loved her.

Vienna, 18 May 1789

'I have caught up with Mozart, at last!' Geytrand announced.

'About time, too! Where is he?' asked Joseph Anton.

'In Potsdam, where Frederick Wilhelm II commissioned several pieces. Then, on the 12th, he gave a concert in Leipzig. It didn't go down very well and he left for an unknown destination, although I think I know where he went.'

'Out with it, then!'

'According to one of our informants at the court of Potsdam, Mozart could be starting a new career in Berlin with the support of the king, who is a keen advocate of his music and doesn't mind about his Masonic allegiance.'

'That monarch mixes with alchemists, occultists and all manner of secret society members! All the same, I was hoping he had a grudge against the Freemasons for letting in the Illuminati.'

'The King of Prussia moves in various and unpredictable ways,' Geytrand said, thoughtfully. 'The head of the Illuminati has been silenced and his movement obliterated. And the Masons claim to be hostile to the ideas he put about. So Frederick Wilhelm II must feel reassured.'

'Mozart in Berlin . . . Of course, he no longer feels safe in Vienna. He is no longer free to do as he likes there and he wants to develop new lodges with impunity!'

'Then, he is making a big mistake, because the King of Prussia is not exactly a liberal.'

'Raise the alert with our Berlin network. They must track Mozart down.'

'They are already on the case, my lord.'

9

Berlin, 19 May 1789

Mozart was granted hospitality by a friend he could trust, the trombonist, Möser, who lived near the National Theatre. Meanwhile, Thamos went in search of Brothers who, under the seal of secrecy, were willing to participate in one or more research meetings. He also wanted to identify policemen charged with spying on the composer. Berlin was no more secure than Vienna.

'Do you know which opera is playing tonight? Möser asked Mozart. 'You'll never guess: *The Abduction from the Seraglio*!'

Wolfgang went to the theatre incognito. It was not his favourite opera but it was better than Paisiello or Salieri. Alas, the singer who took the role of Blonde, the Englishwoman enamoured of freedom, sang a terrible wrong note. The composer could not restrain himself and sprang from his seat, calling out: 'Please sing a D!'

In the interval, the singer, Madame Baranius, had a fit of hysterics and refused to go back on stage. Mozart was obliged to intervene and offer soothing words before she consented to finish the show.

Before he went to bed, Wolfgang wrote a letter to Constance to tell her about the problem of letters being destroyed by the censors. *I cannot write much, this time, because I have a lot of visits to make.* From this, his wife would understand that he was seeing his Berlin Brothers in secret. Soon, Wolfgang would take her in his arms. *But first*, he promised,

> *I have a bone to pick with you: how can you think, or only even suppose, that I have forgotten you? How could I possibly do that? That naughty thought is going to cost you a good spanking on your charming little behind that is meant for kisses.*

Berlin, 21 May 1789

The Berlin lodges, once so powerful, were wavering; Illuminati and Rose-Cross had fled the city; Strict Observance was in its death throes: which way should they go?

Having uncovered a major police operation, Thamos arranged for a small number of Brothers to meet in the total safety of the homes of one or two.

Mozart described the difficulties Viennese Freemasons

had had and then presented the results of the research they had come up with under the direction of Thamos and von Born. The three degrees of Entered Apprentice, Fellow Craft and Master Mason formed the true path to knowledge and the Light, but their rituals had to be correctly prepared and celebrated. In Berlin, they needed dusting down, purifying and restoring to the central tenets of the Egyptian tradition, the mother of initiation. Then Thamos spoke of the deplorable deviations of the higher grade systems, meaningless ceremonies and continual digressions for the sake of glory and pompous titles.

Several Brothers were so impressed, they were all but convinced. But how, they asked, could they start a new lodge with authentic rituals without provoking the wrath of official Masonic administration and the authorities? Working underground demanded too much courage and determination.

Berlin, 23 May 1789

Berlin was turning out to be disappointing and no more liberal than Vienna, and Mozart would have done better to have left already. However, he had received an invitation to the court on the 26th, while two letters from Constance, dated the 9th and 13th, raised his dejected spirits for the time being. He drew up a detailed list of the letters he had sent her and the ones she had sent him. For seventeen interminable days, he had had no news at all!

He went to dine in an inn near the zoological gardens, distressed to think how little money he would be bringing home after such a long absence. He wrote to her to say that he was yearning for her and asked her to prepare her darling little nest for her naughty knave, who had been very well behaved throughout his long trip.

After an unavoidable stopover in Prague, which Constance would understand him making, Wolfgang expected to be back in Vienna on 4 June. But he had to deal with customs. Because of the composer's financial problems, he was at risk of being refused entry, or worse still, clapped in prison. So he asked his wife to send to the border a trusted man who could vouch for him, if needs be.

Vienna, 25 May 1789

Joseph Anton was fretting about the situation in France. The Estates General had met in Versailles to try to solve the economic crisis that was dogging a rich country with a population of twenty-five million. The aristocracy refused to listen to calls for equality, the high clergy was cloaked in the haughty rigidity of its doctrine, the bourgeoisie was crushed by taxes and staging vigorous protests, and the peasants, despite good harvests the previous year, were no less outspoken.

The whole country was thus gripped by violent unrest, and the king, with his detested Austrian wife in tow, seemed incapable of finding a workable solution. Nothing good would come of this Estates General.

According to the Count of Pergen's agents in France, the Illuminati were still a force to be reckoned with and were gradually inciting feeling against the Church and the royal family. They had infiltrated the lodges and, careful not to make any reference to their founder, Weishaupt, they had embarked on a mission to undermine the state using adepts like Mirabeau who had the public's ear. Their secret and all but unassailable power was intent on demolishing the government, overthrowing the monarchy and creating a new society.

The Viennese Freemasons were involved in this movement and Mozart was becoming one of the prime agitators. Now it was down to Joseph Anton, Count of Pergen, to reduce him to impotence.

'Mozart really seems to be living in Berlin,' Geytrand told him. 'Frederick Wilhelm II has given him another audience. There are rumours of a well-paid position.'

'It wouldn't be a bad solution. Vienna would be rid of that confounded Freemason at last, and the King of Prussia would see to his disappearance if he made too many waves.'

Berlin, 26 May 1789

In the presence of Princess Frederica, who listened attentively, Mozart played one of his Piano Concertos[*]. This invitation and the high-ranking audience proved that the court appreciated his talents and was showing their esteem.

When the concert was over, Duport took the man of the moment to see the king.

'Splendid performance, Mozart. I confirm my commission and I should like you to work for me as a permanent composer with an annual salary of 3600 florins.'

In Vienna, Wolfgang earned eight hundred. Such a sum would be ample to pay off his debts and put an end to the lawsuit that was playing on his mind. But he could not abandon his lodge in Vienna and betray Ignaz von Born's faith in him.

'I am flattered, Your Majesty, and I cannot thank you enough for such an honour.'

'So, do you accept?'

'Would you forgive a lover of Vienna for taking time to think it over?'

'I appreciate the answer of a mature and responsible man. I hope to see you again soon.'

[*] K537.

10

Wolfgang's decision, as he left Berlin, was final and Thamos' revelations confirmed his opinion.

'Prussia is turning into a state run by the military and the police, and its attitude towards the movement of ideas will only harden over time. The army will soon dictate to the regime. There will be no flourishing of the ideal of initiation here.'

After stopping in Dresden, they arrived in Prague where they were welcomed by the Freemasons at Truth and Union Lodge. Knowing that they were under surveillance, Count Canal and Father Unger deliberately attracted the attention of the police to leave the way open to other Brothers.

A long meeting was held in an apartment in the old town, while a Tyler stood guard outside to alert them at the first hint of danger. The Brothers studied the pilgrimage the Master Masons had made to look for the tomb of Hiram, assassinated by the bad Fellow Crafts. The place was revealed to them by the miraculous sprouting of an acacia tree. Thamos then described the rites of Osiris and emphasized the role played by the Widow Isis, for it was she who unleashed the process of resurrection.

Again, Wolfgang deplored the absence of a proper ritual for women and preached the need to restore to women their spiritual role. He would soon be involved in research with his Sister, Countess Thun, who was sure they would radically alter Masonic attitudes.

He could not help thinking about his third ritual opera, which would describe the passage from Fellow Craft to Master Mason. *La Clemenza di Tito* was certainly not the subject matter he needed, although the commission meant he had an official excuse to return to Prague. But how could he evoke the secret of transmutation? He had described the ritual assassination of the Master of Work and the just punishment of the wicked Fellow Craft in *Don Giovanni*. Now, he needed to show the action and power of the secret fire where the 'completed' Fellow Craft disappeared to be reborn as the Master Mason. Where would he find a narrative he could use?

Prague, 31 May 1789

As soon as he had made a start on the first Quartet for Frederick Wilhelm II, Wolfgang wrote to Constance telling her that he would be arriving at eleven or twelve noon on 4 June, at the first or second staging post. There, he would meet his wife with their little boy and Gaukerl. His family was essential to his wellbeing and this long absence had become unbearable. In Prague, they might have found even more perfect happiness. But his lodge in Vienna and the legal proceedings made exile impossible. He was determined to stay and prove his good faith, his righteousness and his innocence. Being called Mozart had become an honour that nothing should tarnish.

He had spent nearly all his time in Prague attending to his Masonic commitments, and the trip culminated in a final meeting in the degree of Master Mason. Wolfgang thought of the wonderful life of the priests and priestesses of the sun, whose lives had been regulated by the rhythm of daily rituals.

As he pictured them in their long ceremonial robes, he felt very close to them, and he seemed to enter their minds and join in their processions.

Vienna, 4 June 1789

Mozart left Prague on the 2nd and reached Vienna customs on the 4th shortly before midday. Thamos was travelling not far behind.

'Has Constance followed my instructions?' Mozart wondered, anxiously.

The composer got down before the checkpoint and saw a trio formed of his wife, Karl Thomas and a trusted companion. Wolfgang strolled across to his wife and son as though he were a curious onlooker, while his substitute presented himself at the customs office and announced that he had come from Prague. He gestured to Mozart's borrowed carriage and answered the guards' questions. Satisfied, they let the vehicle through.

'We had better not linger here,' advised Constance.

When they had crossed the border, Gaukerl jumped up to lick his master's face, and Karl Thomas prattled happily about his latest exploits.

'How are you, my darling?'

'I had to call a doctor but fees for consultations and medicines have gone up. The war has resulted in inflation and everyone is feeling the pinch.'

'The King of Prussia commissioned six Quartets and Sonatas from me. I'm beavering away at them.'

On 15 June, Wolfgang finished the first Quartet in the series*. He took special care with the cello part, because Frederick Wilhelm was a keen cellist. The piece was based on old drafts and was gentle and poetic with neither tragedy nor tension. He found the work laborious because it did not answer to his deepest aspirations, and he still had five Quartets to go!

His Brother Anton Stadler liked the music but reminded Mozart that the manufacture of the bass

* K575, in D major.

clarinet needed new investments, and a little loan to keep his big family fed would not be unwelcome. How could Wolfgang refuse?

Vienna, 25 June 1789

The court decried the recent developments in the situation in France ten days earlier: faced with an entrenched nobility and clergy, the Third Estate had become the National Assembly. Now any taxes collected without its consent would be illegal.

The threat of serious unrest was growing more intense. How would the king react to so much discontent? If Louis XVI was not extremely determined, the situation was likely to get out of hand. On the other hand, too brutal a response might set the people against him.

Meanwhile, Emperor Josef II was mired in a war with the Turks and did not seem sufficiently interested in the French morass. The Freemasons were divided; while some defended the royal family, nobility and clergy, others advocated universal brotherhood and equality among men. The Illuminati had left their mark, and rare were those who, like the Count of Pergen, were fully aware of the danger and terrible fall-out that an overthrow of current values would cause. Austria was bound to be affected. How could sound bulwarks be established?

The officer guarding the building where the secret

service had its headquarters appeared in Joseph Anton's office.

'A distinguished visitor to see you, my lord. Should I let him in?'

'Who is it?'

'The emperor's private secretary.'

What could the unwelcome dignitary be doing here? He could only be the bringer of evil tidings. In the thick of the turmoil, Josef II must have decided to dissolve Joseph Anton's secret team. It was a terrible mistake and one that would have worrying consequences.

Joseph Anton cast a last look at the files he had patiently accumulated but which he was sure he would shortly be asked to destroy. His tireless labour, so valuable for his country, was about to be swept away and there would be nothing he could do to avert disaster.

'My lord,' announced the private secretary, 'I have brought a decree from the emperor.'

'I am his faithful and obedient servant.'

'His Majesty fully believes it and is appointing you Minister of Police.'

11

Vienna, 6 July 1789

On the 2nd, Hofdemel had assigned his promissory note to Matthias Anzenberger, owner of the clothing shop 'The Mermaid' on Kohlmarkt, and it was to this merchant that Mozart now had to pay back the hundred florins, on 2 August. Thanks to the commissions for the re-orchestration of Handel's works, meanly paid by Baron van Swieten, the composer was earning money again and the future looked rosier.

He composed a light-hearted aria for the singer Adriana Ferrarese del Bene, 'To the desire of the man who adores you', where wind instruments and voices flirted with one another, and the first of a series of six 'easy' Piano Sonatas intended for Princess Frederica of Prussia, a simple piece with a slow movement tinged with melancholy.

Then suddenly the financial crises began again and Mozart found himself facing possible ruin and decline.

To add to his worries, Constance had an abscessed foot, and he had to send her to Baden, not far from Vienna, to take the waters. The costs for these treatments were considerable, of course, but the money had to be found to save his adored wife, whose courage and stoicism he so much admired. She made no complaint and accepted her plight with calm resignation. This detachment became one of the pillars of Wolfgang's thought.

Vienna, 14 July 1789

Wolfgang felt humiliated at having to ask his Brother for money again, and at first he prevaricated. Eventually, after a few days, he wrote him a letter on the 12th.

> *Very dear, excellent friend and very honourable Brother! God, I wouldn't wish my situation on my worst enemy; and if you, my best friend and Brother, abandon me, I shall alas and through no fault of my own be lost, together with my poor sick wife and child. Only recently, when I visited you, I wanted to pour out my heart, but I did not have the courage and I still don't – I can only do so in writing with a shaking hand – however I am certain that you know me and are aware of my position and fully convinced of my innocence as far as my unfortunate and utterly miserable situation is concerned.*
>
> *Fate is unfortunately so against me, though only*

*in Vienna, that I can earn nothing, even though I
want to. I sent around a list for two weeks and the
only name on it is van Swieten!*

*You know my circumstances, but you are also aware
of my hopes. In a few months, my fate will be sealed
in the business you know about, and there is therefore
no risk to you if you lend me five hundred florins, if
you want or can. I shall pay you back ten florins per
month until my business is over. Then, I shall pay you
back in full with interest, according to your wishes,
and declare myself furthermore your debtor for the
rest of my life. Without your help, the honour, peace
and the life of your Brother may well be obliterated.*

In his pride, Wolfgang said nothing to Thamos about
the nightmare he was living, and he did not talk to von
Born or Stadler about it, either.

Would Puchberg agree to his request?

Paris, 14 July 1789

Seeing a howling mob bearing down on the Bastille,
Angelo Soliman, a renegade Freemason who had betrayed
his Viennese Brothers, cried out in hatred and satisfaction.
He was the sworn enemy of Venerable Ignaz von Born
and von Born's favourite disciple Mozart, and now he
chanted to himself Camille Desmoulins' prophecy: 'The
red, white and blue cockade will travel the world.'

Aggrieved at the high cost of living and intolerable prices of basic necessities, the people had taken to the streets to protest against the oppressors and enemies of the nation. On the 9th, the National Assembly had been renamed the National Constituent Assembly and was calling for a Declaration of the Rights of Man and the application of the motto *Liberty, Equality, Fraternity*. Among its members were a number of Freemasons.

In the opinion of Soliman and his friends who had infiltrated the lodges, and according to the Illuminati encouraged from outside the Order by Bode, words were no longer enough: the time had come to take up arms, bring down royal absolutism, wipe out its partisans, proclaim the sovereignty of the people and make Paris the centre of the Revolution.

The Bastille was stormed by the angry crowds. The governor of Launay and his soldiers were massacred and the few prisoners inside were released. Soliman predicted that this victory would be the first of many and that nothing and no one would withstand the wave of violence.

Vienna, 17 July 1789

Puchberg had not replied to the urgent letter it had cost Mozart so much to send him. Did he doubt the composer's sincerity and integrity?

Wolfgang wrote again, hoping to make himself clearer:

You must be angry with me, as you haven't replied to my letter! When I compare the proof of your friendship with my current requests, I can see that you are quite right. But when I compare my misfortunes (for which I am not to blame) with your friendliness towards me, I think I deserve to be excused. As I told you quite openly in my last letter everything that was in my heart, I can only repeat what I said, but I must add:

1. That I wouldn't need such a big sum if I didn't have to pay the huge costs of my wife's treatment, especially if she has to go to Baden;

2. As I am sure my situation will soon improve, the sum I have to repay is a matter of indifference, but for the present, I'd prefer it to be a large sum, to make me feel more secure;

3. I must ask you – if it is absolutely impossible for you to lend me this sum at the moment – please have friendship and brotherly love for me by supporting me now with as much as you can spare, because everything hangs on it. You surely can't doubt my loyalty, you know me too well for that. You cannot doubt my word, my attitude and my behaviour, because you know my lifestyle and conduct.

Again, yesterday, my wife was in a piteous state.

Today, she was bled and is a little better. I am constantly torn between fear and hope.

These arguments persuaded Puchberg, and that same day, he sent his Brother Mozart one hundred and fifty florins.

Vienna, 20 July 1789

'Louis XVI appears to have made peace with his people and they still show him great affection,' Geytrand told the Count of Pergen, the new Chief of Police now invested with full powers to keep the peace on the empire's territory.

'That is an illusion that will soon be dispelled,' Joseph Anton answered, coldly. 'The peasants will raze the palaces to the ground and endless violence and disorder will follow. France has nothing less than a revolution on her hands and there will be a bloodbath. Documents and reports prove that the unrest will spread abroad mainly at the instigation of the Freemasons. We are no longer obliged to act furtively and we have all legal means at our disposal. The storming of the Bastille has infuriated the regime and everyone is worried about what will happen to Marie-Antoinette. My task is now to nip any revolutionary movement in Austria in the bud, and I have every intention of doing so with the utmost force.'

'Mozart is in the doldrums,' added Geytrand, with a smug smile. 'The legal proceedings against him have broken him and his wife is ill. I do not think we shall be hearing about him much more.'

12

Lyon, 22 July 1789

Although they were prepared to confirm their faith in
Jesus Christ, the Supreme Initiate, some of the Grand
Profess asked their superior, Jean-Baptiste Willermoz, to
take a clear stand on the new situation produced by the
storming of the Bastille. The event clearly represented
revolution that would destroy the social order and affect
Masonic lodges, where there were already deep divisions.

Now aged fifty-nine, Willermoz continued to be a
spiritual leader. He and he alone would dictate what
course of action to take. He saw himself as a revolutionary bourgeois who approved of the initiatives of the
patriots and he presided over one of their committees.

In this way, his brand of mysticism was not suspected
of being on the side of the people's oppressors. On the
contrary, he was thought to be helping them achieve
emancipation.

Vienna, 22 July 1789

Very dear friend and Brother! Wolfgang wrote to Puchberg. *Since you gave me such great proof of your friendship, I have been so sunk in despair that I could not go out or write. My wife is now calmer, and if only her ulcers hadn't reopened, she would be able to sleep. We are afraid that the bone is affected. She accepts her fate with astonishing forebearance and waits to recover or die with a tranquillity that is truly philosophical. I am writing to you with tears in my eyes. If you can, excellent friend, come and see us. Help me with your advice in the business you know about.*

What was at the root of this 'business'? Was it the financial proceedings against Mozart?

It was lucky that there were Masonic meetings. Of course, during the official part they had to make do with praising the emperor and advocating charity. Then they would pretend to disperse, but a few Brothers would follow a lodge member back to his house where they would be out of sight of the prying eyes and ears of the police. If any traitor infiltrated the little circle directed by Venerable Ignaz von Born, they would provoke the wrath of the authorities. So, they had to be extremely cautious about co-opting new adherents to their underground activities.

'Because of the turmoil in France,' von Born announced,

at the banquet, 'the new Police Chief, Joseph Anton, has been given full powers. He will stamp out protestors altogether. We who practise initiation have become suspect because we encourage freedom of thought and advocate lucidity. We must step up our efforts to be prudent and keep absolutely silent about our works.'

When the ritual was over, Thamos gave Wolfgang two pieces of news. In the interests of the war effort, the emperor was reducing to a minimum any spending that was not strictly necessary and had ordered the closure of the debt-ridden Italian Opera House. But he had agreed to run *The Marriage of Figaro*, despite the hostility of the Director of Shows, Salieri, provided Mozart could rehearse the company.

'My wife is ill and has to go to Baden for treatment,' he said, 'but I agree.'

'You have been looking very worried, lately.'

'It breaks my heart to see Constance suffer. Then this revolution in France . . .'

'It will soon be perverted by the atrocities of the worst of political programmes: egalitarianism. And the champions of a doctrine aimed at levelling society will be the first to assume the privileges seized from their opponents. Maybe hope will come from the New World, the United States of America, where our Brother George Washington was elected president on the 30th of April.'

'How I hate blind violence,' sighed Wolfgang. 'Nothing good ever comes of it.'

'Our former Brother, Angelo Soliman, is fuelling the

people's anger,' added Thamos. 'He is manipulating the Freemasons and stirring up tensions among them. Like any renegade, he is intent on destroying what he once worshipped.'

Vienna, 2 August 1789

The gold merchant, Goldhann, was an evil-looking fellow, but he was rich and happy to lend money at exorbitant rates. Puchberg only lent small sums, so Mozart decided to resort to the services of this uninspiring character. He needed to pay for Constance's trip to Baden, maintain the family lifestyle and stop the proceedings brought against him by a court of the government of Lower Saxony.

If the emperor won the war against the Turks, if Viennese cultural life took off again, if he could organize concerts, if success smiled on him once more, the composer could wipe out his debts and set off again on the right foot.

He composed a pretty aria* for the singer Adriana Ferrarese del Bene and another† for her sister, Louise Villeneuve, to sing in an opera by Cimarosa. He had not stopped composing for the voice, and in time, he hoped to come up with the subject of his third ritual opera.

---

* 'I feel moved by joy', K579.
† *Alma grande*, 'A great soul and noble heart', K.578.

Having Constance away preyed on his mind. Baden was only twenty-five km from Vienna, but Wolfgang was taken up with rehearsals for *The Marriage of Figaro* and needed to make sure each performance was as polished as possible. He sent his wife powders and potions for her foot and advised her to look after herself and act coldly and with restraint if any philanderers tried to flirt with her. Wolfgang was jealous and added: *A woman must be careful to be respected, otherwise she becomes the topic of conversation of ill-intentioned persons*. And he told her that he would soon be coming to Baden where he could kiss his adored wife.

Vienna, 15 September 1789

Joseph Anton railed against the new performances of *The Marriage of Figaro* on 31 August, 2 and 11 September and scheduled for the 19th. Nevertheless, the opera was hardly a full-blown success, since it was being put on a mere twenty times, which was nothing compared to the triumphant works of Sarti, Martin y Soler or Salieri and Paisiello, whose shows ran to over a hundred and fifty performances! The modest turn in Mozart's prospects earned him little money and did not extricate him from his legal and financial difficulties.

News from the Emperor's military base was far from encouraging. Months spent pushing back the enemy had exhausted Josef II's troops and his health was visibly declining. The doctors treated him as best they could but without much hope. If he had to return to Vienna, his army would miss him and it was not obvious that his generals were competent and stalwart enough to win the war.

Over the border, France was foundering. Since the fall of the Bastille, the disturbances had spread to the countryside where, despite the abolition of privileges on 4 August, the revolutionaries had set about assassinating nobles in the most barbaric manner, in the name of 'the rights of man and citizens' proclaimed on 26 August by the National Assembly.

Such conclusions were bound to lead to a change of regime, doubtless at the cost of considerable bloodshed. Louis XVI did not seem to have the necessary standing to contain the riots.

In Vienna, Freemasonry was careful not to hail the French Revolution or be seen to approve its leaders, some of whom, however, were Brothers and Illuminati.

Their strategy did not fool the Chief of Police.

13

Vienna, 17 September 1789

After composing 'Gentle spring is already laughing', an aria* to be included in an opera by Paisiello and sung by his sister-in-law, Josepha Hofer†, Wolfgang went to his lodge where, during the Officers'‡ Entry, his Adagio for cor anglais, two horns and bassoon§ was played. That evening, the Brothers of Crowned Hope forgot the ban on music, thought to make the sessions too appealing, and afterwards, they studied one of the main symbols of Freemasonry, the Great Architect of the Universe.

Thamos described how the divine builder from Ancient Egypt had crafted time and space by combining mind with matter. Taking in height, depth, width

---

* K580.
† The future Queen of the Night in *The Magic Flute*.
‡ 'Officers' were those who held an official function.
§ K580a, with a theme from his *Ave Verum*.

and length, the Great Architect drew the circle of the universe with his compass and revealed to initiates the plans and instructions hidden in the darkness.

Vienna, 20 September 1789

Wolfgang and Gaukerl's favourite walk took them down Raubensteingasse, along the Stubentor and into the Glacis, a wooded area and a no-man's land that lay beyond the fortifications.

It was while Mozart was talking to his dog that the idea came to him for his third ritual opera based on one of the most secret aspects of the degree of Master Mason. *Così fan tutte**, 'So do they all', he hummed to himself, remembering a phrase from *The Marriage of Figaro* and thinking of the lodges worthy of the name.

'There are two lifestyles it is essential to avoid,' said Thamos, suddenly appearing at Mozart's side: 'the first is a life of pleasure, because it is base and hollow,

---

* Some musicologists understood the true nature of the work: '*Così* exudes a subtlety of such exquisite purity that it is hard not to hear in it the echo of some spiritual message,' says Roland-Manuel. '*Così* is a ritual opera in the same way as *The Magic Flute*,' thinks Roger Lewinter (*Avant-Scène Opéra*, Nº 16–17, p. 145); 'the most mysterious and the most esoteric opera ever written' considers Massin (p. 1115); 'Behind the mask of *opera buffa*,' considers Marie-Françoise Vieuille, who sees *Così fan tutte* as a 'celebration of the pure number', 'surely the opera opens the way taken by the future initiates, Tamino and Pamina.' (*L'Avant-Scène*, 104, ff.)

and the second is a life of mortifications, because it is pointless and hollow. So, you must show how the Fellow Craft, Don Juan, emerges from the Secret Fire and is metamorphosed to cross the threshold of the Master Mason.'

'I shall describe* what happens inside the athanor, the alchemical furnace where the fire consumes the profane man and the phoenix is reborn. And I thought of the Cabbalistic teaching that you introduced me to. When the world was created, light blazed on the masculine side, on the left; but right and left must take over from one another.'

'The offering of the fire,' Thamos confirmed, 'is indeed the union of the male and female principles†.'

'The degree of Master Mason teaches us to reconcile opposites by observing the rule of Divine Proportion‡. But the Cabbalah tells us that all marriages are difficult. Only the righteous can achieve union and spread peace in this world. So I am going to show two couples who fall apart before coming back together in a way to make them aware of their union.'

'You need a third couple: the alchemists who guide the operation. Do you think that would be too abstract for the audience?'

---

* Concerning the fact that Mozart chose the libretto, see Stricker, op. cit., p. 25.
† *Zohar, Genesis*, Vol. I, p. 355.
‡ The ratio of the whole line to the large segment is the same as the ratio of the large segment to the small segment.

'Don't worry,' Wolfgang assured him, 'I'm going to embody the inversion of the lights in characters who experience a total upheaval, but there'll be plenty of opportunity for comedy. And Lorenzo Da Ponte can add the necessary disguises.'

Vienna, 22 September 1789

Antonio Salieri, Court Kapellmeister and President of the Musicians' Society, looked Mozart up and down witheringly.

'Have you been summoned by the emperor?'

'Indeed, yes.'

'His Majesty is ill and cannot receive you.'

Josef II's private secretary approached Mozart.

'I am sorry, the emperor cannot talk to you but he has sent me to tell you his decision. He will pay you two hundred ducats to compose a new opera. These are troubled times and the Viennese need amusements. Try to give us something less tragic than *Don Giovanni*. Now, get to work, Mozart!'

Wolfgang was speechless. An official commission, and he had only just found his subject. The magic of initiation was not an empty word.

Vienna, 29 September 1789

Before starting work on *Così fan tutte*, Wolfgang put the finishing touches to his Clarinet Quintet*, a piece of such other-worldly beauty that it moved Thamos and Anton Stadler to tears: at last, the Great Magician had explored the clarinet's full palette of sound. The calm, solemn Allegro, and above all the luminous, profound Larghetto, suggested the sublime at the heart of the circle drawn by the Great Architect of the Universe.

Whatever the ordeals, his creative power overcame them.

The piece was performed by Brother Master Masons at a secret meeting, and Stadler gave his all to this heavenly music that expressed the mystery of Masonic thought.

Afterwards, the words of the ritual were also suggestive of immortal music and spoke of the soul of the gods. That evening, 'everything was just and perfect'.

Not content with this miracle, Anton Stadler added,

'We must work on the clarinet. Just think how much more beguiling you could make the instrument!'

Vienna, 30 September 1789

A weakened Josef II returned to Vienna with relief. He had not managed to put the Turks to rout but he had

---

* K581, in A major.

contained the threat, kept up his men's morale and left the army in the charge of generals who could hold it together and prepare the offensive.

Meanwhile, another rift was opening up in the Netherlands, where the people wanted to throw off the Austrian yoke. Repression was the only answer. The emperor's soldiers met with considerable resistance, and after the conflict there could be no doubt: the Netherlands was poised to regain its independence.

Josef II's fine liberal hopes were crumbling, and he was worried about the French Revolution. It now looked inevitable that it would spread to the rest of Europe, and Austria needed to form an impenetrable barrier.

The emperor thought of Mozart, that strange genius who had dared to compose *The Marriage of Figaro* in defiance of the aristocracy, and *Don Giovanni*, so poorly received in Vienna. He decided to give the composer one last chance, in the hope that the librettist, Lorenzo Da Ponte, would provide the musician with an amusing subject.

14

Vienna, 6 October 1789

'On the face of it, *Così fan tutte*, "So do they all", will be about the behaviour of women,' Mozart told Thamos, 'and Da Ponte can have some fun.'

'We, however, will be thinking of the lodges, which do everything according to ritual in order to promote initiation.'

'Most of the Freemasons know nothing about the teaching of the Ancients and refuse to understand that initiation is both male and female. Now, since his first steps on the road to knowledge, the Entered Apprentice has been moving towards his marriage with Wisdom. And if the brother is not united with the Sister, the temple cannot be built. True spirituality radiates from this ritual union.'

'So, we need both a female and a male Venerable to organize the ritual,' suggested the Egyptian. 'The male

79

Venerable will be an old philosopher, Don Alfonso[*], who has many secrets; the female Venerable will appear to be a servant, Despina[†]. In reality, she guides the two Sisters, Fiordiligi, "fleur-de-lys", who embodies purity, and Dorabella, "the gilt beauty", who represents the goddess Hathor. Together they form pure gold, which will be subjected to the ordeal of the fire of alchemical marriage.'

'On the other side,' went on Wolfgang, 'are two Brothers, metallic Ferrando and stony Guglielmo[‡], who symbolize the metals needed to realize the Great Work. Six characters on stage and seven – one of the Numbers of the Master Mason – if you include the orchestra, which will be very important. Of course, the clarinet as the supreme voice of the lodge will be given a starring role!'

---

[*] The word comes from *alfanz*, 'joker' according to Autexier. In several traditions, the wiseman plays 'good tricks' and highlights the absurdity of human pretensions the better to light the way to knowledge. 'Don Alfonso,' writes Stricker, 'guides the couples to freedom, not freedom over the power of the Other, but freedom based on self-knowledge.'

[†] From the Greek, *despoina*, 'the mistress of the house'. She directs the action together with Don Alfonso and is the Handmaid of Wisdom, like Susanna in *Le Nozze di Figaro*.

[‡] *Guglia* means 'cathedral spire, obelisk'.

The Beloved of Isis

Thrilled to be writing a new Masonic opera, Wolfgang composed two arias for Louise Villeneuve*.

Suddenly, Vienna had cause to rejoice: Belgrade had at last been liberated and the empire claimed a resounding victory over the Turks.

All night, the Viennese sang and danced in the streets, and even Constance, who was eight months pregnant, joined in the celebrations. They extolled the hero, Baron Gideon von Laudon. Under the influence of wine and beer, one noblewoman hoisted her skirts over her arms and head, while a young bourgeois lady was stripped naked by the crowd.

Victory, peace, the end of inflation, the return of a pleasant, carefree life . . . hope was reborn in Vienna and everyone sang a *Te Deum* in St Stephen's Cathedral, confident that the Turks would be crushed.

The Freemasons were not the last to toast the emperor's triumph, this time with no reservations.

Vienna, Così fan tutte, *Act I, Scenes 1 to 10*

'Venerable Don Alfonso summons Ferrando, the man of metal, and Guglielmo, the man of stone,' said Thamos.

---

* 'Who knows, who knows what will happen', K582, and 'I am going, but where?', K583, pieces included in an opera by Martin y Soler.

'Ferrando is in love with Dorabella, the gilt beauty, and Guglielmo with Fiordiligi, the fleur-de-lys. To their impassioned declarations, the Venerable retorts that he speaks "ex cathedra", or with authority, because of the supreme position he has been given by ritual.'

'Guglielmo and Ferrando draw their swords against old Alfonso, because he challenges the fidelity of their fiancées. The situation is similar to *Don Giovanni*, but this time there's no combat or assassination because this is another degree. "I am a peaceful man," declares Don Alfonso, "and don't touch duels except at table." The ritual banquet will be the culmination of the opera, as at every meeting.'

'The Venerable has his own agenda. Because the two men present their fiancées like the phoenix, the bird reborn from the ashes and a symbol of the regenerated Master Mason, their claim must be ascertained. Constructive doubt is essential to the practice of initiation, so Don Alfonso makes a solemn bet and demands they keep it secret. The two Brothers take an oath and comply with his instructions. Then the terms of the ritual are declared: "And many a toast we'll offer to the god of love*".'

'In a garden by the seashore, Dorabella and Fiordiligi, feeling a certain fire, are getting ready for their marriage. Enter Don Alfonso, bringer of new anxieties.'

'Have their fiancés died?'

'No, but it's not much better! A "royal command" – the command of Freemasonry – has called them to the

---

* A theme to these words is used in Mozart's last Masonic Cantata (K623).

battlefield. Fearing a fatal outcome, the two women want to die. "Joy is in the end," Alfonso recalls, "and not death."

'Duty summons the Brothers,' Wolfgang added. 'Before a union can take place between the alchemical components, there needs to be a separation. Ferrando and Guglielmo board the community ship and depart. Together, the Venerable and the two Sisters celebrate the plenitude of the work to come: "May the wind be gentle, may the breeze be calm and may every element smile favourably on our desires*."'

'The primary matter is purified,' observed Thamos. '"All is well," Don Alfonso concludes and reflects on the folly of human illusions: ploughing the seas and sowing in the sand!'

'Now the "servant" Despina enters,' Wolfgang went on. 'Not without reason, she complains how hard her work is and comforts the two Sisters, especially Dorabella, who is in despair. So their fiancés have gone off to war? It's not as bad as all that! If they are men of valour, they will come back laden with medals. They are both as good as one another, since neither is worth a thing. And if they are really alive, they will come back alive!'

'There's no better way to describe the elements of the Great Work,' commented Thamos. 'Don Alfonso meets Despina, his female counterpart, and shares the secret by showing her a gold piece, "to sweeten the pill". The two alchemists prepare the inversion of the two poles which our good Da Ponte will treat merely as a crossover of couples.'

---

* Act I, Scene 6, one of the high points of Mozart's work.

15

Vienna, 1 November 1789

Cheered by the emperor's return and the victory of Belgrade, Vienna recovered some of its *joie de vivre*. Joseph Anton, Count of Pergen, used this moment's respite to find his way around the structure of the police force, now that he was its chief. He made as much use as he could of his deadly sidekick, Geytrand, and ordered him to compile confidential files on the heads of service and make a note of any useful gossip.

Reports from France were decidedly alarming. This time, the Revolution was aimed directly at the king. Louis XVI and his family were being forced to live in Paris and he found himself a prisoner of merciless dogmas that, sooner or later, would obliterate the man and his function. Only the most naïve still believed that a constitutional monarchy would be instituted, as certain members of the National Constituent Assembly hoped.

The nobility were leaving France before the inevitable wave of violence. When the revolutionary fury erupted, it would spare no one, not even ardent partisans. Egalitarians, anti-clerics or Freemasons: no one would escape. Then, of course, there was that detested Austrian woman, Marie-Antoinette Queen of France, and there was no knowing how she would be treated.

Many of Josef II's advisers accused Joseph Anton of exaggerated pessimism and believed the storm would abate. They saw Louis XVI as cautious and level-headed and were sure he would find a compromise solution and show the revolutionaries that there were boundaries they could not cross.

'Mozart is composing another opera commissioned by the emperor,' Geytrand revealed. 'Da Ponte is writing the libretto. It's a trifling comedy to amuse the Viennese.'

'Coming from a Master Mason of his calibre, that would surprise me!' Anton retorted. 'This is the third time he is using Da Ponte to cover up his real intentions. He will reveal the initiation of the Fellow Craft, Don Juan, into the degree of Master Mason in a way no one has ever done before. Furthermore, Mozart appears to be surviving our legal and financial assaults! Does he know one of his Brothers is behind them?'

'I doubt it, my lord. Our best informant, Hoffmann, tells me Freemasonry is raising its head again in Vienna. There is even talk of some of the lodges re-opening.'

'At the instigation of Mozart and his cronies! If he oversteps the limit, I shall ruin him.'

Vienna, Così fan tutte, *Act I, Scenes 11 to 16*

'Don Alfonso and Despina introduce the two girls to two young Albanians, who are really their fiancés but so well disguised that the girls don't recognise them,' declared Wolfgang. 'They are introduced as the old philosopher's best friends, and without more ado they declare their love for the two Sisters, who are outraged.'

'Fiordiligi remains as faithful as a rock,' put in Thamos. 'She possesses the purity of the alchemical flame and stands firm against wind and storms. Death alone can alter her heart's devotion.'

'It seems things might stop there, but Venerable Don Alfonso and his female half, Despina, are not to be put off so easily. The ritual must be played out above and beyond the world of human passions. The two Sisters, incidentally, realize the importance of the ordeal they are about to undergo.'

'Guglielmo and Ferrando are ready to sacrifice themselves for the beauties that reject them,' suggested Thamos. 'So they swallow arsenic and collapse. Don Alfonso calls a doctor who happens to be a gifted linguist: Despina in disguise. Using Brother Mesmer's famous stone, which contributed to your own initiatory awakening, she rescues them from the jaws of death.'

'And it doesn't take long,' Wolfgang added, 'for the fire of anger in the Sisters' hearts to be transformed into love. For they find these two men alike yet different, inside the alchemical melting pot that is the Master Masons Lodge.'

The Beloved of Isis

Vienna, 16 November 1789

Wolfgang trusted one of his illustrious Brothers, Dr Johann Hunczowsky, a surgeon and professor of gynaecology at the hospital in Vienna, to attend at Constance's confinement, and she gave birth to a bonny little girl, Anna-Maria.

But the musician was not allowed to kiss her.

'Why not?' he asked the midwife in alarm.

'Don't worry, Dr Hunczowsky is the best specialist in Vienna.'

'At least tell me . . .'

'Please be patient.'

When, an hour after the birth, the doctor emerged from the bedroom, his face was grave.

'I am so sorry, my Brother Mozart. Your little girl is dead.'

'Dead . . .'

'The hand of fate . . .'

'Fate? How can you, a scientist, possibly invoke such a word! Surely you have made a terrible mistake.'

'How dare you!'

'Leave my house immediately!'

'My Brother, I . . .'

'You are no longer my Brother. My child has died because of your incompetence.'

Hunczowsky left, slamming the apartment door in disgust.

Wolfgang ran in to comfort his weeping wife.

Overcome by the doctor's terrible error, the composer consoled himself as best he could with his son, Karl Thomas, and even his dog, Gaukerl, who was as dejected as his master.

A lovely little girl had lived for no more than an hour; now, only one child survived out of five. Life had not spared the couple, yet adversity brought them closer with every blow.

They buried Anna-Maria the next day.

Neither Wolfgang nor Constance felt any sense of revolt. What was the point? The will of the hereafter was being worked out and they had to accept it and understand.

16

Vienna, Così fan tutte, *Act II, Scenes 1 to 13*

The power of the human chain gave Wolfgang the strength to go on with his work. He even managed to smile at the jokes with which Lorenzo Da Ponte peppered a libretto he was enjoying immensely.

'Act II,' said Thamos, 'opens with the games mistress, Despina, reminding the two Sisters that they are on earth, not in heaven, and should pay heed to two suitors who are brave enough to lay down their lives for them. And they needn't worry about being found out, because she will spread the word that the two men are courting her, Despina, like a queen on her throne.'

'The Sisters agree to receive the men. I'll make the music solemn here to reflect the seriousness of the moment when the couples meet. Guglielmo, the man of stone, seduces Dorabella, the gilded beauty, and slips a heart into the young woman's locket in place of her fiancé's portrait. Thus, the small segment of Divine Proportion is formed. The large segment will consist of the man of metal, Ferrando, and Fiordiligi, the fleur-de-lys, who accepts his love, even if it means suffering guilt and remorse, and implores her real fiancé to forgive her betrayal. Mortified, the two tormentors admit that Don Alfonso has won his bet. There is no such thing as fidelity, feelings don't last and human beings are fickle!'

'Not so fast!' interjected Thamos. 'Yesterday's peace can be regained if Guglielmo and Ferrando keep their oath and continue to obey it.'

'Fiordiligi decides to go and find her real fiancé and tries to convince her Sister to do the same. She orders Despina to bring her two hats and two swords – the Master Masons' ritual regalia. Fiordiligi and Dorabella will put on their respective fiancé's clothes and go and fight at their sides, like men and officers.'

'They perform this gesture in imitation of Isis, who turned into a man in order to bring Osiris back to life, but their plan doesn't come off because the time to approach the Great Mystery has not yet come. Invoking the help of the gods, the fleur-de-lys, representing the purity of the alchemical work, allows Ferrando the possibility of doing what he wants with her, after he has forced her to choose between his love and death.'

'Ferrando and Guglielmo are furious! Fiordiligi? The devil's flower! Don Alfonso suggests a way to punish the faithless girls: they should marry them! The lovers protest in horror that they'd rather be united with the boat of Charon, ferryman of the dead or Vulcan's forge or the gates of hell!'

'The very stages required for initiation! Otherwise, Don Alfonso declares, Guglielmo and Ferrando will stay single forever and never have access to the supreme mystery.'

'Why don't the lovers go and look elsewhere?' asked Wolfgang. 'Because, as they confess in their capacity as ritualists, they feel forever bound to the two young women who together form the purity of gold.'

'Love of Wisdom, the Master Masons' pillar, is necessary in all things, says the Venerable. Wisdom will put things right. So do they all, the real lodges at least, isn't that right?'

'The union between the two couples will be based on seduction, illusion and inversion. Will it also lead to the discovery of the alchemical gold and the Philosopher's Stone?'

Vienna, 25 November 1789

At a secret meeting at the house of the Countess Thun, the countess had her own contribution to make to *Così fan tutte*. Fiordiligi and Dorabella were not profane but Sisters whose role in developing the Great Alchemical Work was at last given its proper place.

The little group devised an initiation ritual based on the main Number associated with women, according to documents provided by Thamos and Ignaz von Born. Both men knew that *Così fan tutte* would not be Mozart's last word on the subject and that, given a suitable libretto, he was capable of instigating nothing short of a Masonic revolution through his music.

'Prince Karl von Lichnowsky and my daughter Christine are getting married,' the countess told Wolfgang. 'Don't you think we should admit him to our circle?'

'Thamos is suspicious of him, and I didn't care for his behaviour on our journey to Germany. To be quite frank, my Sister, I don't believe his commitment to initiation is sincere. All the same, I wish your daughter every happiness.'

Wolfgang said nothing about the rumours surrounding the prince; fidelity did not seem to be a virtue Lichnowsky set much store by.

The countess looked disappointed and troubled, but she did not insist.

Vienna, 3 December 1789

Not to be put off by the obvious dangers of moving about and the warnings of his Viennese Brothers, Thamos had responded to Dom Pernety's invitation by going to Castle Thabor, where he and a handful of disciples studied the Great Work. Obedient to an invisible power known as the Sainte-Parole, which had ordered him to leave Berlin and go to Avignon, the seer was now the head of a small brotherhood of Illuminati from Germany, England and Poland.

At sixty-three, the author of *Egyptian Fables* and the *Dictionary of Hermetic Lore* seemed disheartened.

'It is kind of you to come,' he said to Thamos, whom he saw as an Unknown Superior, 'but it is too late. I was hoping to pursue my research away from the profane world but I have made a bad mistake. Why did the Sainte-Parole not warn me that this French Revolution was going to sweep everything away? Two years ago, there were a hundred of us and we celebrated rites in the correct manner and according to true Freemasonry, with the emphasis on alchemy. Then came all this fear and these rifts and fights. I had hoped to keep up a mini-mum of research but the authorities clamped down on our meetings altogether.'

'If you are not militating in favour of the Revolution,' Thamos judged, 'then you are fighting it.'

'But I am not interested in politics and power!'

'Yes, but they are interested in you! And they need homogenous citizens who will subscribe to an intangible doctrine.'

'What will become of this world if folly gets the upper hand?'

'In Vienna, a Great Magician called Mozart is building a temple that will withstand the horror and massacres. The ideal of initiation will not die out.'

'Take the results of my alchemical research. I am too old, now, to battle on and launch into new ventures.

Maybe the Sainte-Parole will guide me again one day . . .'

Abandoned by his followers, the old man disappeared back into his chapel and the Egyptian set out for Vienna, carrying a thick wad of manuscripts to give Mozart to read.

17

Vienna, 10 December 1789

When he had composed twelve Minuets* and twelve
German Dances† for the La Redoute ballrooms, Wolfgang
wrote an enthusiastic contredanse for orchestra in the
joyful key of C major to celebrate the victories of Empire
Field Marshal the Duke of Saxe-Coburg‡, who had driven
back the Turks in a vigorous campaign. The Ottomans
were beginning to realize that they had met their match
and might not conquer Europe.

'The emperor is very appreciative of your latest piece,'
Baron van Swieten told Mozart.

'I am but a humble warrior!'

'Your public support for Josef II's action has had
implications for the whole of Viennese Freemasonry.

* K585.
† K586.
‡ *Hero Coburg's Victory*, K587.

I am now convinced that the new Minister of Police, the Count of Pergen, was the head of the secret service that did the lodges so much damage; he would love to see them wiped out. Because of your attitude, the emperor has recommended more moderate action. In any case, Freemasonry is Josef II's unswerving ally.'

Gottfried van Swieten, head of censorship, had saved the Brothers from considerable trouble.

Vienna, Così fan tutte, *Act II, Scenes 14 to the Finale*

'Lorenzo Da Ponte is delighted,' Wolfgang told Thamos. 'He's tickled pink by all the business with couple-swapping and Albanian disguises. He thinks Viennese audiences will be thrilled.'

'Let's get back to our ritual: we're now in the lodge where preparations are under way for the alchemical marriage. The Venerable, Despina, orders lamps to be lit and the works to be opened. The Choir, consisting of Brothers and Sisters, gets into position. The banqueting table is groaning with good food and drink.'

'Our two "new" couples come in, determined to celebrate the work of dear Despina in the crossing of marriages!'

'Now we come to the crucial point in the opera and the inversion of lights,' Thamos said. 'Human beings will taste divinity, and divinity will temporarily illuminate humanity. Symbolizing the brief period when the energies are exchanged without merging, will the two false couples really commune at the banquet?'

'And now for the toast,' decided Wolfgang, 'Fiordiligi, the purity of the Work, wishes: "In your glass and in mine, may every thought be drowned, and may no memory of the past remain in our hearts." Her prayers are echoed by those of Dorabella and Ferrando. Guglielmo, meanwhile, would rather have a deadly draft, or more exactly, a draft of transmutation, like the cup of bitterness which the aspirant drinks at initation.'

'Despina has changed out of her doctor's disguise and is dressed as a notary.

'Now she brings in the marriage certificate. Will this temporary interlude and the inversions be made to last?'

'No, because the Venerable keeps the document! In the background, the sound of drums heralds the return of the real fiancés. Seized with panic, the two Sisters beg their future Albanian husbands to vanish. They're not the ones they love; in truth, they love two heroes returning from war. Whatever will become of us, they ask, in dismay.'

'"Trust me," Don Alfonso reassures them, "all will be well."'

'Having changed out of their Eastern costumes, Guglielmo and Ferrando come proudly into the banqueting hall and feign surprise at the marriage preparations, especially the marriage contract signed by the faithless girls! There is only one fitting punishment for them: death!'

'Fiordiligi and Dorabella accept their fate so readily that they clamour for the ritual sword to pierce their hearts immediately.'

'Then everything is revealed. Ferrando and Guglielmo admit that they dressed up to trick the two young women and seduce each other's intended. Despina reveals her role and Don Alfonso provides the key to a drama that nearly turned to tragedy. I deceived you but my deception undeceived your lovers. Now they will be wise and do as I wish.'

'Together,' added Thamos, 'they close the lodge works, proclaiming: *Happy is the man who looks at everything on the right side, and, through trials and tribulations, makes reason his guide. What always makes another weep will be for him a cause of mirth and amid the tempests of this world he will find sweet peace.*'

'This "right side" is the side of Divine Proportion. Master Masons only obtain it on condition they reverse the light, see light in the heart of darkness and head towards the alchemical marriage. By going to see the other side, the four partners that form the two couples have become aware of their hidden reality. Before this terribly harsh ordeal, they were content to go along with ordinary passion and ordinary happiness. Having narrowly avoided disaster and been through the alchemical death under the guidance of the Venerable Alfonso and his female counterpart Despina, the two couples achieve the truth of genuine love, in other words, the Great Work*.

'The metals of Ferrando and the minerals of Guglielmo have been given to pure gold, Fiordiligi and Dorabella's union. So, without giving it away, you can describe one of the mysteries of the Middle Chamber. Let us hope our Brothers and Sisters perceive the horizon you are opening to them.'

On 22 December, just as Mozart was putting the finishing touches to *Così fan tutte*, his Brother Anton Stadler gave the first performance of the Clarinet Quintet† at a Musicians' Society concert which Thamos attended. The piece was inextricably linked to the light of the opera and proved how far the Great Magician had risen in initiation. With his ritual trilogy, formed of *The Marriage of Figaro, Don Giovanni* and *Così fan tutte*, Mozart cast extraordinary light on the path from Entered Apprentice to Master Mason via Fellow Craft.

But he had not yet exhausted his capacities and would push back the boundaries of Viennese Freemasonry still

* 'Once the masquerade has been uncovered and order is restored, there is no reason to think that the partners will harbour a guilty nostalgia for the fallacious world of passionate love they experienced in fiction. On the contrary, what they take away from the adventure is a kind of paradisal bliss, like that of the Toast, which transcends love and the beloved and thus transcends all expression of fidelity. Mozart therefore agreed, without any hesitation, to the *dénouement* of the libretto: the initial matching of the couples was the only one that was really viable' (Hocquart, *La Pensée de Mozart*, p. 493).
† K581.

further. Now he was free to tackle another conception
of initiation, in line with the brotherhood of priests and
priestesses of the sun.

18

Vienna, 29 December 1789

Convinced that, with the first performance of *Così fan tutte*, he would receive the money the emperor had promised and be paid by the King of Prussia on delivery of the Quartets and Sonatas, Wolfgang asked his Brother Puchberg to lend him four hundred florins for immediate reimbursement. The musician had to settle the bills of pharmacists and doctors and pay the gynaecologist and Freemason Hunczowsky, who had proved such a poor specialist.

Puchberg was invited to the first rehearsal of the new opera, together with Joseph Haydn and Thamos, and he lent Wolfgang three hundred florins. Although he preferred lighter music, the merchant thought the arias charming.

'My Brother,' Haydn told his young colleague, 'you have attained a perfection no words can describe.'

'Unfortunately,' Wolfgang deplored, 'Salieri is still plotting to stop *Così* being put on.'

'He won't succeed,' the Egyptian assured him, 'because he will come up against the emperor's will. He won't do more than spread slander and gossip.'

'You shouldn't underestimate him,' advised Joseph Haydn. 'He has real powers and there seem to be no limits to his malice.'

'I am not unaware of Salieri's capacity for harm.'

Thanks to Da Ponte and some influential Brothers, *Così fan tutte* would indeed be put on in Vienna.

Vienna, 15 January 1790

The Director of Shows, Count Rosenberg, wore his bad-day face, though it was not so different from the way he looked on good days.

'What do you want, now, Da Ponte?'

'To fix a definite date for the performance of *Così fan tutte*. *The Marriage of Figaro* is on and Mozart's new opera will amuse the Viennese.'

'There's no criticism of the nobility this time?'

'Good heavens, no! It's a lively little number involving couple-swapping and . . .'

'Nothing immoral, I hope?'

'Certainly not. It's a delightful farce that ends with a glorification to marriage and good manners.'

'Very good, very good . . . Alas, the emperor wants

to put a stop to Italian opera in Vienna.'

'My composer friends will persuade His Majesty that that would be a regrettable mistake.'

'Can you take charge of that without involving me at all?'

'I take it upon myself, my lord.'

Vienna, 21 January 1790

After drafting the dark first movement of a Quartet in G minor*, Wolfgang received a hundred florins from his Brother Puchberg whom he had invited to the theatre with Joseph Haydn to attend the first orchestral rehearsal of *Così*.

The two men were enchanted by the composer's rich palette of sound. Haydn marvelled at how Mozart expressed his knowledge and mastery so effortlessly that listeners forgot the complexity of the piece.

'I was an Entered Apprentice Freemason at a single meeting,' he recalled, 'but I have the feeling that this absurd story with its improbable adventures, which one barely notices because of the purity of the music, hides a message about initiation. You've written an opera about Sacred Numbers, haven't you?'

Wolfgang merely smiled.

* K587a.

Vienna, 26 January 1790

Tomorrow, Mozart would be thirty-four. And tonight was the first performance of his *Così fan tutte, ossia: la scuola degli amanti* at the Burgtheater in Vienna. 'So do they all, or: school for lovers*', an *opera buffa* written for the sum of nine hundred florins, money that was particularly welcome in these difficult times. Wolfgang felt confident that the piece would be played again, at least on 28 and 30 January.

But the evening turned out to be difficult. He found the performers generally unconvincing and felt they were missing the hidden meaning of the roles by too far. He was demanding and a perfectionist and he lost patience with a host of slips and oversights.

The audience was not as amused as Da Ponte would have liked. Thamos, however, was transported to a universe of a beauty that took his breath away. After the violence of *Don Giovanni, Così fan tutte* was limpid and ethereal, combining comedy and grace, tragedy and supreme elegance. If the Freemasons understood the need for this ritual in order to discover the Great Work, then their lodges would be less unworthy of the lodges of Ancient Egypt.

'Mozart's natural musical genius may be greater than any other composer's now or at any other time,' Lorenzo Da Ponte muttered in Thamos's ear. 'It is all thanks to me that he has burst onto the Viennese scene.'

* K588.

The Egyptian refrained from comment and instead gave himself up to the music, feeling it fill him with light from another world, the world of the alchemical melting pot where the forces of creation were interchanged to become fully themselves.

Vienna, 30 January 1790

'Baron van Swieten has taken the curious step,' Joseph Anton remarked to Geytrand, 'of asking the emperor to give Mozart a better position at court, either Vice-Kapellmeister or music teacher to the imperial family. Coming from the head of censorship, who cannot be unaware of Mozart's Masonic allegiance, his behaviour is suspicious!'

'Van Swieten doesn't belong to a Viennese lodge,' Geytrand confirmed.

'His support for Mozart suggests he sympathizes with Freemasonry.'

'But he does nothing but criticize the Order!'

'A crafty traitor, that's what I think Baron van Swieten is! Though we still need proof. In the meantime, I have advised the emperor to be cautious, though he has said that he has no intention of promoting Mozart. His *Così fan tutte* has had a decidedly mixed reception and it will soon be off the programme. In the minds of most people, he would do better to settle for composing dance music and give up opera.'

'Is that what you think, my lord?'

'*Così fan tutte* is sublime. It is the most abstract piece Mozart has written and the closest he has come to the invisible. His characters are not humans but symbols of the mystery revealed by Don Alfonso and Despina, the mystery that reconciles opposites. No Master Mason has gone so far in the process of creation. And he won't stop there.'

Vienna, 4 February 1790

'I have to go back to Ezterháza,' Joseph Haydn told Mozart. 'The opera season is about to start and Prince Nikolaus Esterházy will be there.'

'Do you know that he is Master of Ceremonies in my lodge?'

Haydn sighed.

'I have turned a page forever with Freemasonry. You will always be my Brother, Mozart, but I cannot constantly shuttle back and forth between Ezterháza and Vienna, and I do not want to go down the path of initiation.'

'I should have liked to see you among the columns again,' Wolfgang mused, 'but I respect your decision. My admiration and my friendship towards you remain intact.'

'I am immensely touched by your words. Sometimes, I wonder if Freemasonry isn't too narrow a setting for you.'

'It brings me so much!'

'And you bring it so much more! An awful lot of Freemasons seem terribly dull to me.'

'Initiates are often disappointing,' Wolfgang agreed. 'But initiation never is.'

The two musicians took leave of each other according to the Masonic custom.

19

Vienna, 5 February 1790

The imperial and royal Chamberlain, Count Johann Esterházy, was chairing the works at Crowned Hope Lodge for the initiation of the twenty-nine year old intellectual Karl Ludwig Giesecke. Born in Augsburg, he had studied Law in Göttingen before crossing Emanuel Schikaneder's path and starting to write adaptations for the theatre. An enthusiastic mineralogist, he dreamed of writing a libretto for an opera and even of directing a show.

There were two hundred Brothers on the lodge register, but only thirty turned up.

The Venerable stood in the Orient.

Behind him was a panel showing a sun, Solomon's seal and a rainbow that lit up the sea.

The hall had a high ceiling and was lit by a large chandelier, lamps and candles.

Among the decorative figures was the God Hermes, heir of Thoth, master of secret sciences.

Mozart gazed at the two large stones either side of three steps leading to the Orient. The first, the brute stone, represented the initiate's potential and the primary matter of the Great Alchemical Work; the second, the cubical stone, symbolised the universe in harmony and harboured the just proportions that presided at the birth of any life.

Participating at an initiation was always a moment of extraordinary intensity. A mortal, limited individual became a Brother and, from now on, belonged to the golden chain of initiates, forged at the birth of Light.

After the ritual, Mozart and Giesecke struck up a conversation.

'It was Schikaneder who recommended me to join the Freemasons,' the new Entered Apprentice told Wolfgang.

'Why is he not here, tonight?'

'Last May, he was excluded from his lodge in Ratisbon* because of bad behaviour. I don't know any more, but how can you resent such a wonderful man just because he is sometimes too outspoken and demonstrative? Personally, I am delighted I know him!'

Count Canal had come from Prague, and now he took Mozart to one side.

'Venerable Ignaz von Born is organizing an urgent meeting on the 14th. We are fighting for our future and the future of our rituals. We cannot do without you.'

* Karl of the Three Dice.

Vienna, 11 February 1790

Two further performances of *Così fan tutte* on the 7th and another one tonight had not been greeted with enthusiasm in Vienna, but Wolfgang's mind was on his impending trip to Prague. Thamos came to visit him.

'I think we ought to cancel this journey,' the Egyptian advised. 'Van Swieten has had word of a massive police operation, but he doesn't have any more details.'

'Perhaps the Freemasons of Prague won't be affected.'

'You shouldn't take any risks. When the Minister of Police, Count of Pergen, cracks down, he isn't joking. And the emperor has given him full powers. These days, all movements of thought are strictly controlled. The political and religious authorities refuse to tolerate the secrets of Freemasonry. I am going to Prague to assess the extent of the danger.'

Prague, 14 February 1790

Plainclothes policemen were on duty outside Truth and Union Lodge. Keeping a prudent distance, Thamos watched them come and go.

When he spotted a big man, heavy-jowled and unprepossessing with a lustreless expression, he remembered the description one of the hitmen trailing Ignaz von Born had given of his boss.

The Egyptian went to the house of Count Canal only

to find that the nobleman's home was under surveillance. There was nothing for it but to make his way to the emergency meeting point, a small house in the old city once occupied by alchemists.

Count Canal was expecting him.

'A disaster,' he declared. 'On the orders of Geytrand, the Police Chief's devoted crony, a special brigade is after us.'

The Egyptian described the man he had just seen at the lodge entrance.

'Yes, that's Geytrand all right. He does the dirty work.'

'He and Pergen are both creatures of the shadows and have been targeting Freemasonry for years,' said Thamos.

'He has placed several Brothers under surveillance and, in the name of state security, he has ransacked the lodge and its outbuildings.'

'What was there to find that might be compromising?'

'Nothing, really. Sadly, one of our Brothers made the grave mistake of leaving behind documents that should never have been left on our premises – lists of Masons, including adepts of our secret lodge.'

The Egyptian was aghast.

'A stupid administrative instinct,' the count said, shaking his head, 'but the damage is done.'

'Was everyone's name on it?'

'Not visiting Brothers, like Ignaz von Born, and you and Mozart. They are on another list which the idiot came to give me in a panic.'

Thamos ran his eye down the list then tore it into a thousand pieces, which he threw into the fire.

'I want to try to intercept Geytrand. If he gives those documents to the Chief of Police and if the emperor gets to know of them, the consequences could be disastrous.'

Thamos could tell Geytrand was a noxious element, as soon as he set eyes on him: a fearsome and insatiable predator.

When he got back to Truth and Union Lodge, the plainclothes policemen had gone. The Egyptian questioned the Serving Brother who was clearing up.

'When did they leave?'

'Over an hour ago.'

'How many were there?'

'About a dozen.'

Geytrand was not taking any risks. Even if he overtook him en route to Vienna, Thamos would not get anywhere with him.

20

Vienna, 17 February 1790

'Fascinating,' Joseph Anton acknowledged, when he saw the list Geytrand brought him. 'So, there is at least one secret lodge in Prague, attended, what's more, by some notorious Illuminati, like Count Canal, several top functionaries and a number of Mozart's friends and acquaintances. What a pity Mozart and von Born are not here!'

Suddenly, Anton's face tensed.

'Well, look at that: Number 14 is none other than the head of censorship, Baron van Swieten!'

Vienna, 18 February 1790

Although very weak, Emperor Josef II received Baron van Swieten.

'I know everything.'

'Your Majesty . . .'

'Don't interrupt! I am soon to meet my Creator and there are things that I must impart. In spite of your allegiance to the Masons, which you have carefully kept secret, you have given me loyal service and I have been satisfied with your good work. I am sure there is more to this Freemasonry than just evil, although the society remains a mystery to me. Of course, you cannot continue with censorship. Go on improving the imperial library, one of the jewels of our beautiful city. Your first duty is to the empire, Baron van Swieten. Never forget that.'

Vienna, 18 February 1790

Geytrand cowered under Joseph Anton's cold rage. In that moment, he felt as though he might kill him.

'Van Swieten has saved his skin! He is denying everything and talking of fake documents and false accusations against him aimed at ruining his career. And the emperor believes him!'

'He is ill and not in his right mind, my lord. All the same, he has appointed you head of censorship. The baron has had his hands well and truly tied. Once the inevitable happens, as it must, who will succeed Josef II?'

'His brother, Leopold.'

'Will he tolerate Freemasonry?'

'Like the Grand Duke of Tuscany, he stamped out the Inquisition and, I fear, a certain liberalism. But he hates the French Revolution and its proponents. I shall give him the files proving Viennese Freemasonry constitutes a real danger.'

Vienna, 19 February 1790

Having checked that the place was safe, Thamos beckoned van Swieten to come into the inn he had chosen. Mozart was waiting for him. The three Brothers ordered strong beer.

'I can no longer be of help to the Freemasons,' the Baron told them, regretfully. 'The Minister of Police will now have me under permanent surveillance and I cannot risk making any false move. It's nothing short of a miracle that I got away with my life.'

'Go on commissioning music from Mozart,' Thamos advised. 'A sudden break in your professional and social relations would prove that you feel guilty.'

'You're right,' van Swieten admitted. 'But I can't do more than that.'

Vienna, 20 February 1790

Wolfgang bought his Brother Puchberg a tankard of beer and borrowed twenty-five florins for urgent expenses. Just before dinner, Thamos made an announcement.

'Josef II died this morning at five-thirty. The official

115

mourning means all the theatres will be shut until 12 April.'

'That's *Così fan tutte* doomed to failure!' the composer lamented.

'Da Ponte will suggest more performances.'

'His chances are slim!'

'Josef II did not understand the importance of initiation as a set of principles that might have saved Europe from disaster. And I don't have much faith in his successor, Leopold II.'

'Do you think he is hostile to the Freemasons?'

'I am afraid so.'

Vienna, 13 March 1790

Leopold II, Marie-Antoinette's brother, arrived in Vienna with very clear ideas. His predecessor, Josef II, had left the nation in a shambles. He had never managed to win a decisive victory over the Turks in a costly war he should never have started and which was dragging on interminably. The only way to end it was by skilful negotiation, even if it meant riding roughshod over the fighting spirit of a few battle-hungry generals.

Another serious problem was the call for independence in the Austrian Netherlands. There once again, military intervention had proved catastrophic. The only answer was to abandon the use of force.

Now revolutionary ideas were making ripples in

Hungary with the encouragement of Prussia who hoped to weaken the Austrian Empire. Leopold II would not rush in but would favour diplomacy.

But worst of all was the French Revolution which threatened every throne in Europe and left no scope for negotiation. The empire was holding out, thanks to its army and the police.

Not surprisingly, Joseph Anton, Count of Pergen, was one of the first ministers to be granted an audience with the new emperor.

'Everything is under control, Your Majesty, and I shall work night and day to make sure it stays that way.'

'Don't hide any domestic dangers from me.'

'There is just one, and that is Freemasonry. It is currently being closely monitored, and if they overstep the limits, I shall clamp down immediately.'

'Do the lodges of Vienna support the French fanatics?'

'They wouldn't dare, Your Majesty, but, more or less on the quiet, some Brethren advocate subversive ideas, like the musician Mozart.'

'Does he have a position at court?'

'Only a minor one. He composes dance music for the La Redoute ballroom parties.'

'Make sure the Freemasons stay calm,' ordered Leopold II. 'Otherwise, weed out the trouble-makers.'

21

Vienna, 15 March 1790

At a meeting at Crowned Hope Lodge, an Italian Freemason made an announcement that caused his Brothers a good deal of consternation. Cagliostro had been arrested by the Inquisition in Rome, where he was trying to set up his Egyptian rite, on charges of magic, necromancy and Masonic allegiance. When he came before the judges at the Court of the Holy Office, he had launched into a series of resounding confessions.

According to him, the Freemasons of Strict Templar Observance and their allies wanted to overthrow every throne in Europe, starting with the King of France. They would then take on Italy and even the Pope. With subscriptions from 1,800,000 Brethren, the Freemasons enjoyed considerable wealth and had the means to dominate Europe.

'These tales will lead to harsh repression,' was

Thamos's prophecy. 'Now, the current regimes will be suspicious of the lodges and some will persecute them. Cagliostro is doing us a terrible wrong with his grandiloquence.'

'Let's tell Leopold II that we don't approve of the French Revolution,' Mozart suggested, 'and that we are his loyal subjects.'

Hoffmann, the traitor, would report these words to Geytrand. Nevertheless, he was disappointed that the musician had not perjured himself with an impassioned speech against the emperor.

Vienna, 29 March 1790

The situation was improving.

Mozart had sent Puchberg a biography of Handel to show him what a genius he had been, and the baron now lent him one hundred and fifty florins. More debts were thus wiped out.

Wolfgang felt that he would soon be back on an even keel, and he was buoyed up by fresh possibilities: Gottfried van Swieten, who had allayed all suspicion about him, believed that Leopold II might be about to offer Mozart a better situation at court as Vice-Kapellmeister.

Vienna, 2 April 1790

Joseph Anton was staggered.

According to information supplied by Brother Hoffman and the spies of the Archbishop of Vienna, Viennese Freemasonry was rising from the ashes.

Saint Joseph Lodge, where Joseph Lange, Mozart's brother-in-law was active, was 'rekindling its fires'. A new Lodge to Love and Truth had formed, which proclaimed its attachment to Leopold II, invoked his high protection and promised to combat perverse systems, which, under the mask of Freemasonry, were fostering impiety, criticizing religion, encouraging loose morals and challenging authority.

'Clap-trap!' thundered Joseph Anton. 'These corvettes are trying to persuade the emperor that the admiral vessel, Crowned Hope, is harmless. We must not be duped! Crowned Hope should be our main target.'

'Will His Majesty listen to you?' worried Geytrand.

'It is up to me to convince him.'

'We don't have concrete proof and documents. Venerable Count Esterházy is the emperor's faithful servant.'

'Esterházy is a puppet! The real leaders behind the scenes are Ignaz von Born and Mozart. Sooner or later, they are bound to make a fatal error.'

Vienna, 9 April 1790

Although suffering from a bout of rheumatism and violent headaches, Mozart took part in the concert given at the house of Count Hadik, where Stadler performed in the sublime Clarinet Quintet in A major*. Puchberg, who had just lent his Brother twenty-five florins, was pleased to be invited.

'Emperor Leopold II is restructuring the management of music at court,' Thamos told Wolfgang.

'Do you think he has my promotion in mind?'

'I am afraid not.'

'But, van Swieten . . .'

'He has saved his skin, but he is no longer in favour.'

It was a cruel disappointment.

'Am I going to be sacked?'

'I don't think so. Lorenzo Da Ponte's position, on the other hand, looks less secure. He wrote a florid letter to the new emperor but at the same time is issuing pamphlets against him. The Chief of Police will be quick to pick up on them and you will have to find another librettist.'

Lyon, 13 April 1790

The Unknown Agent, now no longer unknown, had a bruising interview with the Grand Profess, Jean-Baptiste Willermoz, the spiritual guide of mystic Freemasonry.

* K581.

'How dare you put about pro-Revolutionary opinions?' Madame de la Vallière demanded.

'History is on the move, my dear.'

'Coward! Hypocrite! All you think of is how to protect your fortune.'

'Madame!'

'The truth makes uncomfortable listening sometimes, doesn't it? In the past, you used to follow my instructions and pretend they came from God to establish power over your Brothers. Now you are worried about the Revolution and you are neglecting Christ and his Holy City.'

'Don't think that!'

'I am taking the archives of the Elect and Cherished Lodge away from you,' declared Madame de la Vallière, the Unknown Agent, 'and I am going to give it to a nobleman who will have the courage of his convictions.'

'Think it over, please.'

'Farewell.'

Willermoz did not take this rupture too seriously. He would tell his disciples that the noblewoman had gone mad.

Vienna, 1 May 1790

Still as busy as ever with Masonic activities, Mozart was tinkering with his *La Clemenza di Tito*, the opera he was writing for Prague on a theme that didn't interest him. At the same time, he was composing a Quartet for the King of Prussia. Persistent toothache and migraines sapped his inspiration, and in spite of his aversion to teaching, he was thinking about taking on more pupils. Next summer, health permitting, he would try to give subscription concerts, but he was not sure the Viennese public was interested in him.

He needed at least six hundred florins to write in peace and not have to think about debts and court proceedings. And now Constance was ill and had to go back to Baden, and the owner of a fancy goods shop was hammering on his door for overdue payment amounting to one hundred florins!

The merchant had his shop at the crossroads between Cathedral Square and the Graben, on Stock-im-Eisen, so-called because a tree trunk stood there ringed by an iron band that had been forged by the devil. Before leaving Vienna to tour the lodges of Europe, Fellow Crafts had stuck the trunk with nails to make sure it stayed put and to attract good luck.

Puchberg was sympathetic and sent his Brother Wolfgang one hundred florins to reimburse the merchant.

22

Vienna, 15 May 1790

The Marriage of Figaro received three more performances on the 1st, 7th and 9th. Mozart had not been totally forgotten. He had barely composed anything since *Così fan tutte* and was struggling to finish the second Quartet dedicated to the King of Prussia*, an arid piece in which the final Allegro provided the only light note.

Wolfgang wrote to Archduke Franz appealing to him to use his influence on his behalf with his father, Leopold II:

> *The ambition for glory, a love of action and awareness of my knowledge prompt me to ask for the position of Vice-Kapellmeister, especially because the very talented Kapellmeister, Salieri,*

* K589.

*has neglected church composition, whereas I have,
since my youth, been a master of the form. The
few honours which the world has done my piano
playing encourage me, too, to beg His Majesty to
entrust the royal family to my musical teaching.*

The composer never received a reply.

Vienna, 16 May 1790

Joseph Anton's case against the Illuminati who had
infiltrated the lodges was damning. Of course, their last
leader, Bode, now safely out of the way in Weimar, had
published a pamphlet refuting the theory that they were
preparing a universal revolution. But some of his friends
said the opposite, like von Knigge, who had retired to
Bremen where he had written a three-volume apology for the French Revolution. The *Hamburg Political
Review* had no qualms about accusing the Illuminati
and some of the Freemasons of engendering French
Jacobinism and hatching underground plots to bring
down the German Empire and all the European monarchies. Former Illuminatus and renegade Leopold-Aloys
Hoffmann used his periodical, the *Wiener Zeitschrift*,
to make insinuations, while the *Magazin der Kunst
und Literatur*, originally run by Jesuits, also propa-
gated malicious rumours. The Archbishop of Vienna
confirmed the danger.

Day by day, using documents and newspaper articles to support his arguments, the Count of Pergen was shaping Leopold II's opinion. In these troubled times, surely such a powerful secret society represented a peril that should not be tolerated?

Vienna, 17 May 1790

Legal proceedings recommenced. With only two pupils when he needed at least eight, Wolfgang had to borrow from money-lenders. He was finding it hard to finish his third Quartet for the King of Prussia. Another loan of one hundred and fifty florins from Puchberg enabled him to stay afloat, but working in such conditions was almost more than he could manage, and had it not been for the solace of his Masonic meetings and Constance's help, he might have given up the struggle.

As he was leaving the lodge, a Brother lawyer spoke to him in an undertone.

'The government of Lower Austria is giving you trouble, I hear?'

'Something like that,' Mozart concurred.

'They're taking legal action and demanding a huge sum and threatening to seize your salary, aren't they?'

'It's terribly unfair!'

'Do you know who is behind these proceedings?'

'I have no idea.'

'Our Brother, Prince Karl von Lichnowsky. I need not tell you that we haven't had this conversation!'

Vienna, 22 May 1790

Mozart gave a concert of chamber music in his apartment*, attended by Puchberg and his wife.

He could not get over Lichnowsky's betrayal! How could a Brother be so duplicitous? And why did he want his downfall? Had he been dastardly enough to ally himself with enemies of the Masonic lodges?

He could not talk to his Sister, Countess Thun, about it, now that Lichnowsky was married to one of her daughters. And there was no point alarming Puchberg. As for Ignaz von Born, his health was frail and Wolfgang's discussions with him turned on the symbols and he did not want to burden him with his money troubles.

But there was Thamos. At the thought of telling him, Wolfgang was overcome with shame and decided to extricate himself alone. Given what a wicked accusation it was, his innocence would be proved sooner or later.

---

* Quartets K575 and 589 were played.

Vienna, 2 June 1790

Constance had gone to take the waters in Baden. Still struggling to compose, Wolfgang sketched out some piano pieces* in which he somehow managed to put form to his despair. Then he set to work on the third Quartet dedicated to the King of Prussia, a wild, sorrowful, almost brutal piece shot through with protestations against injustice. This meditation on adversity made him better able to confront it and recover his energy after the battle.

Technically, Wolfgang still had three more Quartets to compose for his illustrious commissioner, but the project was too far from his true calling and they never saw the light of day. Instead, a fourth Masonic opera began to take shape in his mind, a work that would convey his vision of the Great Mysteries and the future of initiation.

Baden, 6 June 1790

Wolfgang and Constance clung to each other.

'I missed you so much,' he told her. 'And I wanted to tell you the good news: tonight, they're doing *Così*! My opera has been scheduled for the 12th and 22nd, as well.'

'One of your admirers, the tanner, Rindum, gave me a boiled leather bath for my foot. It aids treatment, although it would work still better if you were with me.'

---

* Fragments K590 a, b and c, and *Allegro in G minor*, K312.

'And that's what I intend, my darling! It is just meetings and the performance on the 12th that are calling me back to Vienna. How many baths has the doctor prescribed?'

'About sixty, with another cure in the autumn. The cost . . .'

'Don't worry about that. Your health comes first.'

Life with Constance gave Mozart incomparable happiness. Without her equanimity and strength of mind, Wolfgang could not have gone on with his work.

Vienna, 12 June 1790

Before conducting *Così fan tutte*, Mozart wrote to Puchberg and received twenty-five florins by return of post. He told his Brother frankly that he was having to sell the three Prussian Quartets it had cost him such an effort to write for next to nothing. But he needed the money so badly that he was not going to argue. To improve his situation, he was planning to compose some piano sonatas, and he was delighted when, the following day, one of his Masses* was performed in Baden.

* K317.

Vienna, 24 June 1790

In defiance of the prohibition of the deceased Josef II, Mozart composed three pieces for the Midsummer festivities at his Lodge to Crowned Hope.

First, for the ritual Opening, the choir sang *Lay down your tools today*, appealing to the Brothers to stop their usual work and celebrate the triumph of the light with joy; then a short *Song for the poor* recalled the Freemasons' charitable vocation, which justified their existence in the eyes of authority; finally came *The song of the Human Chain*, to words by Brother Aloys Blumauer.

Together with Anton Stadler, the Jacquins, Puchberg and Thamos, Wolfgang experienced moments of wonder when the sun of brotherhood shone with all its might.

23

Vienna, 17 July 1790

Although *Così fan tutte* was only coolly received, the Burgtheater agreed to two further performances on the 6th and 16th, neither of which elicited much enthusiasm. On Thamos's advice, Baron Gottfried van Swieten commissioned Mozart to write two arrangements of pieces by Handel*.

These modest assignments earned the composer some money and took his mind off the fact that at his last lodge meeting, he had seen his persecutor, Karl von Lichnowsky. The prince had looked quite unperturbed and had had the gall to swagger over to Mozart and ask after his Brother's health.

All he got in reply was silence and a black look. The

---

* *Alexander's Feast* or *The Power of Music*, K591, and *Ode to the Feast of St Cecilia*, K592.

hypocrite had turned away and chatted easily with the nobility there.

Wolfgang could not understand how a Brother could behave in this way. Yet the ignominy of a Freemason must not lead him to doubt initiation, the path to Enlightenment that transcended human nature.

Anton Stadler emptied another tankard of beer.

'Our clarinet manufacturer is getting on splendidly, but his research is a costly business.'

'How much does he want?'

'At least five hundred florins.'

'That's extortionate!'

'It's worth the challenge, believe me.'

'Very well, I'll see what I can do.'

Wolfgang knew that some of the money would be used to support the Stadler family, where seven children now strained their father's slender resources; the rest would help finance the manufacture of the wonderful instrument of his dreams. He had no option.

Vienna, 25 July 1790

Joseph Anton was reading a detailed report from one of his agents based in France. On 14 July, Paris had celebrated National Federation Day on the Champ-de-Mars in the presence of the royal family. The Revolution seemed to have taken a peaceful turn and be leading to a constitutional monarchy as Leopold II, among other sovereigns, would have liked.

The truth was less reassuring. Several counter-revolution protests had been violently dispersed, and on 12 July, the Constituent Assembly had voted in the Civil Constitution of the Clergy, which amounted to selling off Church property and destroying one of the pillars of French society.

'The Revolutionaries want to force Louis XVI to give in,' the Head of Police told Geytrand.

'That would mean the end of the monarchy!'

'That's exactly what the trouble-makers intend! And the Freemasons support them, as that song they sang at Federation Day proves: "The Lodge of Freedom arises with aplomb. Many a tyrant despairs. People from everywhere, the same lessons will make you Brothers and Masons. That is our comfort. "'

'Leopold II will realise what is going on,' was Geytrand's opinion.

Lyon, 26 July 1790

Jean-Baptiste Willermoz, the undisputed head of mystical Freemasonry, felt duty bound to give his followers his interpretation of the decision of the National Constituent Assembly. His allegiance to the Christian tradition made it imperative to defend it tooth and nail.

'The Revolution may not be wrong,' he ventured. 'The Church itself was condemned for having overlooked

Christ's esoteric message. If an official religion is instituted, why might I not become the grand priest and you, my Brothers Profess, my assistants? You would be given the positions of the sacked priests and spread our doctrine throughout the new France.'

This time, Willermoz's patter did not have the desired effect, because most of the Grand Profess were opposed to dismantling the traditional clergy. After the Church, the Revolutionaries might attack royalty itself and the lodges in the name of Christianity.

Disconcerted, Willermoz abandoned the idea of becoming the supreme priest of the Revolution. He might as well stay in Lyon to observe the course of events and adapt to the circumstances.

Vienna, 29 July 1790

The Secretary of Crowned Hope Lodge read out a curious letter from the Bordeaux Brethren to their Brothers in Vienna[*]:

> *"'Although our great Society rarely takes part in political events, it cannot remain insensitive to those that might strengthen it. Such are the principles of the New Constitution in the French Empire. They are entirely in harmony with the bases of*

---

[*] Cf. P. Autexier, *La Lyre maçonne*, p. 110.

Freemasonry: freedom, equality, justice, tolerance, philosophy, charity and good order, and they thus promise the most salutary effects for the good and for the propagation of the Royal Art.

'"Indeed, any good French citizen will now make a worthy Mason because he will be free and virtuous.

'"At the recent Midsummer Festival of St John, this hopeful prospect filled the hearts of our fellows with unadulterated merriment and civic enthusiasm, and they were the first to drink to the health of the Nation, the law and the king; the tribute was made in earnest, and a disciplinary lodge was immediately organized to decide whether, in future, the same toast should be the first.

'"The matter was discussed at length and it was decided that the custom observed hitherto in French lodges relating to the first toast, in the name of the king and his august family, was an acknowledgement of the tacit protection which the monarch granted our works and a mark of the wisdom of our laws which, although republican, nevertheless concur with the laws of monarchies, such that there can, in no case, be a clash between them.

'"But the current form of the government under which we exist has naturally led us to consider that all the lodges of France are only sections of the Universal Grand Lodge that extends across the whole globe; that in all the lodges established

> *in other free countries where Freemasonry is*
> *most in force and respected, there is never a toast*
> *to the health of kings; that the custom practised*
> *hitherto in the lodges of our empire could not*
> *accord with the new Constitution, and that we are*
> *therefore guided by wisdom in all circumstances*
> *to pay the first homage to the gentle influences of*
> *the nascent liberty."'*

Most of the Brothers, including Mozart, were scandalized. Such attitudes implied, in the short-term, the disappearance of royalty in favour of a dictatorial regime where the only law would be the doctrinal madness of its leaders.

Crowned Hope decided not to answer the letter. The traitor Hoffmann immediately sent it to Geytrand to fatten his file on the Freemasons.

Vienna, 14 August 1790

Così fan tutte was performed for the last time on 7 August: the public had liked it even less than *Don Giovanni*. Mozart's career as a writer of opera was over, and the Burgtheater never again put on a work by a composer so little appreciated.

Sick at heart and unable to work, Wolfgang had nothing but his lessons to live from. Again, he was obliged to write to Puchberg.

Very dear friend and Brother, he wrote, *although my condition was bearable yesterday, I am in a very bad way today. I cannot get a wink of sleep, I am in such pain. I must have got overheated yesterday as I rushed about and caught a chill without realizing. Could you possibly support me with a little something?*

The ten florins he received that same day were welcome, and an excellent dinner with Thamos had beneficial effects.

'You don't seem in very good health,' remarked the Egyptian.

'Just passing fatigue.'

'There's nothing serious bothering you?'

'Other than the future of initiation, nothing important.'

'Tomorrow we will go and see our initiated Brothers from Asia. Their founder, Ecker-une-Eckhoffen, has just passed away, and they seem to have come unstuck.'

24

Vienna, 15 August 1790

Mozart and Thamos the Egyptian attended the last meeting of the Rose-Cross Royal and True Priests, the high degree of the initiated Brothers of Asia, whose numbers had dramatically declined. The death of their founder had struck a fatal blow to those researchers who associated the esoteric tradition of St John the Evangelist with the Hebrew Cabbala. Rejecting both the literal interpretation of the Talmud and the Bible, the Brethren opened the door of their lodges to scholarly Jews who revealed the treasures of the *Zohar, The Book of Splendour* to them.

In striving to reconcile Jews and Christians and research the Philosopher's Stone, the adepts had attracted considerable enemies. The dignitaries yielded to the threat of the Chief of Police, judging it better to end their activities and dissolve the Order.

Before closing the last meeting, they entrusted some precious texts to their visitors.

Vienna, 3 September 1790

The revival of *The Marriage of Figaro*, the only opera by Mozart in the Viennese repertory, coincided with Leopold II's first real successes. To begin with, he concluded the armistice with the Sublime Porte, the Ottoman Court in Constantinople, thereby ending the war with the Turks; then, he negotiated the future of a large part of Europe with Frederick-William II, King of Prussia.

Only the deteriorating situation in France cast a shadow over the otherwise bright outlook; but perhaps Louis XVI would still find a way to soothe his most agitated subjects . . .

However, Leopold II was not to be prevented from planning a journey to Frankfurt to have himself crowned on 9 October. The court sent out invitations to, among others, Antonio Salieri and sixteen musicians, asking them to attend the ceremonies.

'My name is not on the list!' Mozart exclaimed, in disgust.

'I should have been surprised if it had been,' Thamos replied. 'Salieri and his friends hate you and your Masonic allegiance does nothing to help your case.'

'I must go to Frankfurt.'

'At your own cost?'

'Every musician not at the coronation will be marginalized at court. And there will be so many grandees there that one owes it to oneself to put in an appearance and try to win commissions, or even a decent job.'

His argument was not unreasonable.

'But I have other things on my mind, too,' Wolfgang admitted.

'Your next ritual opera?'

'You know me better than I know myself!'

'You will soon be ready to write the Great Work, my Brother. In spite of the difficulties, it will come to you.'

Vienna, 11 September 1790

Emanuel Schikaneder gave Mozart's slim hand a vigorous shake.

'Could you write an aria for me, for my new show, *The Philosopher's Stone*? I need something amusing and uplifting, a comic duet for soprano and bass called "Now, my dear little wife, come with me!"'

'The Philosopher's Stone . . . Do you think a show is the place for such a serious subject?'

'Out in the suburbs where I run that theatre owned by one of our Brothers, audiences flock to see fantasy. Why not treat them to our favourite themes? I'm good at adapting works by famous authors, and I can easily mix comedy and tragedy. Our friend Benedikt Schack can write the music and the plot will involve an Egyptian magician and his comic side-kick who are prepared to face the ordeals of the elements in order to find the Philosopher's Stone.'

'Forgive my asking, but I have to know: have you left the Freemasons?'

'Me? Good heavens, no!'

'Rumour has it you've been expelled from your lodge in Ratisbon.'

'Idle gossip! I'm still a member, I assure you.'

'Why don't you visit Crowned Hope?'

Schikaneder ran his hand through his hair.

'The theatre is my whole life! I've been discreetly told that if I want to stay in Vienna and work in peace, I shouldn't have anything to do with the Masons. And your lodge has a very bad name with the police.'

'I'll write that aria for you,' Wolfgang promised.

'While you wait for something better, I hope!'

Vienna, 23 September 1790

Gaukerl had the crestfallen air of an abandoned dog.

'This time,' Wolfgang told him, ruefully, 'I can't take you with me. You can keep house and look after Constance and Karl Thomas.'

On the 15th, Mozart had again been humiliated by Leopold II. The King and Queen of Naples, Ferdinand and Maria-Carolina, the emperor's brother-in-law and sister, were in Vienna to celebrate the engagements of their daughters to the Archdukes Franz and Ferdinand, Leopold II's sons. Several musicians, including Haydn and Salieri, had been invited to the court concerts.

But not the Freemason Mozart.

And on the 20th, at his first public appearance at the theatre, Leopold II had chosen an opera by Salieri, the court's principal musician.

Mozart, meanwhile, had to make do with his minor, subordinate role.

The only solution was to attend the coronation ceremonies, display his talent and make up for so much injustice.

This time, however, he could not ask Puchberg for help, for the banker would have thought the enterprise crazy.

As for Constance, her main concern was to see her husband recover his zest for life and start composing again.

Wolfgang sold his silver and furniture, borrowed a thousand florins from the money-lender Heinrich Lackenbacher to be repaid over two years and obtained a guarantee of two thousand florins from one of his publishers, Brother Hoffmeister, in exchange for luxurious sheets and future compositions. With this financial backing, he could cover his travel costs and enjoy the comfort of his own carriage so as not to get over-tired.

His brother-in-law, the violinist Franz Hofer and his servant Joseph went with him.

'This journey won't be in vain,' he promised Constance.

'Take the time to enjoy yourself a little and come back to me full of enthusiasm and new plans.'

'Our move to another apartment . . .'

'I'll look after that.'

'Dear, excellent little wife! What would I do without you?'

25

Frankfurt-on-Main, 28 September 1790

Mozart was half in love with the splendid carriage he had hired for a pleasant six-day journey, which included some gastronomic stopovers. In Ratisbon, the guests dined in style, drank an outstanding Mosel wine, and were entertained by divine *Tafelmusik* and served by charming waitresses!

Nuremberg he considered a dreadful city, but Würzburg was superb!

As soon as he arrived in Frankfurt, Wolfgang wrote to Constance to tell her his travel stories and assure her that he would manage his affairs with firmness. Then, what a wonderful life they would lead! *I shall work and work*, he promised, *so that we don't fall back into such a desperate situation, even in unforeseen circumstances*. Thanks to the latest financial arrangements before he left, all his debts would be written off and he could get on with the business of composing.

As agreed, Thamos and Mozart met outside the inn.

'No spook,' the Egyptian said. 'Given the numbers of police deployed to look out for the emperor and his guests, they will soon know you are here. I shall contact as many Brothers as possible to find out if any of the lodges are fully functioning.'

Frankfurt-on-Main, 30 September 1790

Wolfgang and his travelling companions lodged at the house of the actor and impresario, Johann Heinrich Boehm. The rent, at thirty florins per month, was modest.

In *Lanassa*, the 'Hindu' play Boehm had just put on, Boehm had had no compunction about using passages from *Thamos, King of Egypt*.

'This story about the priests of the sun is fascinating, Mozart. Have you thought of developing it?'

'Oh, yes, it's been in my mind for years.'

'Then don't hesitate: it will be a great success.'

Wolfgang wrote to Constance again to tell her he could not stop thinking about money troubles and to confirm his intention of working hard. Away from her, he felt sad and lost.

I feel like a child, I am so looking forward to seeing you again, he confessed. *If people could see into my heart, I'd almost be ashamed. Everything looks frozen and icy to me. If you were beside me, I might take more pleasure from people's attitude to me. As it is, it is all so empty.*

Constance, Karl Thomas and Gaukerl moved to an apartment at 970, Rauhenstiengasse, on the first floor of a 'miniature emperor's house' close to the city centre. With a surface area of one hundred and forty-five square metres, the four-room flat was rather dark, but it had one pleasant, light and airy room with two corner windows, which Constance decided to keep for her husband's studio. A glazed door opened into the billiard room, the couple's favourite pastime.

A large fireplace in the entrance hall and a pipe leading to the stove in the drawing room meant this space also served as the kitchen. In it, they put two tables, two beds, a cupboard and a screen behind which the two servants would sleep. In the first room were two chests of drawers, a sofa, six chairs and a night table. In the second, three tables, two divans, six chairs, two lacquered cupboards, a mirror and a chandelier. In the third, the billiard table with five balls and two cues, a table, a lantern, four candle sticks, a stove, the couple's double bed and a child's bed. In the fourth, the studio, a pedal pianoforte, a viola, a table, a sofa, six chairs, a desk, a clock, two book cases, a bureau, sixty pieces of porcelain, five candle sticks two of which were made of glass, two coffee grinders and a tin teapot.

As she folded away five fine tablecloths, sixteen serviettes, sixteen towels and ten sheets, Constance hoped the new setting would please Wolfgang and that he would find inspiration in it.

Frankfurt-on-Main, 2 October 1790

'What are you working on?' Thamos asked Wolfgang.

'An Adagio* for mechanical organ with small high-pitched pipes. It's a commission that will make me a tidy sum, but it's a labour of love! I work on it every day, but I keep having to put it aside.'

'You aren't worried about money, are you?'

'I'm managing.'

'Would you agree to meet Franz Schweitzer, the richest merchant in town? I had a recommendation from the Countess Hatzfeld and asked him to advise you.'

The name of the Brother Hatzfeld who had died so young and whom Mozart had loved so well was decisive and he agreed.

The midday dinner was cordial. Schweitzer was a frank, straight-talking businessman and Mozart took him into his confidence. He told him about his latest financial

* K594.

backing and the debt he owed Heinrich Lackenbacher, with the totality of his furniture as guarantee.

'I don't like this fellow, Mr Mozart, and I advise you to clear your debt without delay.'

'Alas, I'm in no position to do so.'

'Some of your friends are, and those thousand florins will be found for you.'

'I could never agree to that!'

'Don't be ridiculous. From what you say – and I promise this won't go any further than this room – your struggle is far from over. The money will unfortunately only go part way to filling the yawning gulf at your feet.'

'Who is helping me in this way?'

'Friends . . . Don't worry about Lackenbacher, I shall take care of him*.'

'Please pass on my heartfelt thanks to Countess Hatzfeld. I shall always hold the memory of her son in great affection.'

The merchant took his leave.

Frankfurt-on-Main, 3 October 1790

So far I have been living a very retiring life, Wolfgang wrote to Constance, *and I don't go out all morning but stay in this hole that is my room,*

---

* At Mozart's death, this money-lender did not appear among Mozart's creditors.

composing. My only relaxation is the theatre where I see many friends from Vienna, Munich, Mannheim and even Salzburg. I fear a busy life is about to begin – people are already asking to see me everywhere – and although I don't like expos-ing myself to being stared at to left and right, I can nevertheless see the need for it, and, in the name of God, I shall have to go through with it. I suppose my concert will not go too badly and I want it to be over only in order to hasten the moment when I shall embrace you again, my love!

Frankfurt-on-Main, 8 October 1790

On the 4th, Leopold II had entered his coronation city to the blare of trumpets, with a retinue of 1493 carriages, each one drawn by four or six horses. Antonio Salieri swaggered among the guests.

Contrary to expectations, it was not *Don Giovanni* that was performed by the visiting company from Mainz but an opera by Ditters von Dittersdorf, *Love in Exile*. The company's impresario hated the Freemasons and refused to help Mozart shine.

Still anxious about his financial future, Wolfgang begged Constance to wind up the business begun with his Brother Hoffmeister and to seek help instead from Anton Stadler, if needs be. In that way, they would soon have plenty of money.

With the help of Schweitzer and Countess Hatzfeld, he was soon able to give a concert, although there was scant hope he would make a fortune because the good people of Frankfurt were even more penny-pinching than the Viennese.

On his return, he would offer some quartets for subscription and take on more pupils.

If only you could see into my heart, he told her, *I am torn between wanting you and desiring to see you and kiss you again, and the urge to bring home a lot of money. I love you too much to stay away from you too long. And there is so much ostentation in the cities of the Empire!*

Wolfgang was aware how much he had changed. Travelling, glory, applause, superficial contacts: such things no longer interested him.

Another life was calling him.

26

Frankfurt-on-Main, 15 October 1790

To mark Leopold II's coronation on the 9th, Vincenzo Righini's *Solemn Mass* was sung in the Cathedral under the baton of Antonio Salieri. On the 12th, Boehm's troop gave a lively performance of *The Abduction from the Seraglio*, and on the 15th at eleven o'clock in the morning, Mozart finally appeared in the concert he had so much been hoping to give at the municipal theatre. Until early afternoon, dressed in a fine satin suit, he played two concerti and conducted a symphony before rounding off the concert with improvisations.

The audience was thin on the ground and revenue was meagre, because the sovereign was giving a great banquet that day and the troops of Hesse were starting manoeuvres. Despite these other distractions, Frankfurt was eager for another concert. Nettled, Wolfgang wanted nothing more than to return to Vienna, but he agreed to play for them again.

On the 16th, he left the coronation city with relief, stopping off at the house of a famous music publisher, Johann André.

'Your pieces have become too difficult, Mozart. You really must try to give the public what they want.'

'I would rather starve to death than go against my own vision of music.'

Mannheim, 22 October 1790

After playing at the Palace of Mainz in the presence of the Prince-Elector, for which he received one hundred and sixty-five florins, Mozart stayed in Mannheim. On the 24th, his *Marriage of Figaro* was to be performed there for the first time.

Outside the door to the hall where rehearsals were taking place, Backhaus, a young actor, stood guard. But Wolfgang did not like what he heard.

'May I go in?'

'Entry is forbidden,' Backhaus answered, tersely. 'Come back on the 24th and pay for your ticket.'

'Won't you let Mozart listen to his own opera?'

The actor trembled from head to foot.

'You surely aren't . . .'

'I should just think I am!'

The door opened. Singers and musicians begged the composer to advise them, and so he attended the dress rehearsal; afterwards, he went on his way.

Munich, 4 November 1790

On the 29th, Mozart had lodged with his old friend Albert, 'the scholarly innkeeper' of the Black Eagle, and that same evening he went to see his Brothers Cannabich and Marchand, together with Thamos.

No one was following him.

Wolfgang had only expected to stay for a day, but the Freemasons organised a special meeting and invited him to take part in a concert in honour of the visiting King Ferdinand IV of Naples and his wife, in the Emperor's Hall of the Residence.

The entertainment was much appreciated and proved excellent for his renown. Above all, the atmosphere at the meeting was friendly and there was plenty of music played by superb musicians who did much to lift the spirits of the downhearted composer.

He wrote a short note to Constance, describing these happy moments and suggesting they repeat the journey together the following summer and try another cure. A change of air would do them both good.

Vienna, 10 November 1790

Karl Thomas, now aged six, ran to kiss his father. Gaukerl was jealous and insisted on being petted. With these first duties accomplished, Wolfgang was at last able to clasp Constance in his arms.

'How do you like our new apartment?'

'Splendid!'

'Come and see your study.'

It was the lightest room in the house and the composer liked it immediately, already envisaging the reams of manuscript paper that he would cover with black ink.

'Thank you for managing our affairs so efficiently, my darling, and seeing to the move. With a little surprise help in Frankfurt and the small sums I've earned, we can sign a loan for a thousand florins straight away by mortgaging our furniture.'

Constance approved of this step. Gradually, the Mozarts were emerging from financial turmoil.

'You've had a letter from England.'

He opened it and to his astonishment read:

'To Mr Mozart, the famous composer in Vienna.
Through a person associated with His Royal Highness the Prince of Wales, I have come to hear of your intention to travel to England, and as I wish to make personal contact with people of talent and am in a position to contribute to their livelihood, I should like to offer you, Mr Mozart, a position as a composer. If you could arrange to be in London from the end of December until the end of June 1791 and compose at least two serious or comic operas, according to the choice of the Directorate, I can offer you three hundred pounds sterling, with the advantage of writing for the Professional Concert

*or any other concert hall, with the exception only
of other theatres. If this proposition is agreeable to
you and if you can accept it, kindly reply in writing
and this letter will act as a contract.*

I remain, Mr Mozart, your obedient servant.

*Robert Bray O'Reilly, Manager of the Italian
Opera in London.'*

England, the country of freedom, new glory, two
operas, money . . . But he would have to comply with the
decisions of the Directorate and leave Vienna for several
long months which he intended to devote to work on
his next ritual opera, in collaboration with Thamos and
Ignaz von Born.

In London, he would be protected and far from the
police and the jealousy and pettiness of Salieri and his
cronies. But ought he to abandon his lodge and flee like
a coward?

The offer came either too late or too early. Before being
initiated, Mozart might have answered in the affirmative. Still, if the persecution of the Freemasons became
intolerable, he would know where to take refuge.

Vienna, 5 December 1790

With the agreement of Prussia, the Austrian army once
more occupied Brussels. Hungary was calmer and the
Turks were accepting peace. Triumphant, Leopold II

could forget foreign politics for a while and concentrate on restoring order to the different sectors of the government and turn his attention to agriculture and ecclesiastic matters.

Everyone felt the strong arm of their sovereign, whose decisions and actions were influenced by his Minister of Police, the Count of Pergen, now master of his army of functionaries and informers.

Mozart, meanwhile, was earning his keep more easily, thanks to two new, high-placed pupils. 'Please play me something,' he had asked Dr Frank, and the amateur pianist had played his best for the composer.

'Not bad! Now listen to this.'

Wolfgang's strong, nimble fingers developed dazzling improvisations on the theme hesitantly begun by Frank.

'What a miracle!' the doctor exclaimed. 'Under your fingers, the piano turns into several different instruments at once!'

It was the only way Wolfgang knew how to teach. Lessons bored him so much that he spent most of the time improvising, laying the groundwork for future compositions. And it was not that confounded Adagio and Allegro for mechanical organ that was going to reignite his passion for creating! However, he was bound to finish the commission from Count Joseph Deym, a curious fellow also known as Müller, who had once had to leave Vienna for a shady business involving a duel. Once back in the capital, he had founded a kind of gallery, where he displayed wax figurines of recently deceased personalities, such as

Field-Marshal Laudon, who had died on 14 July. And it was at the public exhibition of his statuette that Deym's mechanical organ, described as a 'musical clock', was going to play Mozart's funeral music.

'I sometimes wonder if I'll ever get to the end of it,' he groaned to Constance.

'Get rid of this millstone as quickly as you can.'

'I'll get back to it.'

Constance hid her anxiety, but privately she wondered when her husband would show his true genius again.

27

A well-intentioned colleague had sent Wolfgang an article from the serious Berlin *Musikalisches Wochenblatt*: '*There can be no connoisseur who holds Mozart to be a serious artist or even simply correct. Still less could the discerning critic believe him to be a subtle composer.*'

'Forget about those fools and their like,' Thamos advised.

'But I'm becoming a laughing stock!'

'Your operas are already performed in many countries by strolling players who earn money from them, although unfortunately that doesn't benefit you. Your compositions will soon transcend the bounds of your existence.'

'But that's the point: I've stopped composing! I've composed next to nothing this year.'

'Our Brother Johann Tost, a Hungarian amateur

violinist, likes your chamber music. He wants to buy a big score for a handsome sum.'

'A string quintet. I haven't written one for three years.'

Wolfgang immediately seized his pen.

Seeing him absorbed already, Thamos withdrew.

'How did you find him?' Constance asked him, anxiously.

'He is composing.'

The young woman's smile showed her profound relief.

At last, her husband was coming out of the darkness!

Vienna, 10 December 1790

'Good news!' exclaimed Anton Stadler, raising his tankard.

'Your new child?' Wolfgang asked.

'The birth went well! I wanted to talk to you about old Leopold Hoffmann, Kapellmeister at St Stephen's Cathedral. He is seriously ill and this is the moment to ask to replace him. With a career like yours, you'd be snapped up by the city council. You like playing the organ, so the job should be more to your liking than teaching!'

'You're not wrong, but . . .'

'I've written an application in administrative terms. All you need do is sign it. You should at least apply.'

Vienna, 14 December 1790

Before dining with an impresario from London, Mozart, Joseph Haydn and three other Brothers played through the Quintet in D major* that finally broke a long silence and marked Wolfgang's return to composition.

The first movement was characterized by anguish and strife. Everyone remarked on the creator's ability to organize such a raging whirlwind before launching into an Adagio of such searing intensity that it sounded as though it might have destroyed him. The Menuetto suggested lucid serenity, the final Allegro, incredible energy. Youth was absent, now, yet the composer's strength remained intact.

Johann Peter Salomon, the London impresario, imperiously graced with his presence the sumptuous banquet Mozart offered.

'I am delighted to be engaging the illustrious Joseph Haydn,' he announced, 'to give several concerts for a handsome remuneration! Following the death of Prince Nikolaus Esterházy, his successor Prince Anton is giving him an annual pension of two thousand florins, and above all, his freedom!'

Mozart was distraught to hear that Haydn was leaving.

'Dear Papa, you aren't built to travel the world, and you speak so few languages!'

'The language I speak is spoken the world over.'

* K593.

'How right Haydn is!' declared Salomon, approvingly. 'You should come to London, too, Mozart. Glory and fortune await you there!'

'Pressing obligations are keeping me in Vienna.'

'I shall find a way to convince you, you'll see!'

The moment came to say farewell.

'Are you really so upset?' Haydn asked, anxiously.

'I feel as though this is the last time I shall ever see you.'

'Don't talk nonsense! I am no longer as young as I was and I hate travelling, but I shall come back and tell you all about my experiences in London. It will soon be your turn to stun the English.'

Vienna, 25 December 1790

Christmas morning, Karl Thomas' shining eyes as he opened his presents, Gaukerl's delight at the festive fare, Constance's love: so much happiness consoled Wolfgang for his grief.

'I dared to call Haydn "papa", my Brother for just one evening! He has always supported me and never let me down. Our separation is hard to bear. I understand his move and I approve of it. In London, he will at last be appreciated as he deserves, and the whole of Europe will salute his work. But no longer being able to talk to him and make music with him hurts terribly.'

'I share your feelings,' Constance said, 'because

Joseph Haydn loves you like a father. Maybe I can help you bear his absence.'

Wolfgang clasped his wife's hands affectionately in his.

'I'm pregnant,' she murmured.

Paris, 26 December 1790

'I am rejecting the Civil Constitution of the Clergy,' Louis XVI told Marie-Antoinette. 'The priests are no longer appointed by the Pope and have to take an oath to profane authorities.'

'Won't that provoke the wrath of extremists?'

'Their aim is less and less veiled. They want to wipe out the monarchy and impose military and police tyranny in the name of grand ideals that will plunge France into turmoil.'

'How can we avoid it?' asked the queen.

'I was hoping to find common ground with the Constituent Assembly. But that was nothing but an illusion. I now know that our duty is to fight this Revolution. We must therefore leave Paris, which has become an open-air prison, and cross the eastern border to join our German and Austrian allies. Once abroad, we will start a war to win back our country.'

'I approve, Your Majesty.'

28

Vienna, 29 December 1790

'Let me introduce our Brother Franz-Heinrich Ziegenhagen,' said Thamos to Mozart. 'He comes from Hamburg and is hoping to reform Freemasonry.'

'The Freemasons cannot go on like this,' said Ziegenhagen. 'Our lodges are full of dull nobility, bourgeois gentlemen who just want to network and intellectuals puffed up with vanity, not to mention the curates and their spies!'

'What do you suggest?' asked Wolfgang.

'Forget the old fossils and let's look after the younger generation. They are the ones we ought to be training. Firstly, their minds: we should exclude all dogmatic religion and develop genuine spiritual freedom. Then, daily activity: stop kow-towing to fake thinkers who spread trouble and disorder and let's restore the dignity and grandeur to manual labour. And lastly, the body:

thanks to the Church and bourgeois morality, hypocrisy is the order of the day. Let us practise naturism and see ourselves as we are, without vanity or false modesty. That, in my view, would be a peaceful revolution.'

'What do you think?' Thamos asked Mozart, when Ziegenhagen had gone.

'New ideas, at last! But our Brother is overlooking an essential point: the Royal Art and the communion of Brothers with their Sisters who have been so mistreated by Freemasonry. Without the priestesses of the sun, the priests are nothing but puppets.'

'Ignaz von Born is expecting us. Your grand plans are taking shape, I see.'

Mozart smiled.

'And you are its real author.'

Vienna, 4 January 1791

On the day of a repeat performance of *The Marriage of Figaro*, Joseph Anton, Count of Pergen and Minister of Police, struck a decisive blow. He handed the emperor a report accusing Freemasonry of spreading pernicious ideas aimed at undermining the reputation and power of the monarchy. The Freemasons were responsible for inciting French revolutionaries to dire extremities.

'Is the danger really so serious?' asked Leopold II.

'I have spent most of my life studying the Freemasons, Your Majesty, and my conclusions are based on hard facts.'

'King Frederick William II of Prussia and I are asking the French authorities to instate a monarchical regime compatible with the wellbeing of their country.'

'With respect, Your Majesty, you will be disappointed.'

'So far, Count of Pergen, I have been successful in privileging negotiation over confrontation. Your hatred of the Freemasons is blinding you. I take on board your warnings but I must remind you that it is I, and I alone, who governs.'

Vienna, 5 January 1791

Mozart finished a remarkable Piano Concerto[*]. No revolt, no combat, just almost total detachment and limpid fluidity. Such pared-back beauty reflected the grace accorded to the tiny minority of men capable of perceiving the invisible and giving it a voice.

Superficially, the music would appeal to everyone; at a deeper level, it represented a distant voyage that stirred feelings of anxiety in Thamos: would Wolfgang return from this wonderland and want to complete the Great Work?

Mozart was a stranger on this earth. His life was not like other people's and yet he gave them unexpected light. Unconcerned by the material world, his mind genuinely elsewhere, he embodied perceptions so that

---

[*] K595, Nº. 27, his last Piano Concerto.

Wisdom based on strength and harmony should not be masked by the folly and stupidity of the human race.

Some creators sometimes reached the sky; but Mozart came from the great beyond*.

The mission the Abbot Hermes had sent Thamos on was not yet accomplished: Mozart, the Great Magician, had yet to become the alchemist who could lay the foundations for the building of a new temple.

Vienna, 14 January 1791

Twenty-five-year-old Franz Xaver Süssmayr, Mozart's new pupil, was a composer, singer, violinist and organist.

'I don't like him at all,' Wolfgang told Constance.

'He seems polite and agreeable enough.'

'That's just a veneer. Underneath he is terribly ambitious.'

'Is that so very bad?'

'Not always, maybe. But when it comes to Süssmayr's intelligence, he has considerable progress to make! Anyway, we'll see if he keeps up with my lessons.'

Wolfgang had recovered some of his *joie de vivre*

---

* So said the conductor Joseph Krips (cf. Hildesheimer *Mozart*, p.19, note 9). Saint-Foix, II, 591: 'When we interpret Mozart's work from the latter part of his short life, we find an ascension in which it is difficult not to see a spiritual, almost supernatural dimension, to the extent that external events have no dominion.'

and, in the depths of winter, was composing three songs*
celebrating springtime, the return of new life and carefree children who find amusement in a thousand and one
things. Karl Thomas and Gaukerl were his first audience, and they loved them.

And Constance dreamt of giving birth to a child who
would be as robust as Karl Thomas.

Vienna, 27 January 1791

Wolfgang celebrated his thirty-fifth birthday at an
exuberant banquet where the Champagne flowed freely.
Stadler, the Jacquins, Constance and Thamos wished
their hero every happiness.

'Your *Figaro* is playing again on the 20th,' Stadler
reminded him. 'Salieri is beside himself with rage! Have
you finished your new dances for the balls of La Redoute?'

'Six minuets†, and I'm working on six jolly allemandes‡.'

'All those revellers whooping it up to Mozart! If only
they understood the true greatness of your music. It
makes me mad to think of you lowering yourself with
this work.'

---

* *Come sweet May*, K596, which re-used the theme from the final
rondo of his last concerto; *When spring comes*, K597, and *The children's game*, K598. Alberti published these three *Lieder* in a collection
for children.
† K599.
‡ K600.

'It helps me keep my family, and I do it as well as I can.'

'As long as Vienna enjoys his music,' observed Gottfried von Jacquin, 'Mozart's good name is bolstered in circles close to the emperor and with it, the good name of Freemasonry!'

'I should not be too sure,' Thamos advised. 'No argument will dissuade the Chief of Police from spying on us and seeking to stamp us out. And our Brother Wolfgang is still more exposed than any of us.'

29

Vienna, 1 February 1791

Anxious and uneasy, many Brothers were leaving Crowned Hope, where numbers were falling as the months went by. The latest notable Mason to resign was the lawyer Franz Hofdemel. His wife, Maria Magdalena, continued taking lessons from Mozart.

'I now have several indications to suggest that we have a traitor in our midst,' Thamos told Mozart. 'We know the Archbishop of Vienna's spy, but he is too simple-minded to be much harm. The real informant, on the other hand, is doing us serious damage. I am sure he is talking to the police about our rituals and the subject of our works.'

'How can a Brother behave like that?' Wolfgang asked, indignantly.

'Remember the myth of the Master Mason: treachery is an integral part of the life of initiation.

169

Overlooking that element has led many brotherhoods to disaster.'

'Do you have precise suspicions?'

'In recent weeks, certain behaviour has come to my attention. Sooner or later, I shall find out.'

Vienna, 1 March 1791

*Minuets, allemandes, contredanses and Ländler by Mozart were the delight of the three thousand dancers in the small and great hall of La Redoute in Vienna's imperial palace. They ate, drank and made merry until five in the morning in their fancy-dress costumes. Above all, they adored the trio from the *Sleigh Ride*, with posthorn and bells, and *The Triumph of the Ladies*.

Leopold-Aloys Hoffmann left the small hall shortly after midnight and went to meet Geytrand, who was impervious to the cold night air.

'Any news, Hoffmann?'

'Nothing major. The lodge is ticking over.'

'Come, come, my friend, don't try to be clever with me! We have a very compromising file on you. Are you not Brother Sulpicius, one of the Illuminati?'

Hoffmann immediately revealed the events of the latest meeting at Crowned Hope. Satisfied, Geytrand disappeared.

* K601 to 607.

Chilled to the bone, Hoffmann drew the flaps of his greatcoat closer around him.

'Good evening, false Brother.'

Thamos the Egyptian barred his way.

'You . . . have you been here long?'

'I followed you.'

'But this is madness!'

'On the contrary, now I know who you are.'

'I don't know what you're talking about!'

'May it be your lot to suffer dire punishments, you louse! Don't ever set foot in a lodge again.'

Sensing that Thamos was not speaking lightly and was longing to wring his neck, the traitor turned on his heel and vanished into the night, determined to have nothing more to do with the Freemasons.

Vienna, 2 March 1791

Count Deym had sent Mozart a new commission for the mechanical organ in his museum of wax figures. This time, Wolfgang set to work with more enthusiasm and quickly composed a Fantasy* that was nothing like a little genre piece. A majestic Andante was preceded and followed by a Fugue marked 'Allegro'. The influence of Bach was apparent in the rigour and sense of tragedy. When Constance heard this short piece, she

---

* K608, in F minor.

thought she perceived a new development in Mozart's style*.

'Excellent news, my darling. Three publishers have sold several scores of Quartets and the ever-popular dance music. We've made six hundred florins: what a relief! The future looks brighter, at last.'

'What about your grand opera?'

'It is gradually coming to me. I shall soon be ready to sketch the outline.'

Vienna, 3 March 1791

'We have just lost our informant,' Geytrand announced to Joseph Anton. 'Apparently, his conscience smote him and he has left the Freemasons.'

'Hoffmann, a conscience! Didn't you offer him a rise?'

'Not even a hefty bonus would have changed his mind.'

'There's only one possible explanation: his Brothers found him out and threatened him.'

'Crowned Hope has a hard core that will be difficult to crack,' sighed Geytrand. 'There are now very few initiates and they have closed ranks.'

'This is all Mozart's doing, needless to say! He must be delighted with the situation: as a conductor, he knows

* The Minuet in D Major for Piano, K355, may date from this period.

the benefit of weeding out the dross and keeping the soloists. In any case, we have lost our eyes and ears.'

'I shall try to bribe a new informant,' Geytrand promised, 'but I can't promise success.'

The Count of Pergen had had so much success while he had carried on his activities under ground, but now he felt thwarted. Mozart's lodge had been considerably weakened but it was holding out, and there was every sign of a resurgence of Freemasonry in Vienna. As for Leopold II, apparently so hostile to secret societies, he was demanding deplorable moderation from his Chief of Police.

Was it a temporary hitch or the hand of fate? Either way, Anton would not give up the struggle.

The influence of Mozart, the real leader, was continuing to grow. His capacity to withstand multiple blows was extraordinary, as though he were indestructible like the Stone Man in *Don Giovanni*. With no traitor to inform on him, what plot could he be hatching?

Vienna, 4 March 1791

Mozart was unenthusiastic about performing at a concert where the star was the clarinetist Joseph Bähr, a musician at the court of Russia who was hoping to arrange a grand tour for the composer of *The Marriage of Figaro*.

In rooms made available by the purveyor of grand banquets, Ignaz Jahn, Wolfgang played one of his Piano

Concerti*, but he barely noticed the applause. No longer interested in stunning audiences with his showmanship, he could think of nothing but the ritual opera that would lead to the heart of the Temple. He still had to go on writing dance music, like *The Mischievous Girls†*, but his thoughts now increasingly turned to Egypt.

* K595, Mozart's last Concerto.
† Contredanse K610.

30

Vienna, 5 March 1791

'Thank you for this audience, your Majesty,' oozed Lorenzo Da Ponte, at his most unctuous, bowing low before Leopold II. 'I am entirely at your service and promise to write highly entertaining opera libretti.'

'Indeed, your style is not always so very . . . entertaining. I don't like your pamphlets or your critiques. You will therefore no longer belong to the court staff.'

'Someone is out to harm me, Your Majesty! I can assure you of my total loyalty, and I . . .'

'Get out!'

The emperor's cold rage left Da Ponte no option. As he left the imperial presence, he wondered how he could restore Leopold's faith in him.

By the time Mozart called to see him, he was suffering from a migraine.

'What a disaster!' the abbé exclaimed. 'Leopold II has

sacked me! Salieri is behind all this and wants to bring me down. But I shall fight back! No one has the right to trample on Lorenzo Da Ponte!'

It was pointless, Mozart realized, to think of collaborating with the abbé again. Now he would be interested in nothing but trying to win back his position. As Thamos had predicted, he would have to find another librettist.

Vienna, 6 March 1791

Although worn out by relentless pain, which kept him a prisoner in his room, Venerable Ignaz von Born was glad to welcome Mozart and Thamos. He showed them the letter from the American Freemason Benjamin Franklin congratulating him on his study, *The Mysteries of Egypt.*

'I have decided to write an opera about the mysteries of Isis and Osiris,' Mozart announced.

'What a splendid project! But are you aware of the risks? The authorities and the police will see you as spreading terrible propaganda; the Church will accuse you of paganism, and Freemasons will think you are breaking the rule of silence. Some will be jealous of you for getting so far along the road to initiation, while others will blame you for giving women such an important role.'

'"When you build the House," I was told, "when Male and Female are united, then the stone is perfect"'.

---

* *The Zohar, Song of Songs*, p.65.

Freemasonry has forgotten the vital necessity of female initiation*, and the moment has come to restore the harmony.'

'You really are putting yourself in very great danger,' von Born insisted. 'In the current climate, undermining the powers that be will win you sworn enemies.'

'I don't care. We are going to build a temple together where we can perform works that will reveal the great secret and bestow the true light of the Orient†.'

'The Great Work, the union of the king and queen, the initiation of the royal couple beyond the three degrees,' murmured von Born. 'So, you will be passing down the key to the Great Mysteries.'

'Will you agree to work with me?'

'As long as my strength permits. We must make haste.'

Taking his inspiration from several sources‡, Wolfgang had already drafted the basic libretto§.

---

* Article 3 of the Constitutions for Freemasons, written by Anderson in 1723, states: 'The persons admitted members of a Lodge must be good and true men [. . .] no bondmen, no women, no immoral or scandalous men, but of good report.'

† Texts from the Masonic Cantata, K623.

‡ For instance, *Lulu or the Magic Flute*, an Arabian tale translated by Wieland; *The Philosopher's Stone*, by Schack; Abbé Terrasson's *Sethos*; Brother Paul Wranisky's *Oberon*; Heliodre's *Ethiopics; The Golden Ass* by Apuleius, and several alchemical and cabbalistic books.

§ Concerning Mozart, the real author of the libretto of *The Magic Flute*, see H. Abert, *Introduction to the score of The Magic Flute*, London-Zurich-New York; J. and B. Massin, *Mozart*, p.1145 and 1138, note 1; C. de Nys, *Mozart*, Paris, 1985, p. 158; J. Chailly, *The Magic Flute*, p.25.

'I'm going to call this opera *The Magic Flute*. The magic instrument in question was made of wood taken from the heart of a thousand-year-old oak, after it was struck by a thunder bolt of celestial fire during a raging storm, and it will symbolize the Rules and Regulations. The sound of it soothes the savagery of men and beasts and pacifies violence. Its music enables men and women to experience the Great Mysteries together.'

'Have you chosen your librettist?'

'There's no point asking Da Ponte. I thought of Brother Schikaneder for several reasons. Firstly, he is deeply attached to the Masonic ideal and will understand my demands; secondly, he is a true professional and will produce a drama that answers to my wishes, and finally, his troop are old hands and he runs a theatre that belongs to my Brother and friend Joseph von Bauernfeld. I realize it is out in the suburbs and its audiences are largely uneducated, but it is none the worse for that. They may be more receptive than Viennese nobility, who can be dreadfully superficial. Schikaneder will help me realize my vision.'

'Excellent idea,' Ignaz von Born said, approvingly. 'And our Brother Alberti can publish the libretto.'

'Unlike the three operas that dealt with Apprenticeship, Craftsmanship and Mastery,' Wolfgang added, 'this text will be written not in Italian but in German. And the recitatives will be spoken not sung.'

The Venerable took a gulp of the potion Thamos had concocted for him. It relieved his pain and would prolong his life by a few weeks, or months if he was lucky. As an experienced alchemist, von Born was in no doubt about his approaching end and he was glad he would be able to contribute to his disciple's Great Work.

But Thamos was overcome by an emotion of an intensity he had not felt since leaving his Brothers in the monastery in Upper Egypt, before it was destroyed by fanatical Muslims. Since finding the Great Magician, he had come a long way, right to the door of this temple of the priests and priestesses of the sun, which was about to be built note by note.

31

Vienna, 7 March 1791

'What a nightmare it is being an impresario!' Emanuel Schikaneder groaned dramatically. 'I am having to crack the whip. From now on, anyone who steps out of line or turns up late will be liable to a fine that will go to the strolling actors' charity. Don't you think that's a fine application of the Masonic principle of solidarity?'

'I like your sense of discipline,' Mozart agreed, 'and it makes me want to collaborate with you.'

Schikaneder's eyes lit up.

'Do you have a project, a serious one?'

'Very serious.'

'Do you have a libretto?'

'I am working on it at the moment, and you can help me bring it to fruition, so long as you agree to follow my instructions.'

'Give me your hand!' declared Schikaneder, striking

Mozart's palm with his own. 'I'll bring you some great ideas and audiences will love them.'

Vienna, 8 March 1791

Wolfgang composed an aria for bass* for Franz-Xaver Gerl† to sing, then he went to call on his Brother Artaria to discuss the forthcoming publication of twelve German dances and twelve minuets arranged for piano, before going to see von Born.

Thamos joined them.

'No policemen on the prowl,' he declared, with relief.

'Why does Leopold II want to spy on an old, sick scholar who has lost his influence?'

'Because the Minister of Police does not see you like that, Venerable Master. In his view, you are still the mastermind behind a secret society and Mozart is its operational arm. He is awesomely efficient and we cannot afford to drop our guard.'

Ignaz von Born nodded. Just when Mozart was about to embark on a fabulous adventure, they owed it to him to keep him out of harm's way.

'The ritual will involve three characters,' Wolfgang announced. 'At the top of the triangle is the Venerable, and I suggest we call him Sarastro.'

---

* K612, with *contrabass obligato*.
† He was to be *The Magic Flute*'s first Sarastro.

'A reference to Zoroaster and the "prince of stars", the sun*,' observed Thamos. 'He will dispel the prejudices, gossip and lies that beset the lodges and, in the face of criticism from some Masons, prepare both man *and* woman for initiation. The royal couple will succeed him and revive the tradition of the Great Mysteries.

'You need to think about the names of your two heroes,' von Born said to Thamos.

'We shall call him Tamino and her, Pamina. Both names have *min* as their root. In Egyptian hieroglyphs, it means "stable, lasting being", and it refers to soundly built monuments. This couple must construct the new temple after the celebration of the sacred marriage. Min is also the name of Osiris revived when he had risen again from the sleep of death. Tamino, "the Man of Min", and Pamina, "the Woman of Min", have to go through this ordeal together. Also, I've reversed the articles: *Ta* is feminine and *Pa* is masculine, because in *Così van Tutte* we learned how to reconcile opposites and reverse the lights. Their names show that Tamino and Pamina are indissociable. Menes, another way of writing the root *min*, was the first pharaoh, the unifier of the Two Worlds and the wise monarch in *Thamos, King of Egypt*. Tamino also means "my king" and Pamina "my queen"†: here, we're talking about the only real

---

* Cf. Autexier, *Mozart*, p.173.

† For these interpretations, see Autexier, *Mozart*, p. 173 (who refers to Nettl) and Veyssière-Lacrose, *Lexikon Aegyptiaco-Latinum*, published

high degree of initiatory Freemasonry, the accomplishment of the Royal Art.'

'Tamino embodies the long way of alchemy strewn with ordeals,' added von Born, 'and Pamina represents the short way. Consequently, she will receive Sarastro's teaching directly. He will grant the divine blessing on the couple and at the end of their initiation, they will be accorded happiness and the consecration of Isis.'

'The ritual will consist in bringing Tamino and Pamina together,' Mozart decided. 'They will go through ordeals and purifications in order to transcend their own existence and discover creative love that gives rise to initiation.'

Vienna, 30 March 1791

For the past week, the Viennese had been flocking to visit the mausoleum Count Deym had built to the memory of Field-Marshal Laudon, a peerless warrior who had fought the Turks so valiantly. On the stroke of every hour, the crowd was surprised to hear funeral music by Mozart[*], the talented composer of dances and contredanses.

---

in Oxford in 1775, which gives the Coptic words descended from the Ancient Egyptian. The work was known to Freemasons working on Ancient traditions.
* K608.

Wolfgang finished eight calm and intimate variations on a theme by Gerl*, his future Sarastro, entitled 'Woman is the most wonderful thing'†.

'As long as the initiation of women is not restored,' he told Thamos, 'this world is ill-made.'

'We must recover the thrust of the ancient mysteries and anchor Freemasonry to its original tradition, the tradition of Egyptian thought. That is what is at stake in *The Magic Flute*.'

---

* According to other musicologists, he used a theme by Schack, a friend of Schikaneder.
† K613.

32

Vienna, 30 March 1791

'You have given the empire tremendous service, Count of Pergen, and you deserve a long rest.'

'Your Majesty, I should rather go on with my work as Chief of Police. The dangers are far from over, Freemasonry above all.'

'Your obsession is blinding you.'

'Look at America and France! Other countries will soon join them. The Freemasons want to overturn the monarchies, force people to subscribe to their ideas and seize power. If we don't radically intervene, Austria will succumb.'

'I shall see to it that that disaster is averted. From today, you are no longer Minister of Police.'

Joseph Anton bowed and withdrew.

So, Mozart had won! He had used his network of influences and conspirators to persuade Leopold II not to ban Freemasonry, that charitable society that had so much respect for the emperor!

But the battle was not over yet.

If he went under ground, the count would not be powerless.

Ignaz von Born was ill and Mozart was now the man he had to remove. There was nothing for it but to set about destroying him physically and make sure that any investigations into the business would not lead back to him, Joseph Anton.

As a priority, he would have to lay false trails and set up suspects. How lucky that Mozart had so many enemies!

Vienna, 1 April 1791

'A pleasure to welcome you, Count of Pergen,' Anton Migazzi, Archbishop of Vienna said, stiffly. 'I was sorry to hear of your dismissal.'

'The Freemason Mozart is entirely responsible.'

'Him again! Is he that powerful?'

'Far more than you imagine, your Grace. He is the secret head of Viennese Masonry and plays a decisive role in Prague.'

'I cannot forget that he challenged me on 12 August 1785 when he organized ritual music to be played in his lodge for the initiation of Karl von König, a Venetian Freemason outlawed by the Inquisition.'

'He has come a long way since then! He knows how powerful he is and will confront the Church openly before long.'

'Is he not afraid of losing his soul?'

'Mozart only believes in initiation – Egyptian teaching, to be precise.'

'Great Heavens! He surely isn't a pagan?'

'If you read the *Egyptian Mysteries* by his master Ignaz von Born, you will see for yourself, your Grace. The Catholic faith is under threat.'

'What do you suggest?'

The Count of Pergen thought for a long moment.

'I am praying to Almighty God to protect His flock and I am thinking of the Old Testament. Divine wrath struck down the impious and worshippers of idols.'

'There is never enough reliance on the Holy Scriptures, my Lord. May God inspire the actions of righteous men.'

Vienna, 10 April 1791

After receiving thirty florins from his Brother Puchberg, Mozart had called on Johann Tost, a Hungarian Freemason, and a wealthy business man with a passion for chamber music. Wolfgang played him the String Quintet he had commissioned*, a work infused with the serenity of a creator in full control of his art. Now that he

---

* K614 in E flat major, Mozart's last Quintet.

was deep in preparations for his Great Work, his music expressed optimism and detachment.

Already, Sarastro was singing in his head, the Venerable who would oversee the initiation of Tamino and Pamina and, in so doing, reject the reactionary tendency to reduce Freemasonry to a masculine society and dispel the dark side of the female soul symbolized by the Queen of the Night intent on destruction not initiation. Gradually, the community of priests and priestesses of the sun already suggested in *Thamos, King of Egypt* was taking shape.

Vienna, 17 April 1791

The day before, and again that evening, Antonio Salieri conducted a large orchestra of a hundred players at one of the Lenten concerts that so delighted the Viennese.

'What a nerve the old hypocrite has!' Da Ponte exclaimed to Mozart. 'He loathes you, but there he is conducting one of your symphonies*! Currying favour with the nobility, that's the only thing he's interested in. The rat is bloated with ambition and will bite anyone that gets in his way. I'm sure he was the one who persuaded Leopold II to banish me from court, so he could choose his own libretti. But I shall fight to the bitter end.'

'Are your supporters persuasive enough?'

* K550.

'I'm afraid not,' the abbé sighed. 'And I have to spend my days foiling Salieri's pernicious influence. Whatever you do, Mozart, don't trust that parasite. Like most second-rate men, he can grow violent and dangerous.'

'I don't get in his way.'

'Don't be so sure! You are gifted and have friends in high places. Salieri knows that his big operas will not outlive him and that yours contain more wonders than he can ever aspire to. I say again: be on your guard.'

33

Vienna, 18 April 1791

In his three previous ritual operas, *The Marriage of Figaro, Don Giovanni* and *Così fan Tutte*, Mozart had composed the overture last of all. This time, he discussed it with Ignaz von Born and Thamos.

'Celebrate the Number Three and ternary thought, the basis of our journey towards knowledge,' the Venerable suggested.

'In Egypt,' Thamos added, 'the divine forces are Three: mystery, light and formulation. It is through Three that One, which is inaccessible to human thought, can be passed down.'

'Three will be present in *The Magic Flute**,' Wolfgang assured them. 'The ritual will open with its sublimation,

---

* For instance, the three doors to the temple, the three Ladies and the three sun children.

namely, Nine, the secret Number of the degree of Master Mason. So, at the beginning of the overture, there will be three different chords and in the middle, three times three chords signifying the celebration of the Great Mysteries: the Venerable Sarastro wants to teach the Royal Art to the couple, Pamina and Tamino.'

'*The Magic Flute* will be a work with popular appeal but that is also esoteric,' Thamos predicted. 'It will speak to everyone.'

'I have decided to found a new Order of Initiation,' Mozart revealed. 'It will be called The Grotto and will provide genuine rituals with *The Magic Flute* as the basis. Our Sister Thun and our Brother Stadler have agreed to take part in the enterprise.'*

'The light of Egypt will guide this Order,' said von Born.

Vienna, 21 April 1791

Although hard at work on the libretto, Wolfgang still found time to compose the final chorus for an opera by

---

* A letter from Constance to the Leipzig publishers, Breitkopf and Hartel, revealed Mozart's intentions: 'On the subject of the Order or Society by the name of Grotto that he wanted to found,' she wrote, 'I cannot give you more explanations. The court clarinettist, Stadler the Elder, who wrote the rest of the statutes, may be able to help, but he has to admit that he is afraid, because he knows that the Orders or Secret Societies are hated.' See, too, *Dictionnaire Mozart*, p.169.

Sarti* and to play at a concert at the house of von Greiner, a lawyer and importer of foodstuffs and a Freemason in the Lodge to True Concord.

Always eager for jollifications of the sort, Puchberg, who had been invited to this wonderful soirée, was delighted to be welcomed to a salon that brought together philosophers, poets and musicians. He had brought along a violin for Mozart.

'I hope Greiner has paid you correctly?'

'He promised to pay, but I forgot to ask him for the money.'

'Leave it to me,' was Puchberg's rejoinder. 'What can be distracting you to the point of overlooking the essential?'

'A project. A very big project.'

'Excellent news!'

Puchberg's help came at a good time, because Anton Stadler had just asked Mozart for more money to continue work on the manufacture of the bass clarinet, which the composer would one day put to good use. With Constance's agreement, Wolfgang was still financing the project. He also had dreams of a piano that would make his music resound in a way not even superior models of the fortepiano ever would. In the future, he would pay more attention to improving the quality of the sound by promoting the birth of new instruments.

---

* K615, 'Let us live happily in sweet contentment', a lost work.

The Magic Flute, *Act I, Scene I**

'The scenery will play a big role,' Mozart announced, 'and the stage must be set to resemble the setting for a lodge ritual†.'

'What symbolic universe do you have in mind?' asked Ignaz von Born.

'A rocky landscape with a few trees. On either side of the stage are mountains. One symbolizes masculine initiation, the other female initiation. In the middle is a temple.'

'You will be reproducing the hieroglyph *akhet*,' observed Thamos, 'the sun of the mind rising between two hills, the Orient and the West.'

'Tamino, dressed in a luxurious Japanese hunting robe, rushes down a rock face pursued by a serpent, which he has not managed to kill. His only weapon is a bow that is useless because his quiver is empty; in other words, he does not yet have mastery over his arrows, the sun's rays.'

'The allusion to Japan, the Far East,' commented Born, 'means that Tamino is under the protection of the Light of the beyond, the Eternal Orient. Unaware of his predestination, he is "hunting" knowledge, without the

* See W. A. Mozart, *The Magic Flute*, translation by C. Jacq, Maison de Vie Editeur, 2006.
† Many modern set designs for *The Magic Flute* ignore the indications in the libretto and the ritual nature of the opera and thereby misrepresent the opera and Mozart's conception.

appropriate means. And on the way to his real country, he meets the Enemy.'

'Thinking his end has come, Tamino realizes that he will be sacrificed to the monster but he can no longer fight it off. His efforts to escape are all futile, so he prays to charitable gods and begs them to save him.'

'*The gods*!' thought von Born 'That term is sure to elicit the Archbishop's wrath.'

'Having uttered this cry for help, Tamino falls senseless to the ground.'

'He thus loses all human power to enter into the death of initiation,' said Thamos. 'Now he is at the mercy of the destructive serpent that drinks the water of the celestial river to quench its thirst, deprives the cosmos of life and stops the sun from rising.'

'The temple door opens! Three veiled Ladies appear, each armed with a silver spear, silver being the colour of the moon as a symbol of the right act at the right time. Together, thanks to the power of the number Three, they slay the serpent and save Tamino. The Ladies live in the temple of the Queen of the Night,' said Wolfgang. 'She has lost peace and serenity because she has been split off from the Temple of the Sun.'

'This ritual scene,' added Thamos, 'illustrates an episode in the mysteries of Horus when the initiates harpoon the monster to the ground.'

'The three Ladies are fascinated by Tamino's beauty. They all want to win him, but the trio forms an indivisible entity. So, they go back to the temple to tell the

Queen of the Night. Might not this handsome youth be the bringer of a brilliant future?'

'Tamino comes out of the sleep of initiation,' said Thamos. 'He sees the baleful serpent and knows that it was not he who slew it. What divine power heard his call? Where is he?'

'In the distance, he hears the sound of a flute. An odd-looking fellow is coming and Tamino hides behind a tree.'

34

Vienna, 25 April 1791

Contrary to everyone's expectations, Leopold Hoffmann*, the aged Cathedral Kapellmeister who had been at death's door, recovered. Mozart felt bound to write an official letter to the city councillors to explain his position. Grumpy old Hoffmann earned two thousand florins a year, and that was before the firewood and candles. Wolfgang wished him no harm and was keen to let this be known.

So he took his finest quill pen and wrote:

Very honoured and wise gentlemen of the City Council of Vienna,
When Kapellmeister Hoffmann fell ill, I took the liberty of applying to replace him, on the strength

---

* He did not die until 1793, long after Mozart.

of my musical talents, my compositions and my knowledge of the craft which have become famous abroad. As my name is held in esteem everywhere and as I was privileged enough, several years ago, to be engaged at the very honourable court of Vienna as a composer, I thought that I would not be unworthy of the position and might deserve the kind disposition of the wise City Council.

However, the Kapellmeister has recovered his health and, as I wish and desire with all my heart that he may live a long life, I thought it might be of benefit to the service of the Cathedral and to you, gentlemen, to act as an assistant to Mr Hoffmann, initially without remuneration, so that I might help that excellent man in his duties and acquire the esteem of the very wise City Council with real work which my considerable knowledge of the sacred style leads me to think myself more capable than other men.

The Magic Flute, *Act I, Scene II*

'Tamino now sees a man covered in feathers coming down the mountain and carrying on his back a huge birdcage full of birds,' Wolfgang went on. 'He is playing pan-pipes and singing about his wish to find a wife, and he adds that he has the intelligence of his instrument.'

'We shall call him Papageno,' von Born decided.

'The name is based on the Greek word for "engender" or "generate", because this character embodies multiple desires as opposed to Tamino's spiritual unity. Some people will see an allusion to *Papegei*, or parrot, the basic degree of the Order of the Illuminati.'

'Tamino represents stable, creative power,' put in Thamos; 'Papageno stands for volatile creation. Tamino grasps his hand and declares that he is a king's son, in other words, a prince and predestined. Poor Papageno knows nothing about his parentage or where he was born. All he knows is that he was brought up by a jolly old man and that his mother was a servant to the Starbright Queen of the Night. He now lives by catching all sorts of birds for her, in exchange for food and drink. "Can I see her?" Tamino asks. "What human eye could pierce her veil of darkness?" Papageno asks. "What mortal being can claim to have seen her?" Tamino remembers that he often heard his father, the king, speak of this Queen of the Night whose secret he must discover. He wonders if Papageno is really a man. Oh yes, the curious fellow assures him, and he boasts of his colossal strength which allowed him to strangle the evil serpent with his bare hands!

'Raised by a "jolly old man" refers to the alchemist,' Thamos added. 'And the "volatile agent", Papageno, is charged with uniting the two elements of the royal couple, Tamino and Pamina.'

The Beloved of Isis

Vienna, 26 April 1791

Joseph Anton had shut himself away in the cavernous office of his lonely castle. With the curtains drawn against the light he detested, the Count of Pergen was rereading his files. He alone properly understood Freemasonry; no one else knew how to tackle it.

'Well, Geytrand?'

'I have kept part of our old network and retained the best members. Alas, they have become terrible gluttons!'

'Pay them enough not to betray us.'

'I have naturally restored surveillance of Ignaz von Born's house, of course with the utmost discretion. Mozart often goes there.'

'A new ritual opera, that's what they're working on!' snapped Joseph Anton. 'Mozart is creating a positive Masonic war machine according to von Born's plans. That confounded Venerable still holds sway.'

'His health is declining. Maybe we could speed up the process.'

'How might we go about it?'

'In days gone by, a Freemason named Gugomos threatened to poison any Brothers who displeased him with a highly effective substance called *aqua toffana*. We might be able to administer small doses that would go undetected. On your instructions, I have procured a good quantity.'

Anton seemed to hesitate.

'We are no longer an official service, my lord, and you

are free to decide without referring to anyone else. Our first priority is to eliminate Ignaz von Born. Otherwise, he will return as Freemasonry's leader and restore its old vigour to it.'

'We must make sure we are above suspicion.'

'One of our agents will poison von Born's food every day. If we can get rid of him, we won't have any more trouble from Mozart. Deprived of his master, he will be too distraught and inconsolable to do anything more than compose dances and contredanses.'

35

The Magic Flute, *Act I, Scenes 3 to 4*

'Papageno boasted that he had strangled the serpent,' Wolfgang recalled, 'and now the three Ladies remonstrate and establish the truth. With their faces still hidden, they bring him from the Queen of the Night, not the usual wine and cakes, but pure water and a stone. Instead of sweet figs, a symbol of fruitful multiplicity, the third Lady brings a gold padlock to lock up Papageno's mouth as a punishment for gossip and pretensions; life will be pleasanter without them!'

'The padlock refers to the secret work of alchemy,' said von Born. 'As the embodiment of the agent linking the elements, Papageno cannot and must not reveal it.'

'The three Ladies give Tamino a locket from the Queen of the Night. Inside is the portrait of her daughter. If it moves him, he will be destined for happiness, fame and glory. Tamino instantly conceives a supernatural love for her: this is not a woman he is looking at but a divine image that no mortal ever beheld before. He has fallen under the spell of enchantment and wants to conclude an eternal union.'

'This vision of Isis takes us beyond the degree of Master Mason,' von Born went on. 'We have reached the threshold of the Royal Art, at the point where the Brother realizes the importance of the Sister and the future king goes towards the future queen to recreate the primordial unity.'

Vienna, 28 April 1791

On the previous evening, Wolfgang had played at another concert at the house of his Brother von Greiner, where again, Puchberg, always eager to attend these delightful entertainments, was one of the guests.

He was immersed in work on *The Magic Flute*, when Constance entered his study with a letter in her hand.

'It's from the City Council.'

'That cathedral job . . . Perhaps we are in luck?'

Wolfgang broke the seal. Hopes gave way to disappointment.

'The City Council has rejected my application.'

'Don't be downhearted, darling. Your opera project has given you so much enthusiasm, you really mustn't let this incident put you off.'

'Don't worry, I shall bring it to fruition. It's the cathedral's loss!'

The Magic Flute, *Act I, Scenes 5 to 8*

Ignaz von Born was glad of the chance to take his mind of his sufferings by working on the libretto for *The Magic Flute*. He knew his days were numbered, and he refused to listen to the exhortations of his doctor and his family to rest.

'Now that Prince Tamino has been stirred to initiatory love allied to vigilance,' Mozart declared, 'the three Ladies give him the second major virtue essential to the initiate: perseverance. They tell him that the Queen of the Night is sending him on a mission to rescue her daughter Pamina, the name of the girl in the portrait. They explain that she was abducted by a demon while she was meditating among the cypress trees before attending an initiation ceremony. But she is beyond vice and not even violence can assail her virtue.'

'Since Tamino agrees to deliver his beloved,' put in Thamos, 'the Queen of the Night appears in a clap of thunder.'

'The mountains part,' said Mozart, 'to reveal a splendid hall in which the queen is seated on a throne set with transparent stars. She instructs Tamino to save her daughter. If he rescues her, she will be his forever. Fascinated, Tamino calls on the gods to give him the necessary courage. The three Ladies return and remove the padlock from Papageno's lips on the compassionate orders of the Queen of the Night. He promises never to lie again, and they all sing the moral stanza: love and brotherly friendship would replace hatred, calumnies and bitterness, if all liars had their mouths padlocked.'

'The servants of the Queen of the Night also have another mission, and now they give Tamino a golden flute. It will protect him from evil, make him powerful and turn men's passions into happiness and joy.

'This flute is worth more than gold and crowns,' added Thamos, 'because it represents the Rules and Regulations for initiates.'

'The Ladies order Papageno to act as Tamino's servant and go with him to Sarastro's castle,' Mozart continued, 'and they give him another magic object, a ring of bells.'

'The Queen of the Night gives her most precious treasures to the two men because she thinks she has converted them,' Thamos explained. 'She will use them to defeat the Venerable Sarastro and rescue Pamina from the way to initiation. Rejected, shut out of the temple, the Queen of the Night is intent on destroying him.'

'How shall we find the castle? Tamino and Papageno ask the three Ladies. They cannot guide them but they give the two travellers another threefold gift in the guise of three pure, celestial and clever boys whose directions they must follow.'

'The Queen of the Night will surely be avenged,' commented von Born. 'The community of the initiates to the mysteries of Osiris and Isis is about to lose its leader.'

36

The finances of the Mozart family were improving day by day. Although they still had debts, they continued to dress elegantly, they never went hungry and they took good care to look after themselves.

The rent was not above their means and was paid on time, and everyone, Gaukerl included, appreciated the comfort of a good-sized apartment. As an excellent mistress of her household, Constance saw to it that there were no unnecessary outgoings and began to pay off some of their creditors. Of course, Wolfgang would rather not have had to compose minuets, dances and contredanses and so much music for the masses, but he was disciplined about his official duties because they were an essential part of his livelihood in addition to his publications and lessons.

Above all, *The Magic Flute*, the realization of his

dreams as a musician and a Freemason, was taking shape. At last, the vision outlined in *Thamos, King of Egypt* was becoming a reality. His producer was an initiate, he had a theatre, a troop and the ideal libretto; maybe, this time, the opera would be a success.

The Magic Flute, *Act I, Scenes 9 to 15*

With the help of the elixir Thamos made up for him, Ignaz von Born was coping better with the pain of his illness and continued contributing to the ritual development of *The Magic Flute*.

'The scene changes to Sarastro's stronghold,' the composer announced. 'Unbeknown to him, his servant, Monostatos the Moor, with a soul as black as his skin, is a lecherous traitor. He is supposed to be guarding the precious Pamina, the future of women's initiation, but instead he lusts after her and wants to take her by force.'

'We've come across a fair number of traitors,' the Egyptian reminded them. 'Who are you going to take as your model?'

'Soliman the African! He left Vienna to join the French revolutionaries and fight against his ex-Brothers. In Italian, *soli-mena* means "he who keeps to himself", which is the same as Monostatos in Greek.'

'Let's think of another renegade. How about Leopold-Aloys Hoffmann? The former secretary to Charity Lodge did nothing to help your petition and then betrayed the Illuminati and Freemasons.'

'Does Pamina try to escape?' asked von Born.

'Monostatos catches her and his slaves drag her back in chains. Faced with her jailer, who threatens to kill her, she faints. Papageno saves her by scaring off Monostatos, but the sight of Monostatos gives Papageno just as much of a fright, and the two men run off in opposite directions. Pamina wakes up from death. She calls in vain for her dear mother, the Queen of the Night, and the first person she sees in her new life is Papageno. He checks the portrait that inspired Tamino's love and realises that she is indeed Pamina. Then he reveals to her that Prince Tamino is in love with her.'

'Pamina asks him the time, and he answers "shortly before midday", which is significant because that is when the lodge works open,' stated von Born. 'So begins Pamina's initiation into the Great Mysteries.'

'Papageno bewails the absence of a Papagena, while Pamina hopes Tamino will soon come to rescue her. Together, they sing a hymn to love, still at work in the circle of nature. For a true couple will achieve divinity.'

'But that ideal is still a long way off,' commented Thamos, 'because Tamino must endure many ordeals first. Advising him to be steadfast, patient and discreet, the three celestial boys lead him to three temples. When he tries to open the doors to the temples to Reason and Nature, a voice cries: "Back!" Finally, he knocks at the door to the middle temple, the temple to Wisdom. An old priest appears and tells him the truth: it was not love and virtue that guided Tamino's footsteps here but death and vengeance.'

'The Prince sees Sarastro as the embodiment of evil,' Mozart continued. 'If he is in charge of the Temple to Wisdom, it is all false hypocrisy. The priest warns him that he has been misled about Sarastro by female gossip. He admits that Sarastro abducted Pamina from her mother's arms, but he is under oath to keep silent and refuses to say any more. Darkness will lift if Tamino is led to the sanctuary by the hand of friendship. When will day dawn? he asks anxiously.'

'"Soon or never!" answers the choir of initiates,' said von Born. 'And they tell him that Pamina is alive and well. Tamino plays his flute and charms the wild animals, but the woman he loves cannot hear him. Will his music lead him to Pamina?'

Vienna, 2 May 1791

The professor of women's ailments, surgeon and Freemason, Johann Hunczowsky, was enormously proud of his recent promotion. His appointment to the position of private surgeon to Leopold II had made him one of the city's leading personalities.

He was still smarting from the violent criticisms of his Brother Mozart, after the accidental death of his daughter Anna-Maria who had lived for just one hour. How dared he accuse him, him a famous specialist, of making such a heinous mistake?

'Congratulations,' the Archbishop of Vienna said to him. 'You deserve the trust of our sovereign.'

'Thank you for this audience, your Grace. Although I belong to a secret society that you do not like, I must assure you of my Christian faith and my total respect for the Church. Thanks to you, the moral health of Vienna remains sound and unshakable. Unfortunately, not all Freemasons share my feelings, and some even dare to criticize our Holy Church.'

'Your words worry me, my son. Are you combating this deplorable tendency?'

'You may rely on me, your Grace, and you should show no leniency towards certain leaders whose subversive ideas are a threat to our society.'

'Are you thinking of anyone in particular?'

'Your question puts me on the spot.'

'God orders you to speak, my son.'

'Ignaz von Born is leading the lodges in the wrong direction. He is ill and no longer has any Masonic power. On the other hand, his principal disciple, Mozart, is still an active member and is developing the pagan ideas of his master. He seems to me to be a very dangerous individual.'

The archbishop's honeyed tones hid his inner rage. Mozart, always Mozart! The wrath of God would have to be unleashed and it was his job to see that it struck as it should.

Was the former Minister of Police, the Freemasons'
main adversary, Count of Pergen, still pursuing his
crusade? If so, he would be able to find the appropriate
methods.

37

The Magic Flute, *Act I, Scenes 16 to 19*

Thamos's alchemical elixir was acting to good effect, and Ignaz von Born's appetite had returned and he was able to walk about. But his body was exhausted and there would be no miracle now. Aware of his condition, the Venerable put all his energies into working on the ritual opera that would form a true ground-plan for future Masonry.

'Tamino goes off to look for Pamina,' Mozart said. 'She hears the sound of his flute. Monostatos has caught her and calls his henchmen to tie her up, but Papageno shakes his magic bells and they fall under the spell and start to sing and dance.'

'Trumpets and cymbals announce Sarastro's entrance,' stated von Born.

'Papageno panics and tries to hide. What should they say? "The truth" answers Pamina.'

'Wise, Venerable and universally worshipped, Sarastro gets down from a chariot drawn by six lions,' Thamos went on. 'He stands for vigilance and the transmission of initiation.'

'Pamina asks for forgiveness: her only reason for trying to escape and leave the realm of light was to evade the clutches of the malevolent Monostatos who had tried to rape her.'

'Sarastro soothes Pamina,' von Born added. 'He knows she loves a man she has never seen. All the same, he does not grant her her freedom, because she would go back to her mother, the queen of darkness, and be lost forever.'

'Monostatos now conducts Tamino before the Venerable Sarastro,' said Thamos. 'Thinking he is leading him to his death, he allows Tamino and Pamina to see each other for the first time. They recognize one another at first sight and know they were always intended for each other. They embrace and wonder if they are not about to celebrate their death. Monostatos separates them and reminds Sarastro that he must punish them.'

'It is the Venerable's duty to grant the traitor just retribution,' von Born decreed: 'seventy-seven strokes of bastinado!'

'Monostatos is banished,' Wolfgang took up, 'and the choir, consisting of Brothers as well as Sisters, praises the wisdom of Sarastro. He orders Tamino and Pamina to be led to the temple of ordeals so that they can be purified. Their heads are cloaked with sacks so that they cannot see. Then they are led away by their guide.'

'And the choir concludes Act I,' declared Ignaz von Born: '"If Virtue and Justice spread glory on the path of great men, the world would be a kingdom of heaven and men would be like gods. "'

Vienna, 9 May 1791

After writing a little piece for mechanical organ, which Deym had commissioned for his museum of wax figures*, Wolfgang plunged back into *The Magic Flute*.

Constance's attention to all their material worries meant he could devote himself entirely to the Great Work that would form the basis of the Grotto, the future initiation society where women would be initiated and the Egyptian mysteries would be key.

'You've had a letter from the City Council,' Constance announced, while Gaukerl sprang on to his master's knee.

Constance read out the letter in astonishment.

'First they refuse you, and now they've decided to accept your application. When Leopold Hoffmann dies, you will be made Kapellmeister at St Stephen's Cathedral.'

'Well, now we really will stay afloat with that new salary. But we mustn't wish for Hoffmann's death, even if he does detest Joseph Haydn!'

* K616.

'God will decide,' replied Constance, secretly hoping for a sensible intervention from the Lord.

Wolfgang wrote a *Kyrie* in D minor* so profound it was almost unbearable but in which there was nevertheless a sense of repose.

The Magic Flute, *Act II, Scenes 1 to 6*

'The scene opens in a forest of palm trees,' Mozart explained. 'The tree trunks are silver and the fronds are gold. In the centre, where the tallest trees grow, is a pyramid. Around it are eighteen seats for the Brothers, and on each seat are a little pyramid and a black horn studded with gold. These elements will evoke the Egyptian tradition, the initiates' ability to play the music of the spheres and the alchemical Rose-Cross degree. Carrying palm branches, the lodge members enter in a solemn procession to celebrate this extraordinary meeting.'

'Sarastro tells the initiates, who are servants to Isis and Osiris, that this is one of the most important assemblies of our time,' von Born interjected. 'The lodge first accepts that Tamino is fully able to confront the supreme ordeals, because he can keep a secret and is virtuous and humane. Tamino will be initiated by Sarastro together with Pamina whom Sarastro has been raising himself

---

* K341. The date of this piece was suggested by Monika Holl.

so that he can lead her to knowledge and to Tamino, because the couple will be essential to the lodges.'

'But he has to face the doubt and hostility of the Brothers!'

'Sarastro must appear convincing and win the allegiance of the brotherhood. And if Tamino dies, he will join Isis and Osiris beyond death. These two great gods formed the original couple that gave rise to initiation, and Sarastro asks them to bestow the spirit of wisdom on the new pair and to guide their steps.'

'The scene changes to a courtyard in front of the Temple. It is dark,' Mozart took up. 'Two initiates remove the sacks from the heads of Tamino and Papageno. They will now be subjected to the ordeals of darkness, solitude and silence. Brother Schikaneder will be sure to show Papageno's distress! All he wants is to run away from this terrifying place and eat and drink and find a Papagena! In the name of friendship and love, however, Tamino is ready to risk his life to conquer knowledge and wisdom. He knows his reward will be Pamina. So he gives his hand to his initiator, not the Commendatore who led Don Giovanni to his death at the end of his Fellow Craft's road, but a ritualist who leads the future Venerable to the heart of the Temple. The hardest test will be when Tamino sees Pamina but is not allowed to speak.'

'The forces of darkness try to prevent this initiation,' said the Egyptian. 'The three Ladies reappear and promise Tamino and Papageno death and perdition if they continue on this path. Tamino keeps his word and stays

215

silent. Inside the sanctuary, the voices of the initiates come to his aid and the three enemies are rushed away to hell.'

'The journey continues,' said von Born. 'Tamino's conduct is steadfast and manly and he passes this ordeal. But he has to go on along this thorny path. Pure in heart and with the help of the gods, he may yet succeed.'

38

Vienna, 11 May 1791

The Archbishop of Vienna and Joseph Anton met in top secret in a palace owned by the Church.

'I must say, I am extremely annoyed, my lord. The City Council is clearly in thrall to the Freemasons; do you know that they have promised Mozart the position of Kapellmeister?'

'I was told, your Grace.'

'Hmm . . . Are you continuing your activities under ground?'

'To you, a man of God, I confess that I am.'

'I assure you, I shall not breathe a word. This Mozart . . . How much more will he defy us?'

'He often visits Ignaz von Born,' Joseph Anton revealed. 'It is my opinion that Mozart is preparing a work that will openly broadcast the Masonic ideal. He is a genius, so I fear the worst.'

'A genius? What do you mean?'

'I mean that he knows how to put sublime form to creative thought in such a way as to convey it without betraying its secret. He touches men's hearts and transcends dogma.'

'Transcends dogma! That is criminal of the Freemasons! My lord, we must stop this demon from doing harm.'

'I have been dismissed, your Grace.'

'God is giving you full powers and I grant you absolution.'

'Whatever I do?'

'Whatever you do.'

The Magic Flute, *Act II, Scenes 7 to 12*

To be worthy of Tamino, Pamina has to face several dangers.

'The first is Monostatos' bestial desires,' said Mozart. 'Pamina is asleep under an arbour of roses, the symbol of the secret of initiation. The traitor's dusky face is burning with wicked passion as he approaches her.'

'The Queen of the Night emerges from the shadows,' put in von Born, 'and repels Monostatos, her ally. Where is the young man, Tamino? she asks, testily. He has gone to join the initiates, Pamina replies. The Queen realizes that her plan has failed: Tamino is eluding her and with him, Pamina. So she explains how, when her husband died, she lost her power. He considered her unworthy to receive it and gave it into the keeping of Sarastro, the solar circle with seven rays, symbolizing the union of male and female initiation.'

'The Queen of the Night wants to destroy the temple from which she is barred forever,' added Thamos. 'Pamina protests: why shouldn't she love an initiate who belongs to a brotherhood praised by her father for its wisdom, intelligence and goodness? Is Sarastro not the most virtuous of these exceptional men?'

'The Queen of the Night is incensed by her daughter's lucidity,' said Mozart. 'So, Pamina is in love with an initiate, an ally of Sarastro, her mortal enemy! With her heart boiling with infernal vengeance, the queen of darkness swears to desert her daughter unless she kills Sarastro with a dagger, which she places in Pamina's hand. The young woman is in despair, certain she could never become an assassin.'

'Monostatos has overheard all this,' commented Thamos. 'Now he has Pamina's life in his hands as well as her mother's, because he can betray the plot to Sarastro. The only solution is for the young woman to agree to love him! When she refuses, Monostatos threatens to stab her. She begs him to spare her.'

'Sarastro saves her,' suggested Ignaz von Born, 'and banishes Monostatos. The Venerable knows that the Queen of the Night forged the dagger and is plotting her revenge as she wanders in the underground halls of the Temple. This sentiment is foreign to the initiates, who practise authentic friendship. Sarastro is concerned only to recreate the royal couple, formed of Tamino and Pamina. But the young man has not yet defeated the dark.'

Vienna, 13 May 1791

In June 1787, Crowned Hope Lodge had over a hundred Brothers, most of them absentees. Now there were only thirty-nine on the register.

The Brothers sat on benches covered in fabric and contemplated the flame from the Orient, hoping that it would light up their way.

After the opening of the works to celebrate the recreation of the universe by light and the establishment of order in the world by the Three Great Pillars of Wisdom, Strength and Beauty, the Venerable gave the floor to Count Canal, who had arrived from Prague to warn his Viennese Brothers.

'Our Order is in peril,' he declared. 'There are ever more police about and the Prague lodges are under constant surveillance.'

'It doesn't matter, because we are doing nothing wrong,' judged Count Thun, whose mystical leanings masked some awkward facts about his private life.

'You are right, my Brother,' nodded Thamos the Egyptian, 'but sadly the emperor does not share your opinion. In the eyes of his counsellors, we are concerned only with free-thinking and we blame the regime and the Church for keeping people down. Consequently,

Leopold II loathes and detests Freemasonry for challenging morality, religion and society. We are disgracing the ideal of charity which should have remained our only principle.'

'We must explain to the emperor how things really are,' proposed Count Thun, 'and convince him that we are still his good and loyal subjects.'

'Our high-placed Brothers are doing that every day. It is a difficult task because our adversaries are powerful and determined.'

'What should we do, in the event of danger?'

'Go on as we are,' declared Mozart. 'Nothing is as important as initiation. If the world were deprived of it, it would become a battlefield of envy and violence. We are not above reproach because members have become half-hearted. We must pull together and refuse to be blackmailed. Let us open the doors of our temples to men and women who deserve to be let in.'

'My Brother,' exclaimed a dignitary, 'are you suggesting women should be initiated? The lodges of adoption and a few worldly ceremonies are quite enough for them.'

'We all know that the alchemical work is accomplished through the symbolic union of the king and queen.'

Refusing to engage with him on this subject, other Brothers put forward the necessity of pleading their cause with the authorities in order to avoid disaster.

Without the brotherly glance in his direction from Thamos the Egyptian, Mozart would have felt completely alone.

39

The Magic Flute, *Act II, Scenes 13 to 25*

'I wasn't surprised at how most of the Brothers reacted,' said Ignaz von Born. 'They are creatures of habit and don't like change. Which is a very good reason to build a new temple.'

'Tamino and his loquacious companion, Papageno, go on their way,' said Mozart. 'An old woman claiming to be eighteen years and two minutes old pops up and reveals that he is her lover, then vanishes without telling him her name. The three boys come down from the sky in a flying machine, bringing back the magic objects that had been taken away from the two travellers, the flute and the jingle bells. They offer them a meal and promise that the third time they see them, joy will be the reward for their courage. Papageno tucks in and eats and drinks, but Tamino plays his flute.'

'Because he is keeping to the Rules,' Thamos put

in, 'Pamina appears. She heard the sound of the magic instrument and is looking for comfort and help from her beloved. But Tamino has to stay silent.'

'Even Papageno refuses to speak this time,' added Wolfgang. 'Tamino no longer loves me, is Pamina's conclusion, and this insult is worse than death. Instead of the happiness she had hoped for, she finds only loneliness and despair.'

'Tamino continues on his road of ordeals,' von Born continued. 'Inside the vaulted hall of a pyramid, the initiates form a triangle, the emblem of the creative principle. They all hold lanterns shaped like pyramids. Worshipping Isis and Osiris, they sing of their joy at receiving a new Brother who will devote himself to initiation because he is strong of mind and pure in heart. Tamino, however, still has to go along two perilous roads. Sarastro greets Pamina and takes the sack off her head so that she can see. Then she gazes on her beloved.'

'This is the most cruel test of all,' remarked Thamos, 'because Tamino says farewell to her before facing terrifying dangers.'

'However,' said von Born, 'Sarastro assures them that they will see one another again and find joy.'

'Pamina is sure that Tamino will not get out alive,' Wolfgang emphasized.

'The will of the gods will be accomplished. Although they are sure of their eternal fidelity, Tamino and Pamina separate. "Farewell forever" thinks Pamina, in distress.

'Papageno, meanwhile, is quite happy to renounce

celestial joys reserved for initiates,' noted Wolfgang. 'He gets the cherished glass of wine and plays his bells, begging a pretty little woman to appear and enjoy life with him. And the old woman reappears. If he rejects her, he will be condemned to prison and a diet of bread and water. So he promises her fidelity until the day he finds a more beautiful girl! This false promise is enough to turn her into a ravishing young Papagena, but the Brother Speaker forbids Papageno from touching her, because her suitor is not yet worthy of her. The ground opens and swallows him up.'

'The two couples are temporarily split up,' observed Thamos. 'Now comes the hardest ordeal of all, the ordeal of death.'

Vienna, 14 May 1791

At forty-one, the composer Antonio Salieri was at the peak of his fame and fortune. Chosen by Josef II to be the official musician at the court of Vienna, he had managed to persuade the rigid Leopold II not to strip him of any of his privileges. Thus, Salieri continued to hold sway over Viennese music and entertain the court with operas that were as quickly forgotten as they were written.

'I am one of your most fervent admirers,' Joseph Anton told him. 'Your talent distracts us from the approaching storm clouds over Europe.'

'You are pessimistic, my lord.'

'The emperor will stand firm against the kind of turmoil that is dragging France to the edge of the abyss, but he must muzzle those who put about subversive propaganda, like one of your competitors.'

'Who do you mean?' Salieri asked, in alarm.

'Mozart.'

'Mozart? Vienna has forgotten about him!'

'He is writing another opera.'

'An opera,' murmured Salieri. 'But he didn't have much luck in that field.'

'His setbacks have done his abilities no harm.'

'Mozart . . . If he lives long enough, he will outshine us all.'

'If we act carefully, we can get rid of this subversive element.'

'I hardly dare understand you, my lord!'

'Be bold, dear Salieri, be bold! Otherwise, your star could well be dimmed.'

'I am only an artist in love with beautiful music, and . . .'

'You are a courtier determined to defend your interests, and you are now forewarned. Either you take the necessary action, or you will suffer the consequences of your inertia.'

Leaving Salieri alone with his confusion, Joseph Anton went to find Geytrand. His assistant was brandishing his informants' reports.

'Did your interview go well, my lord?'

'Salieri is not very bright but he is very attached to his privileged position.'

'Do you think he is capable of eliminating Mozart?'

'It is not impossible. The man is pretentious, selfish and scheming. If he feels himself threatened, he will react. In any case, he is a new ally and I have high hopes of fruitful initiatives!'

'I am amazed at Ignaz von Born's resilience,' Geytrand admitted. 'He is still receiving Mozart and working long hours with him.'

'The significance of their ongoing project is giving him the energy to go on,' judged Joseph Anton. 'They are moulding a veritable war machine to restore Freemasonry to its former position. Ignaz von Born is giving his last strength to the battle and passing down to his disciple the spiritual power to make him even more formidable.'

40

The Magic Flute, *Act II, Scenes 26 to the Finale*

Thamos the Egyptian had given his spies the slip again and was visiting Ignaz von Born. The secret police were back on duty to show that they were not to be duped and still saw the mineralogist as Freemasonry's mastermind. Mozart, his chief disciple, was now top of their list of dangerous and subversive initiates.

Given the Venerable's state of health, it was impossible to organize work meetings anywhere but in his house. They were coming to the critical part of the opera and the culmination of the ritual of *The Magic Flute*.

'The three beings of Light descend from the sky again,' von Born declared, 'because death is on the prowl and threatening to annihilate the hopes of Sarastro and the initiates. But the sun will soon light up the golden way and, once more, the serenity of wisdom will be embodied in men's hearts. Then the earth will become a kingdom of heaven.'

Christian Jacq

'Pamina, beside herself with grief, threatens to kill herself with the dagger intended for Sarastro,' said Wolfgang. 'She is therefore refusing to behave like a bad Fellow Craft and assassinate the Master Mason. Since she cannot marry Tamino, because the primordial couple cannot be reconstituted, she would be better dead.'

'The three boys swear that Tamino is faithful,' said Thamos. 'Although he is bound to remain silent, he loves her, and she loves him. And this love gives her the strength to face death. No enemy can separate them because the gods are watching over them. Although they cannot reveal the reason for his silence, the three boys lead Pamina to Tamino.'

'The scene changes to two great mountains,' indicated Mozart. 'Inside one is a raging waterfall, while the other contains fire. The power of these elements is visible through iron grills. Tamino, in bare feet and lightly clad, is led on by two initiates carrying black cutlasses and with lighted torches on their helmets. They read Tamino the inscription engraved on the pyramid that stands centre-stage. "He who travels this road beset by difficult tests will be purified by Fire, Water, Air and Earth. If he conquers the fear of death, he will soar from earth up to heaven. Then he will be enlightened and will be able to dedicate himself fully to the mysteries of Isis. "'

'That encapsulates the initiation to the three degrees,' noted von Born. 'Now, he must go on.'

'Tamino does not quail before death,' Mozart

228

confirmed. 'He joyfully embarks on this perilous road and orders the doors of fear to be opened to him.'

'Without Pamina,' Thamos remarked, 'he would never manage. But she is given permission to travel with him, and she joins him. Now that he can talk to her, he knows that nothing, not even death, will come between them.'

'They walk towards the temple,' went on von Born. 'A woman who fears neither the dark nor death is venerable and will be initiated. The queen is always at the king's side. She will guide him, and love will direct him along a thorny path of roses. Pamina takes Tamino's hand and asks him to play the magic flute carved by her father from the deepest part of a thousand-year-old oak while thunder and lightning raged during a storm. Bolstered by the power of the music, the couple go on their way with joy through the dark night of death. They go through fire and water, and then they come to a brightly lit temple porch and discover the perfection of the light.'

'The happiness of Isis is granted,' commented Thamos. 'The noble couple has vanquished danger and the consecration of the great goddess is granted.'

'Don't forget Papageno!' Wolfgang reminded them. 'He cannot find his Papagena and decides to hang himself. The three boys again descend from the sky and persuade him to desist, advising him to use his magic bells, which he has been wrong to neglect. The sound attracts Papagena and the couple is united and look forward to having lots of children.'

'We still have to settle the case of the Queen of the

Night and her clan,' Ignaz von Born added. 'Carrying black torches, the forces of darkness try to violate the temple, launch a surprise attack on the initiates and destroy them. Once they have done that, Pamina will be given to the traitor Monostatos. But there is a clap of thunder and a flash of lightning and a violent storm is unleashed. The whole stage turns into a sun and the malevolent beings are cast into hell. Light dispels the shadows and destroys the power that was wrongfully wrested by hypocrites. The priests and priestesses express their gratitude and welcome the united initiates who are wearing ritual dress. Strength is victorious and crowns Beauty and Wisdom with an everlasting crown. Wisdom, Strength and Beauty, the Three Great Pillars of initiation, enthrone the royal couple. Sarastro has brought the Great Work to its end and a new era begins based on the primordial tradition.'

A long, very long silence followed the conclusion of *The Magic Flute*, which Venerable Ignaz von Born had directed.

'What would give me the greatest pleasure,' the composer said, at last, 'would be success by silence.'

'You are not writing for our own time,' answered von Born, 'or even for profane Freemasons. Founding a new Order of initiation is the right way.'

Since their first meeting, Thamos knew that the Great Magician would bring the vision of the Ancient Egyptians to light. Now, he needed to write music that would travel through time to convey that light.

41

Vienna, 23 May 1791

Karl Thomas was now six and he could not understand why his mother would not let him sing at the top of his voice.

'Usually, I . . .'

'Your father is working.'

'He's always working!'

'Yes, but he's writing a very important piece,' Constance explained, 'and he is trying to avoid any little noise. He goes about on tip-toe, even in his study, and when he takes Gaukerl for a walk, he goes "shhh" to passers-by if they make too much noise.'

'What is he writing?'

'A grand opera called *The Magic Flute*. We must both be careful not to get in his way. On the contrary, we must help him concentrate and gather his forces.'

Karl Thomas looked unconvinced, but he agreed to the constraints.

When he had finished a Quintet for glass harmonica*, an instrument the Freemason Benjamin Franklin had invented for the blind virtuoso Marianne Kirchgässner, Wolfgang knew that the ritual opera he had carried about in him for so long could at last come to fruition.

After his morning ablutions, he would walk up and down composing melodies, which formed the basis of his music. His mind was constantly alert, he was in an excellent mood and he seemed to observe the external world as though he never really came out of his work. At mealtimes, he sat deep in thought, brushing a corner of his serviette back and forth under his nose and made only anodyne conversation. Although working flat out, he never complained.

'You look pale,' he said to his wife.

'I'm just a bit tired.'

'Don't hide anything from me, darling.'

'My feet and legs hurt. The doctor recommends I take a cure in Baden.'

'Well, you should listen to him.'

'The cost . . .'

'Your health comes before everything else!'

'Where can I stay that won't be too expensive?'

'I shall write to my friend Anton Stoll, the teacher and choir master at the parish church in Baden. He will find you a comfortable, affordable apartment. In your condition, you ought not to go up and down stairs. He is not

---

* K617, for flute, oboe, viola and cello.

terribly astute, but Stoll will do us this favour. I'm thinking of the ground floor flat Goldhann lived in. He's a
kind of banker and sometimes lends me money.'

Vienna, 5 June 1791

Constance, who was seven-months pregnant, had gone
to Baden with Karl Thomas, Gaukerl, a chambermaid
and Süssmayr, a pupil of Mozart who would help her
deal with practical matters.

Wolfgang dismissed his servant Leonore and went to
sleep at the house of the horn player and cheese monger,
'that nonentity' Leutgeb. Mrs Leutgeb did not launder
his neck tie nearly as well as Constance, he wrote to her
immediately, adding that he trembled at the thought of
her taking the Anthony baths and negotiating the steps
and that she must take good care not to slip. Then he sent
her 2999 kisses . . . and a half.

On the 6th, Wolfgang dined at the Ungarishe Krone
with Süssmayr, who was home from Baden, and spent
the evening at the opera. His flat, when he returned to it,
seemed dispiritingly empty.

Vienna, 7 June 1791

Emanuel Schikaneder took a swig from his tankard of
beer to clear his mind, then cut a thick chunk of hare pâté.

'My theatre is going from strength to strength,' he announced to Mozart. 'Burgers and well-dressed folk like nothing better than to be amused by a good show. How is our future opera coming along?'

Wolfgang gave him a detailed progress account of his *Magic Flute*.

'Splendid!' exclaimed Schikaneder. 'I'll write that all in and include as many comic scenes and dramatic effects as I can. And I'll keep Papageno's role for myself. The audience will split their sides laughing!'

'I'll be thinking about every word in your libretto,' Wolfgang warned him.

'Agreed, agreed! Ah, I can already see the birdcatcher, the flying machine with the three boys, exquisite little Papagena and the splendour of the Egyptian temple! Let's get to work, my Brother.'

'My wife's health is worrying me. I am going to join her in Baden tomorrow. All the same, I've made a start on the music.'

'A triumph . . . *The Magic Flute* will be a triumph!'

Vienna, 11 June 1791

When he returned from a brief trip to see Constance, Wolfgang felt anxious and depressed. He thought the daily treatment of baths excessive; surely she should stop them just for a day at least, he wrote to her.

He rose at half-past four and managed to open his

watch but could not find the key to wind it up. Annoyed, he wound up the great clock and, fighting off his despondency, he composed an aria for *The Magic Flute* in which the two priests who objected to the initiation of women roundly criticized them*.

Today, he was to meet the 'banker' Goldhann, an iron merchant and a slightly questionable usurer, whose loan would enable the composer to forget his financial problems.

The saccharine gentleman turned up at Mozart's house in the course of the morning but claimed to be too busy for a proper meeting and promised to return between midday and one o'clock. The musician waited in vain until three, missing a lunch appointment with Brother Puchberg. He was obliged to eat alone at the Ungarische Krone in the now empty dining room before going home and continuing to wait for Goldhann. He could not focus properly on his work in these circumstances, and at half-past six, he at last received a string of excuses. His 'banker' assured him he would keep his word.

Wolfgang went back to the Ungarische Krone, dined and went on to the Leopold Theatre where he attended a performance of a German opera by Wenzel Müller that had the arresting title *Kaspar the Bassoonist or the Magic Sitar*! 'It is causing quite a stir,' he noted, 'but it is nothing to write home about.'

Tomorrow would be a better day.

---

* The priests' duet in Act II, No. 11.

42

Lonely, hassled by day-to-day worries and quite at a loss without Constance's invaluable help, Wolfgang was feeling completely tormented just when he had most need of all his creative energies.

He rose at five, threw on his clothes and went to the house of Goldhann.

He found the door locked. Panic seized him. What if the banker was actively trying to avoid him? Without a loan, Wolfgang could not pay for Constance's cure in Baden. *Who will keep on prodding him on my behalf?* he wrote to her. *For if he is not prodded, he goes off the boil.* And he kissed his dear little wife two thousand times.

A meeting in the degree of Fellow Craft restored his energy. Stadler told him that the bass clarinet was nearly complete and the investments Mozart had agreed to would soon be crowned with success.

The Beloved of Isis

'You look worried,' Thamos said to him.

'Constance's health bothers me. Will this new cure be beneficial, will her pregnancy reach a happy conclusion? We have had so much misfortune. But don't worry, I'm not neglecting *The Magic Flute* for an instant!'

Vienna, 13 June 1791

After dining again with Schikaneder, who was poised to write the libretto according to Mozart's strict instructions, Wolfgang went and hammered on Goldhann's door.

'I should love to help you, my dear Mozart, but what are your guarantees?'

'My salary for composing dance music for the La Redoute balls, the City Council's promise of a job at the cathedral and a new opera put on by Schikaneder. My career was temporarily interrupted but it has taken off again. Oh, and there are my pupils and future concerts.'

'Interesting . . . Let us take a closer look.'

The interview lasted until nine in the evening. Wolfgang was satisfied and wrote to Constance that the 'banker' was going to visit her in Baden and he begged her to give him a hard time! Still just as jealous, he advised her not to go to the casino, on no account to dance because of her foot and not to go about in company.

Baden, 17 June 1791

Anton Stoll was delighted to see Mozart, who provided him with religious music and music by his friend Michael Haydn.

'Thank you for helping out Constance.'

'Don't mention it! Dare I ask . . . We are coming up to the Festival of St John, and if you could compose a little motet . . .'

'Do you have a specific text in mind?'

'The *Ave Verum Corpus*, a Latin text from the fourteenth century. It isn't liturgical but I think you will like it.'

Stoll knew how Mozart had worshipped the Virgin Mary in his youth.

The Master Mason read the few lines:

Hail, true body born of the Virgin Mary, who truly suffered and was sacrificed on the cross for man, whose pierced side overflowed with water and blood, be for us a foretaste of the test of death.

The test of death, the one Tamino and Pamina overcame in order to be initiated.

Mozart, the Freemason, had long ago left behind religion and belief. Nevertheless, this short text struck a profound chord with him. And he was interested in the pagan nature of the Feast of St John, once more permitted now that Josef II's ban had been lifted. On that occasion, the Church and the goddess Earth came together in a marriage promising good harvests and which was celebrated with a procession that stopped four times to symbolize the cardinal points of the cosmos.

'A distant legacy from the Festival of Min,' Thamos said, as, on that sunny 18 June, Mozart was about to conduct his *Ave Verum Corpus** for small choir, strings and organ, in the modest church of Baden.

'Is something wrong?' Wolfgang asked, surprised to see the Egyptian.

'I had a presentiment that a big event was about to take place and I wouldn't have missed it for the world. Go on and conduct, please.'

The *Ave Verum Corpus* seemed to open doors to a land of light beyond death. Thamos was bowled over by this short, limpid piece. Quite clearly concerned with future initiation, the music was suffused with the spirit of the Eternal Orient.

The two Brothers met outside.

'There may be an opportunity to celebrate a genuine Feast of St John this summer,' said the Egyptian. 'Would you compose a short cantata to the glory of the sun, the soul of the universe†?'

'Of course!'

'I wanted to give you the last chapters of *The Book of*

* K618. Mozart only used that part of the text.

† *Dir, Seele des Weltalls*, K429 (468a). The date and author of the words are disputed.

239

Thoth. They will inspire you and help you construct *The Magic Flute*.'

Vienna, 25 June 1791

The midsummer Festival of St John did not take place, and Mozart's Cantata remained unfinished. Most of the Brothers were afraid of attracting the wrath of the Church by holding a rite with so strong a pagan influence.

Composing *The Magic Flute* was giving Mozart tremendous creative energy and nothing could shake it. He rose before five, wrote to Constance at five-thirty, and decided to play a practical joke on the lumbering Leutgeb. Calling at his house, he had a message sent up to him that a dear old friend from Rome had searched all over town for him but had not found him anywhere. The cheesemonger was completely taken in, put on his Sunday best and had his hair elaborately dressed. Everyone had a good laugh at his expense when the farce was uncovered.

Wolfgang asked his Brother Puchberg to lend him twenty-five florins* to pay for Constance's cure in Baden. It was to be his last loan, because he would soon be earning enough. He took the opportunity to thank his Brother for helping to sell sheet music for a total of four

* In all, from 1788, he received 1415 florins from Puchberg, a relatively modest sum, given that he earned an annual salary of eight hundred florins and benefited from additional sources of income.

hundred and fifty florins, of which the composer only took a third.

With his money troubles abating, Mozart was now free to turn his attention entirely to the mysteries of Isis and Osiris.

43

Vienna, 26 June 1791

'Mozart's wife is taking the waters in Baden,' Geytrand told Joseph Anton. 'He goes there now and then and is still attending his lodge but he is not going to see von Born so often. Either the Venerable's health has taken a turn for the worse or their work is nearing completion.'

'I fear the worst, my good friend! Meanwhile, news from France is catastrophic! Louis XVI took fright at the spread of revolutionary insanity and tried to leave the country but was arrested at Varennes-en-Argonne. He refused to use force and let himself be bound hand and foot by fanatics who dragged the monarch back to Paris in tatters. The crowd was raving around the royal couple and threatening to do terrible things to them. They are accusing the king of conniving with the enemies of the Revolution. Disaster is looming, Geytrand. Sooner or later, the dogmatists will call for the execution of the king and queen and sow bloody terror that will spread throughout Europe. And now this intolerable chaos Mozart and his Freemason friends are plotting!'

Geytrand coughed.

'According to our informants, my lord, Mozart is not remotely attracted by the French Revolution.'

'We will accuse him of complicity. Then the emperor will see what a noxious character he is.'

Vienna, 26 June 1791

Mozart's contact with the Piarists[*] was not the result of new-found belief but because he wanted to have his son Karl Thomas educated by their religious community. The little rascal was wayward and disobedient and he hoped that the rather strict discipline of the order's instruction would put him on the right path. His son's future depended on a sound education, no matter what the cost.

Wolfgang asked Constance to send him two summer outfits, the white and the brown one. Then he advised her to take no more than one bath every two days, and only for an hour. The best solution would be not to bathe at all, while she waited for him to visit her again.

Thamos took Mozart to see von Born, who was confined to bed.

---

[*] An order of regular clerics founded in 1597.

'The French situation is growing worse with every passing day,' the Egyptian declared. 'The royal family has been taken prisoner by the revolutionaries, and the Freemasons are suspected of supporting the Jacobins and preparing the ground for revolution in Germany.'

'In other words,' put in von Born, 'this is the worst possible moment to put on *The Magic Flute*. By promoting initiation, our Brother Mozart is at risk of serious trouble with the authorities.'

'Venerable Master,' said Wolfgang, 'I do not care. The time has come to give artistic form to our vision.'

'You should be aware of the danger,' von Born advised. 'You alone will be blamed for defending the Masonic Order.'

Mozart smiled.

'I do not deserve that honour, but I shall try to prove myself worthy of it.'

Vienna, 2 July 1791

Thamos introduced Mozart to several English Freemasons. They wanted to meet an artist who had no qualms about defying people's mistrust of the Order and increased police surveillance, and who openly declared his allegiance.

'Shouldn't you come to London?' one of the visitors ventured. 'There, you could express yourself freely and you would have overnight success.'

'I cannot desert my Brothers in the thick of the

storm. We shall find a way to persuade the emperor that Freemasonry is useful and its ideal noble.'

'Isn't that a rather . . . optimistic view?'

'You only need a few determined men to realize the impossible.'

'Don't do anything rash, Brother Mozart. London will wait for you.'

Twice a day, a mail coach took post between Vienna and Baden, and Wolfgang used the service to write frequently to Constance.

Please tell that oaf Süssmayr to send the score of Act I so that I can work on the orchestration. If he could send the parcel today, it would go off tomorrow morning by the first coach, and I would have it by midday. Even if everything goes wrong, there is only one thing on my mind and that is your health. So long as you are well, everything else becomes a trifle.

Vienna, 3 July 1791

'My dear Brother,' Schikaneder said to Wolfgang, 'I am going to place at your disposal a little summerhouse in the garden near the theatre where our *Magic Flute* is to be put on. You will find it a charming place to work in and very relaxing. Inside, you will find a table and chair and as much manuscript paper and ink as you want. The players will come and encourage you and bring you food and drink.'

As the impresario predicted, Mozart was visited first by Franz-Xaver Gerl, his future Sarastro and married to Papagena, next by Josepha Hofer, Constance's sister and the first Queen of the Night, then by the young Miss Gottlieb who would take the part of Pamina, and finally by Schack, proud to be cast as Tamino and whose wife would be the third Lady.

The singers were a close-knit troop and were very excited by this new opera. During a quiet moment, Wolfgang wrote to Constance to advise her to drink wine, as it was inexpensive and wholesome, whereas the water was horrid.

Puchberg told him that he had just sold some scores to Brother Franz Deyerkauf, a music seller in Graz, the capital of Styria, and a great admirer of Mozart's music to whose glory he wanted to erect a monument in his garden.

The following day, Wolfgang sent Constance three florins and the day after, twenty-five. Work was coming on apace and he visited Baron Wetzlar, a business man who would help him pay off his last debts.

As soon as everything is settled, he wrote to his wife, *I shall be ready to be with you. I mean to rest in your arms, for I greatly need to, for this mental worry and anxiety and all the running around have fairly worn me out.*

44

'Mozart is working day and night in a summerhouse near Schikaneder's theatre,' Geytrand told Joseph Anton. 'The troupe appears to be a hotbed of Freemasons.'

'We need an informant.'

'Gossip is enough, my lord.'

'And?'

'Mozart is composing a grand opera. He wrote the libretto himself after work sessions with Ignaz von Born, and Schikaneder is adapting it for the stage. The plot is a fairy tale with alternate spoken and sung passages.'

'What is the subject exactly?'

'The story of a magic flute and a pair of lovers. Schikaneder seems immensely proud of his role as a comic character dressed in feathers who will amuse his audience. Mozart knows he is banned from the big theatres because of his flops, and now he wants to entertain popular audiences in local theatres.'

Vienna, 7 July 1791

Every morning at seven o'clock, Wolfgang held discussions with Goldhann to update the terms of his loan without crippling himself. He apologized to Constance for not sending her more than one letter per day because he had too much work.

Away from her, he found time dragged, but he had to keep on regardless and finish writing

The Magic Flute. I cannot tell you how I feel, he confided to her, *it's like a painful emptiness, a kind of unsatisfied yearning. It never goes away and grows and grows, day after day. When I think of what childlike fun we had in Baden! Here the hours are dull and boring. I don't even find my work entertaining because I was used to breaking off from time to time to chat to you, and that pleasure is now impossible. If I sit down at the piano and sing something from my opera, I have to stop immediately, because it moves me too much. Basta! As soon as my business is finished, I'm leaving straight away.*

Wolfgang could not be happy without Constance, especially at a time of such concentrated work when he so much wanted to discuss his music with her. Sometimes, he found the experience so intense, he could hardly bear it. The ritual in *The Magic Flute* took him out of himself right to the heart of the mystery of initiation. The notes and melodies came from a light up above, and it was only by an exhausting effort that he managed to commit it to paper. No previous work had made such demands on him.

Baden, 9 July 1791

In Baden, Constance saw a creditor and soothed his concerns with the promise of imminent payment. Wolfgang was worried about the consequences of this step and possible penalties, when the final details of his contract with Goldhann were not yet settled.

Sometimes, he felt so disheartened that he wanted to throw everything up and rush back to Baden to be at peace with his wife. But he knew it would be childish to run away and Schikaneder was begging him not to lose an instant. Producing *The Magic Flute* would be his big break and he had no doubts about the opera's success.

In Baden, Süssmayr acted as Constance's servant. Mozart was prone to calling him 'Sauermayr' – 'sour' instead of 'sweet' – because he thought he was jealous and not very clever. All the same, he was useful to them.

At last, on 9 July, the composer was able to hug Constance in Baden, though not before he had stroked Gaukerl and rebuked Karl Thomas, who was misbehaving.

'You are exhausted,' she remarked.

'And you, how are you?'

'The treatment has done me the world of good.'

'Do you feel fully recovered?'

'Not quite, but I'm coming back to Vienna with you.'

'Think first of your health, my darling. Provided I know you are jolly and smiling, I can put up with every trial.'

'I want to be with you so you can work in peace.'

Vienna, 12 July 1791

As the Piarists were asking Mozart to conduct a mass, and as he was still keen to send the unruly Karl Thomas to be educated by them, he asked his friend Anton Stoll, the Baden choirmaster, to send him the score of one of his pieces of church music he had previously sent him.

Constance's return had put him in excellent spirits and he opened his letter with a flourish: *Very dear Stoll, don't be a poll, you excellent madman! Comedian and drunken sot!*

When he had dispatched the missive, Wolfgang welcomed Thamos and Franz-Heinrich Ziegenhagen, a Freemason, trader and teacher from Hamburg.

The Egyptian was looking for texts for the future

initiation society, the Grotto, and Ziegenhagen, who was delighted to see Mozart again, had come up with an idea of some originality considering how conservative the lodges could be.

'We want the heart and mind to blossom,' the trader said. 'Adepts will be unburdened of all dogmatic religion and learn a manual craft and think freely. I have written a hymn for the new community. Will you set it to music?'

'What does it say?' asked Wolfgang.

'First comes a recitative to the Great Architect: "You who praise the creator of the infinite universe, whether you call him Jehovah, God, Fu or Brahma – listen! Listen through the voice of the trumpet the words of the Master of the Universe! Their eternal sound echoes across the continents, planets and stars. And you too, human beings, listen to this. "'

'Let's hope the Great Architect hears you,' said the musician. 'What comes next?'

'A slow movement advises people to love order, moderation and harmony. True nobility involves an enlightened mind. Then, there's an Allegro that will banish false belief and that bids enlightened beings to join hands, cast off error and discover the truth! Iron weapons will be turned into ploughshares and rocks will be blown open with the dark powder previously used to make munitions used to kill men. A second slow movement proclaims that the reign of evil should never be regarded as inevitable. Reason will win out and conquer disaster and blindness. Be wise, be strong, be Brothers! Our lamentations will turn to songs of joy and the deserts will become gardens of Eden. And the last Allegro states: thus can the true happiness of life be attained.'

'I like your words and ideas,' Wolfgang nodded. 'I shall write you a Cantata* straight away.'

The work was simple, pared back and almost austere.

Mozart was no longer alone: another Mason was trying to drag the lodges out of the mire. If his attempt succeeded, Brothers and Sisters of the Grotto would find precious allies†.

---

* K619. *A Little German Cantata.*

† Ziegenhagen tried to establish a brotherhood in Alsace. When his attempt failed, he committed suicide.

45

Vienna, 12 July 1791

At eleven o'clock in the morning, elegantly but unostentatiously dressed, the Abbé Lorenzo Da Ponte attended a private audience with Emperor Leopold II.

'Your Majesty, my loyalty to you is total I assure you, and I must thank you for the favour you show me.'

'That's enough barbed courtesy, Abbé. You have written and been the inspiration for pamphlets against me.'

'I have been terribly slandered! If I have made mistakes, I beg your pardon.'

'What have you done for me?'

'My talents as a librettist have been used in numerous operas that entertain our dear Viennese, and I can provide you with ample information on this or that person in your court whose words or acts are sometimes suspicious.'

'Do you have any specific examples?'

Da Ponte trotted out all sorts of tittle-tattle, mingling truth and lies and sparing no one, especially his competitors.

'You have often worked with Mozart.'

'I wrote three operas that brought him to fame.'

'What can you tell me about him?'

'Not much! He is passionate about his work and composes at an extraordinary rate.'

'Could he be plotting against the regime?'

'Not to my knowledge, Your Majesty.'

'I think you are ill informed, Abbé.'

'Your Majesty, I . . .'

'Let's leave it at that.'

At midday, Lorenzo Da Ponte left the palace. He knew he had failed to win over the emperor and inveigle his way back into his good graces.

The only solution was to leave the country[*].

Vienna, 14 July 1791

Domenico Guardasoni, impresario at the Prague National Theatre, arrived in the empire's capital in an ugly mood. In Vienna, he met Mazzolà, the official court poet, to discuss *La Clemenza di Tito*, an *opera seria* to be performed when Leopold II was crowned King of Bohemia. At a time when the French Revolution

---

[*] Da Ponte spent some time in London, after which he travelled to New York where he died at the age of eighty-nine having attended the first performance of *Don Giovanni*.

was raging and denouncing all Europe's monarchs as tyrants, the opera stressed the generosity and tolerance of a Roman emperor who would be identified with the Austrian one. By proclaiming Leopold II's benevolence, it would act as splendid propaganda.

In April 1789, Guardasoni had commissioned Mozart to write the music, but there had been no proper contract; the musician's star had faded and the impresario preferred to give the work to the most fashionable composer of the day, Antonio Salieri. Alas, Salieri had refused the proposal four times.

Guardasoni wanted to see him in person and persuade him to take it on. Full of his own importance and scornful of Prague which he saw as a provincial city with little to offer, Salieri nevertheless agreed to receive the obdurate beggar.

'An opera about Ancient Rome . . . the theme is terribly dated!'

'The circumstances demand a noble, serious style, maestro.'

'I am not going to waste my talent on it.'

'It's an official commission.'

'It's 14 July, the coronation is on 6 September. No composer, do you hear, not one, would take on so hazardous an enterprise for such a silly little work that is bound to displease his Majesty.'

'Let me try to convince you . . .'

'I do not let you, no! Deal with your *Clemenza di Tito* yourself and stop pestering me!'

Vienna, 15 July 1791

'Delighted to see you again, my dear Mozart!' gushed Guardasoni. 'Prague will always hold you in great esteem. Do you remember our agreement about *La Clemenza di Tito*?'

'I had forgotten about it.'

'On 6 September, you must be aware, our revered emperor is to be crowned King of Bohemia.'

'I have so much work at the moment that I hadn't given it much thought.'

'But I had thought of no one but you to write this opera to the glory of our sovereign! I am sorry I couldn't contact you sooner. I had a few administrative details to sort out . . . I realize it is now the middle of July and you are the only person capable of an almost superhuman feat.'

'I'm finishing an opera as an absolute priority. I couldn't think about anything else just now.'

'Finish it off, Mozart! Finish it quickly and then write *La Clemenza di Tito*.'

'The 6th of September . . . there's no way!'

'Think how grateful the emperor would be!'

Mozart had believed in Guardasoni's spoken contract and composed several passages for the opera intended for Prague. Since then, they had lain neglected at the back of a drawer. If he worked hard on them, he might manage to put together a reasonable score. It might even open the way to a position at court, bring him back into the limelight and protect Freemasonry.

'Very well,' Mozart said.

Guardasoni went away in relief.

Vienna, 16 July 1791

'Mozart?' spluttered Antonio Salieri, knocking over his wine glass. 'Mozart is writing *La Clemenza di Tito* instead of me?'

'They have already agreed on the matter,' his secretary confirmed.

'He's not got time! The little upstart will fall flat on his face and the emperor will never forgive him. This time the scheming wretch will be trampled under foot and never get up!'

'Let us hope so, maestro.'

'Of course he will! Even if he works night and day, he'll never write a musical tragedy that holds together.'

'And what if he succeeds? Then he'll come out from the shadows where his failures had relegated him.'

The interview with the Count of Pergen returned to Salieri's mind, and he began to take his suggestions seriously. Getting rid of this obstructive rival was starting to become a necessity.

46

Vienna, 23 July 1791

Joseph Anton had just heard bad news from two sources.

Firstly, Mozart had been officially commissioned to write an opera for the festivities in September when Leopold II was to be crowned. Why had Salieri refused the commission? Too short notice, evidently! Everyone agreed that Mozart would never manage it, but the Count of Pergen knew what this fiend was like. He belonged to a race apart; he was the kind of builder who, in defiance of time and tiredness, was capable of taking on more work, even when he already had unfeasible amounts. If he succeeded, the Freemason would be back in the emperor's good books.

The second news item came from Paris. On the 17th, the people had gathered on the Champs-de-Mars to sign a petition calling for Louis XVI's abdication. After violent clashes, the National Guard had opened fire on the crowd and the blame for the disaster had been laid at the monarch's door because he was now seen by his subjects to have betrayed his country. Soon, they would be clamouring for the death of this tiresome adversary, after a parody of a trial where the outcome was already known.

The Masonic lodges, and particularly Mozart's, would follow suit in this wave of destruction.

Vienna, 24 July 1791

'My confinement is near,' Constance told her husband. 'I can tell from the way the baby is kicking that it is going to be a boy.'

'May the gods look favourably on us,' prayed Wolfgang. 'We have suffered so much, we deserve a second child in full health.'

'*The Magic Flute* will bring him luck.'

Thamos interrupted the couple.

'Ignaz von Born wants to see you.'

The Venerable, the model for Sarastro, lay close to death.

Wasted by disease, he had come to look like an old man at the age of only forty-eight, but he comported himself with remarkable dignity.

He gave Mozart his Venerable's apron and his seal with its emblem of a set square.

'May this symbol always be your guide, my Brother.

It is essential in all construction and stands for discernment and righteousness. It will enable you to perceive the laws of the universe and order your material. Every lodge is born of God and of the set square; it will provide the foundations for your community of initiation where Brothers and Sisters experience the Great Mysteries.'

Wolfgang showed von Born a thick manuscript.

'Here is our work, Venerable Master. I have finished *The Magic Flute*. May my music extend your thought.'

'It will surpass my thought, my Brother, and extend throughout the universe.'

Ignaz von Born closed his eyes.

No ceremony was organized in his honour and no journal mentioned his death.

Vienna, 26 July 1791

Still in shock from his Master's passing, Wolfgang walked the hundred paces back to his apartment. This time, there was no lofty professor of medicine in attendance, only an experienced midwife.

With his mind still on Ignaz von Born, whose absence weighed on him already, Wolfgang could only admire the forbearance with which Constance had buried four of her children but had never stopped giving birth.

He must follow her example and never give up, regardless of the blows of fate. *The Magic Flute* would soon be premiered, his initiation society the Grotto would be born and Mozart intended to lead it in such a way that it would instil genuine hope in future generations.

The smiling face of the midwife appeared from the bedroom.

'It's a boy, Franz Xaver. And this one won't die young[*]! Your wife is tired but is doing well.'

The completion of his grand opera, the death of Ignaz von Born, the birth of a son . . . Swept up in a whirlwind, Mozart invited his Brothers Stadler and Jacquin to empty several bottles with him and help him come back down to earth.

Vienna, 28 July 1791

'You wanted to see me, Süssmayr?' said Antonio Salieri, in surprise.

'Thank you for agreeing to see me, maestro.'

'You are a pupil and friend of Mozart who has just stolen *La Clemenza di Tito* from me!'

'His pupil but not his friend! If you knew how he treats me . . . He is so unpredictable, so idiosyncratic! I need a peaceful life.'

'What exactly do you mean, Süssmayr?'

'I should like to come and work for you, maestro.'

Salieri hesitated. If he took on someone from Mozart's circle, he would be party to all manner of precious details

---

[*] Franz Xaver Mozart lived to be fifty-three.

and could make judicious use of them. Too good, much too good to miss!

'Get away with you, young man! Go back to your teacher.'

'I'm serious, maestro! There's no future with Mozart. With you, on the other hand . . . '

'What sort of fool do you take me for? He sent you here, didn't he? Well, the mission has failed. I refuse to be duped by Mozart and I refuse to be made fun of, and you can tell him that from me!'

Vexed, Süssmayr beat a retreat. Acting as Constance's servant was becoming humiliating and Mozart's jibes were irritating; he would have liked to leave their service.

But there was nothing he could do after such a snub, and Süssmayr returned to the daily grind.

47

Vienna, 30 July 1791

Satisfied that his business was running smoothly, Puchberg was not sorry to have helped Mozart, whose financial situation had vastly improved. If his new opera was a success, as Brother Schikaneder promised, Wolfgang's debts would soon be paid off.

At twenty-eight, Count Walsegg-Stuppach, the landlord of the house Puchberg occupied, was sunk in depression after losing his beautiful young wife, Anna, who had passed away on 14 January. He often took refuge in his lonely castle where he could contemplate the sombre mountains of Semmering.

'I should like a *Requiem* to commemorate my wife,' he told Puchberg. 'Though I should have to sign it myself, of course.'

'I know an accomplished composer. Wolfgang Mozart.'

'Mozart?' exclaimed the Count. 'He would never accept!

He is well known and independent and would never agree to my conditions.'

Mindful of the handsome sum his Brother Wolfgang would make for composing, doubtless at speed, a conventional religious work, Puchberg insisted.

'It all depends how the matter is broached, my lord.'

'What do you suggest?'

'We will send an anonymous messenger who will make him a suitable offer.'

'I shall think it over.'

Vienna, 10 August 1791

'Your Majesty,' said Domenico Guardasoni to Leopold II, 'I contacted the illustrious Antonio Salieri several times and begged him to write *La Clemenza di Tito*, but he flatly refused on every occasion. So I have chosen Mozart and he has agreed to meet the deadline.'

The impresario of the Prague National Theatre was afraid the emperor would summarily reject the idea. Engaging a Masonic musician would make tongues wag and he might be sidelined irrevocably.

'Salieri has made enemies of a lot of composers,' Leopold II said, thoughtfully. 'But Mozart will be far less expensive. You can give him two hundred ducats for the opera and fifty more for travel expenses*.'

---

* This amounted to 1150 florins. Mozart's annual salary at the time

The Beloved of Isis

Constance was recovering from her confinement and the baby was in good health, watched over by Karl Thomas who was delighted to have a little brother. Gaukerl stood guard at the foot of the cradle.

'I have accepted Guardasoni's conditions,' Wolfgang told his wife. 'The loans and success of *The Magic Flute*, which Schikaneder has such faith in, will remove all our problems.'

'The deadline is ever so tight!'

'I shall work at the speed of light, but in any case I have already composed several arias and dear Süssmayr will tackle the recitatives.'

'Are you happy with the libretto?'

'I quite like it. Valentini* used the theme in an opera premiered in Cremona in December 1769 and I was lucky enough to attend. Though not beyond reproach, Emperor Titus submits to Wisdom – one of the aims of Masonic initiation – and pardons men who are plotting against him with neither mindless pity nor blind benevolence. If today's monarchs were that enlightened and could be generous and lucid instead of authoritarian, we would know true justice.'

'Who were Titus' enemies?' asked Constance.

'Vitellia is in love with the emperor but is furious

was eight hundred florins.
* 1704–1797.

because he has chosen another woman to be his bride. So she tries to persuade her friend Sextus to lead a group of insurgents to set fire to the Roman Capitol and assassinate Titus. The plan fails because the young man does not want to become a criminal. However, the emperor gives up trying to win the woman he loves because she is in love with another man, and decides to marry Vitellia. Then he discovers the plot; Sextus is arrested and condemned to death. Vitellia admits that she masterminded the uprising. She achieves serenity and waits to be justly punished for her crimes. Titus, recognizing that he was the cause of this terrible process, acknowledges his guilt and pardons them all, and harmony is restored. Is not each of us alone responsible for his mistakes? In any case, we should not blame other people for our weaknesses and imperfections. Sarastro's rigour and Titus' clemency: these are the two most important virtues in a true king.'

Vienna, 15 August 1791

'You were wrong, my dear Geytrand!' said Joseph Anton. 'The death of Venerable Ignaz von Born has not reduced Mozart to impotence. Quite the reverse, in fact. He has finished *The Magic Flute*, ousted Salieri and is back in favour with the emperor, even while he is pursuing Masonic activities! His Master's death has made him stronger. Instead of crumbling, Mozart has found extra energies.'

'It's a flash in the pan, my lord. He is trying to drown his sorrow in work.'

'No, he is taking over as head of the underground Freemasons according to the dictates of von Born! He has an iron determination and is riding high.'

'Since I managed to eliminate von Born without arousing the hint of a suspicion,' Geytrand reminded Joseph Anton, *sotto voce*, 'why don't we apply the same method to Mozart? When it is administered in small doses, *aqua toffana* leaves no traces. Its action is slow and certain.'

Joseph Anton expressed his thoughts out loud.

'The Church wishes Mozart would disappear, as does Salieri, and some of the Freemasons think he is a revolutionary. There will be plenty of potential suspects. In the first place, no one could possibly suspect us, and in any case, one of our allies might do the job first.'

Geytrand smiled.

'If there is one place Mozart would not think to distrust, it is the Prague lodge he will attend during the coronation festivities. He can have his first dose of poison during a banquet.'

'So you are planning to buy a Servant Brother and manipulate him?'

'Indeed, my lord.'

Joseph Anton paused again. If *The Magic Flute* was a disaster, if the composer did not finish *La Clemenza di Tito* in time, if the emperor felt so offended he dismissed him from court, if the Masons banned him from the lodge because of his subversive ideas, if . . .

No, it was better to organize the future.

'My lord,' murmured Geytrand, 'do I have your permission to settle the Mozart problem?'

'Let us set the ball rolling. If things go our way, we can always halt the process.'

48

Vienna, 19 August 1791

Wolfgang felt he would never get over the death of Ignaz von Born. The Venerable had left a huge gap and no one would fill it. His philosophy lived on in *The Magic Flute* and would find full expression when Mozart, Stadler and Countess Thun welcomed the Brothers and Sisters through the doors of The Grotto, the initiation society of the future.

That evening, Wolfgang attended a concert given by the blind virtuoso, Marianne Kirchgässner. She played several pieces on the glass harmonica, including the Adagio and Rondo composed for her*.

As he was leaving the hall, an old man in a dark cloak approached the musician.

'May I speak to you, Mr Mozart?'

* K617.

'Who are you?'

'A messenger from a rich and powerful man. He wants to commission you to write a *Requiem*.'

'A mass for the dead . . .'

The man nodded.

'Is it urgent?'

'All your conditions will be accepted.'

Requiem . . . The word echoed like a roll of thunder in Mozart's head. Suddenly, death, that best friend of man, seemed to wear a more forbidding mask.

'I need to give it some thought.'

'In your own time, Mr Mozart. We shall meet again.'

Vienna, 20 August 1791

The performers of *The Magic Flute* were excited about learning their parts. They had not only to sing well but also to speak well, and, in his eagerness to do justice to the fantastical work he had such high hopes for, Schikaneder proved a hard taskmaster. Although his knowledge of Freemasonry was limited, he nevertheless appreciated that the ritual opera opened the way to a new universe. As an old hand in the business, he made much of the character of Papageno and knew the public would love his comic energy.

When Wolfgang took Gaukerl for a walk, he came across the old man in the dark cloak a second time.

'Have you made your mind up, Mr Mozart?'

'I shall take it on.'

'Does one hundred ducats sound enough to you?'

'Absolutely.'

'In that case, as soon as possible would be best.'

'I am up to my eyes in work . . .'

'I know I can count on you, Mr Mozart.'

All sorts of questions flooded to Wolfgang's mind, but he found that he could not bring any of them out.

The first notes of the *Requiem* were already playing in his heart.

Vienna, 21 August 1791

When the works of Crowned Hope Lodge closed, Prince Karl von Lichnowsky invited two Brothers back to his place: the first, an affluent, dumpy little burger; the second, a tall, thin senior official.

'An odd rumour is going about,' the prince started. 'Mozart has written an opera that betrays our secrets and he wants to found an Order where women will be initiated to the Great Mysteries. Should we tolerate such an outrage?'

'This is preposterous!' blustered the burger. 'And to think some people wanted to appoint Mozart Venerable of our lodge!'

'My friends and I will stop him achieving that status,' the senior official assured them. 'Alas, the death of Ignaz von Born has not reduced his disciple to silence.'

'I have always loathed this Mozart,' admitted the burger. 'If we let this go on, he will do serious damage to Freemasonry.'

'What should we do?' asked the prince.

'First you must re-launch your lawsuit. It was most unfortunate that it foundered. And then, you must tell the emperor that this musician is up to his neck in debts, damaging the court's reputation and seriously failing in his duties as a man of honour.'

'Will that be enough?' asked the burger, anxiously.

'We can't take things any further,' said Lichnowsky. 'We are after all dealing with a Brother.'

'A Brother who is ready to deny us and who is a menace,' objected the senior official.

'He has written music free of charge for our ceremonies,' the burger reminded them. 'The whole lodge has benefited from them!'

'We must not give way to sentimentality,' the senior official advised. 'Viennese Freemasonry has suffered enough already and its future could be gravely compromised by revolutionaries like Mozart. The situation in France is deteriorating and the plague started by the rioters could spread to other countries, including our own. Who will be the first to be blamed? Us, the Freemasons!'

'That would be grossly unfair!' protested the burger. 'We are the emperor's faithful subjects and have no intention of overthrowing society.'

'The police think otherwise,' said the senior official. 'Von Born and the Illuminates of Bavaria have done us a terrible wrong. If we let Mozart take up the torch, we shall be making a great mistake. Trustworthy informants have told me that Antonio Salieri wanted his downfall. And the former Minister of Police, Count of Pergen, will not give up so easily. If Mozart were to fall victim to a blow from fate, one or other of his enemies would be blamed, but surely not us, his Brothers. Let us do what we have to and get rid of this obstructive character.'

Prince Karl von Lichnowsky knew what had to be done.

49

Vienna, 24 August 1791

At eight o'clock in the morning, everything was ready. Constance, whom Mozart could not do without, left Karl Thomas and bonny little Franz Xaver in the care of a boarding school. Süssmayr made sure his boss had enough ink and manuscript paper, and Stadler finished his night's sleep in one of the comfortable carriages bound for Prague.

Another journey and exhausting hours of travel stretched ahead of them.

During the journey, Wolfgang wrote the last pages of *La Clemenza di Tito* in the hope of pleasing the emperor. Fearing Mozart would be followed, Thamos was protecting him. The Egyptian was worried and remained permanently on his guard. At the last meeting at Crowned Hope, some of the Brothers had seemed hostile to the musician. How would the Freemasons greet the extraordinary message of *The Magic Flute*? Most of them were opposed to the initiation of women; at best, they should be content to imitate the initiation of men. And many Masonic women were happy with their worldly folk ceremonies and agreed.

Like Ignaz von Born, his deceased Master, Mozart was refusing to bow to political pressure and was promoting a parallel initiation that would be seen as dangerous.

Mozart was taking huge risks beyond what was sensible.

Just as the composer stepped into his carriage, the old man in the dark cloak appeared.

'Are you going away, Mr Mozart?'

'A business trip.'

'I hope your journey doesn't mean you have to interrupt work on the *Requiem*?'

'Indeed, it does.'

'That is annoying, very annoying.'

'I shall attend to it when I get back.'

The messenger bowed and walked slowly away under Constance's anxious gaze.

'I don't like that odd fellow! What is his name?'

'It doesn't matter. I wanted to compose a *Requiem*, and this commissioner has brought me face to face with death.'

'Don't talk like that, you make my hair stand on end!'

'I'm sorry, I should be thinking about our Prague triumph!'

Wolfgang recovered his good humour and advised Süssmayr not to fall asleep but to carry on writing the remaining recitatives, even if they weren't very good.

Prague, 26 August 1791

The arrival of Antonio Salieri, with his five carriages and twenty court musicians, did not go unnoticed. He had gone on ahead of Mozart and was still the first composer in the empire. He would manage the local artists and the programme of concerts given during the festivities for the coronation.

The perfect alibi: he must organize at least one mass by Mozart, whom he so ardently wanted out of the way! Here in Prague, Salieri felt less sure of his ground, because audiences liked his *Marriage of Figaro* and *Don Giovanni*.

Salieri knew that his own trifling works, trotted out with the regularity of clockwork, would not stand the test of time. Mozart's creations, on the other hand, smacked of eternity. Of course, Antonio was treated like a star and enjoyed the esteem of the critics who praised his accomplishments, but he himself doubted the judgment of flatterers, fools and fops, slaves to the zeitgeist.

Salieri gorged on this food; all he wanted was to preserve his good name at all cost.

The Beloved of Isis

Vienna, 26 August 1791

'You must flee, my lord,' Geytrand advised Joseph Anton. 'If you answer the emperor's summons, you will be arrested. One of our spies must have told him that you are still running a secret service.'

The Count of Pergen grabbed Mozart's stout file.

'I have always been a faithful servant of the state and I am not going to act like a coward.'

Lavishly dressed in a green silk frock coat, Joseph Anton rode to the imperial palace, running over in his mind the main stages of his tireless battle against the Freemasons. In defiance of all the obstacles, he had never given up.

The emperor received him in a small drawing room.

'You are no longer the Chief of Police, Count of Pergen, but you are still using your network to observe the lodges.'

'That is right, Your Majesty.'

'Is Freemasonry really such a threat to the security of the empire?'

'I have no doubt about it.'

'Would the lodges of Vienna and Prague dare to import the insane ideas of French revolutionaries?'

'Unfortunately, yes.'

'I was hoping that these follies would stay in their country of origin!'

'You are deceived, Your Majesty.'

'Since you feel you have a mission to fulfil, Count of Pergen, please accomplish it!'

'What have I to understand?'

'Tomorrow, I am signing a strict declaration with the King of Prussia aimed at the seditious French. If they overstep the limits, we will take military action. You, Count of Pergen, are to oversee the Freemasons. In the event of war, no inside betrayal must disturb the cohesion of the empire. We shall travel together to Prague and you will be responsible for my security.'

50

The peasants were bringing in the harvests, the grapes hung red and golden on the vines, the sky was a brilliant blue, and the valley of the Danube flaunted its glittering charms under the eye of the splendid mansions either side. Constance savoured every minute of their peaceful journey. Wolfgang spent the whole time composing. Now and again, he glanced up at the passing scenery, then turned back to his work.

As they drove into Prague, *La Clemenza di Tito* was almost finished.

The composer's carriage headed for Bertramka, the Duscheks' calm, comfortable villa that Mozart liked so much.

'Back at last!' exclaimed the singer Josepha. 'Why did you stay away so long? Prague has been pining to applaud you!'

'Vienna won't let one go,' Wolfgang apologized.

'And you're soon to be an official musician, I hear?'

'That's a bit of an exaggeration!'

'Salieri is swaggering about, but the emperor has chosen you to compose the opera that will be the high point of the coronation festivities.'

'It has yet to be finished and appreciated by him.'

'Your studio is waiting for you, dear Wolfgang.'

While Josepha and Constance took refreshment under the shade of an oak tree, the musician shut himself away with Gaukerl in the light and airy room. He felt full of energy and picked up a pen.

Thamos, meanwhile, contacted the Prague Brethren, who were eager to welcome Mozart to a meeting. Curiously, they seemed more relaxed. The Egyptian was suspicious and took extra precautions.

In fact, the home of the main dignitaries was no longer under observation.

This leniency seemed odd, just when the emperor was arriving. Security measures ought, on the contrary, to have been stepped up.

Thamos was troubled by the anomaly and remained on his guard.

Prague, 31 August 1791

When Leopold II arrived on the 29th, he resided at the Hofburg on a hill overlooking the city. On the 30th, the

Empress Maria Louisa, settled at the castle of Lieben with some of the court, and on this Wednesday, the procession from the Invalidenhaus headed for the Cathedral of St Guy and hailed the presence of the imperial couple, who entered the cathedral to the sound of music conducted by Antonio Salieri.

Leopold II's bodyguards were numerous and visible. A second, less obvious brigade had received orders to intervene at the first sign of trouble.

As if the regime had lost interest in local Freemasonry, the usual informants had stopped spying on the lodges. In reality, Geytrand's spooks had taken the place of the official police, who were too obvious.

Mozart was bound to use the trip to visit his Brothers and prepare the future. Anton would show the emperor that the musician really was the head of an underground organization with members outside Vienna.

Prague, 2 September 1791

The previous day, arias from *Don Giovanni* arranged for wind instruments had been played at a dinner at court. And on the evening of the 2nd, at the National Theatre in the old town, the opera itself was performed in the presence of the imperial couple, although the whole of Prague knew they did not like this music by Mozart.

A thousand people filled the hall, and many music-lovers had to be turned away.

Such beautiful music delighted the wind players, among them Anton Stadler on the bass clarinet, which had at last seen the light of day after years of work. The arrangements did not allow him to show off the instrument's full range of sonorities, but he was happy to hold back because he knew that his Brother Mozart would compose a concerto for the new instrument.

'It is all quite safe, Your Majesty,' the Count of Pergen muttered in the emperor's ear. 'You can enjoy your Prague stay without worrying.'

'What is Mozart doing?'

'He is playing billiards with friends, drinking wine and working.'

'Has he finished *La Clemenza di Tito*?'

'If I know him, he surely has.'

'What an extraordinary little man he sometimes seems.'

'He is, Your Majesty. And that makes him all the more dangerous.'

Prague, 3 September 1791

After a jolly game of billiards which he won, Wolfgang left the billiard table and withdrew to the back room of the café, where he met Thamos, Count Canal and a dozen Prague Brothers, all aware of the gravity of the situation.

'The French Revolution will flood Europe,' predicted the Egyptian, 'and inspire a host of other dogmatists. In the name of ideology, all crimes will be permitted. A centralized state will impose its law and block all freedom of thought. Before being persecuted, the Freemasons will ally themselves with the new regime. In Austria and Bohemia, they are accused of spreading subversive ideas. And our brother Mozart will be at the top of that list both because he was Ignaz von Born's disciple and because he is the composer of *The Magic Flute*, a ritual opera that will trouble many Brothers.'

'We mustn't dramatize the situation,' advised Count Canal. 'Our Order is going through a hard enough time as it is, but in my view, the French Revolution won't spread beyond the country's borders. If it does, Austria and Prussia will intervene and their armies will easily crush a bunch of ragamuffins hastily mobilised by the adversary.'

They were interrupted by several knocks on the door of their improvised temple from the Brother Tyler on guard outside.

'Our works are suspended,' ordered Thamos.

The Brothers quickly dispersed. Some of them went through the kitchen door, others settled in the snug bar, and Mozart returned to the billiard room.

'There's an odd chap in the tavern quizzing the waiters,' the Tyler informed the Egyptian. 'He's been spotted before hanging around the lodge.'

'The Count of Pergen's secret service is still on our trail,' Thamos said.

51

Prague, 4 September 1791

On this fine late-summer Sunday, allegiance was sworn to the Emperor Leopold II in St Guy's Cathedral, after the celebration of a Mass directed by the ubiquitous Salieri.

Unkind rumours appeared to have done him no harm and he was still clearly the favourite court musician, and he intended to control any intrigues with an iron fist.

But there was still the problem of Mozart. An informant had told him that he spent more time playing billiards than composing *La Clemenza di Tito*. Salieri had shrunk at the news, because the musician's behaviour was unique: while he chatted and had fun, he was planning the outlines of a score before swiftly committing it to paper back in his study later on.

Salieri manufactured music; Mozart exuded it.

'Marvellous performance,' complimented Joseph Anton. 'The emperor is very pleased with your services.'

Salieri drew himself up.

'What brings you to Prague?'

'His Majesty ordered me to take charge of his security and put down any possible disturbances.'

'Not an easy task, my lord!'

'I can handle it. On the other hand, you seem to be showing remarkable benevolence towards Mozart.'

'If he doesn't finish his opera in time, he will be discredited forever! He seems to be playing billiards rather than working.'

'An illusion, my dear! Mozart will be on time, as usual, and he will make a fool of you, yet again. If you continue to close your eyes and ears, you will be eclipsed.'

Salieri was shaken.

'What should I do?'

'Didn't I tell you?'

'I am just a musician and . . .'

'Prague is crawling with alchemists. Some of them use dangerous substances and get rid of their enemies with total discretion.'

'I daren't think what you mean!'

'Don't pretend to be naïve, Salieri. Here is the address of one of these specialists. Go and see him and follow his instructions.'

Christian Jacq

Prague, 5 September 1791

At the banquet after a secret meeting, at about two o'clock in the morning, Count Canal revealed that the police still feared the underground influence of the Illuminati, believed them intent on raising Prague against Leopold II and considered Mozart to be their leader.

To the composer, this information was just confirmation of nonsensical rumours that were already circulating in Vienna, and they did nothing to spoil his appetite. A Brother Servant, renowned for his culinary skills, had cooked them excellent dishes.

So, they forgot the dangers and threats and talked about the mysteries of Isis and Osiris, for they alone could restore full meaning to Masonic initiation.

As he put the finishing touches to *La Clemenza di Tito* before beginning rehearsals that afternoon, Wolfgang suddenly felt unwell. He turned pale, his eyes bulged and he had pains in his stomach. He was barely able to compose.

'Do you want me to call a doctor?' asked Constance.

'No, I'm feeling better already. I didn't sleep properly last night, but the opera is finished.'

Anton Stadler dispelled any doubts.

'The orchestra is excellent and the bass clarinet is ready. When we get back to Vienna, you can give it a masterpiece.'

'Let's concentrate on *La Clemenza*, first!'

'How on earth did you write it in so short a time?'

'By the grace of the gods, no doubt.'

Prague, 5 September 1791

Count Rottenham, Burggraf of Prague and the city's principal authority, was also one of Leopold II's confidants. The emperor lent a willing ear to the opinions of this important personage, who exuded his strong sense of duty and devotion to the imperial family. A staunch defender of the regime, he abhorred the slightest anti-establishment movement in Bohemia and only just tolerated the existence of Masonic lodges, despite their protestations of fidelity to the state and Church.

The day before the coronation, Rottenham's time was fully accounted for; however, he agreed to grant an audience to Count of Pergen, the former Minister of Police.

'I am in charge of the emperor's security,' said Joseph Anton, 'and I am afraid of trouble from certain Freemasons. Revolutionary ideas have gone to their heads.'

'Do you have concrete evidence?'

'A thick file based on long investigations. Love and Truth Lodge is particularly suspect. In my opinion, it is still a hotbed of Illuminati and is plotting against the empire.'

'I have heard terrible things about it,' admitted Count Rottenham, 'but I have no legal grounds for taking action. Its members don't want to attract the wrath of the law and are careful not to step out of line.'

'That makes them all the more dangerous,' countered Joseph Anton. 'And it is flaunting its impunity by receiving its secret leader while the emperor is being crowned tomorrow!'

'Whom are you referring to?'

'Mozart, the composer of the opera His Majesty commissioned.'

Rottenham did not hide his annoyance.

'The emperor is still not convinced of Mozart's guilt,' added Joseph Anton. 'But I have been on the musician's trail for many years. He was quickly raised to Master Mason and has not stopped extending his influence. Mozart was the disciple of the alchemist, Ignaz von Born, and he is leading a secret organization aimed at revolutionizing the way we think.'

Count Rottenham turned over the pages of the file, pausing over some and promising himself he would read the document more attentively later on.

'What do you want me to do?'

'Talk to the emperor; show him that Mozart is dangerously cunning, and you will be helping to protect the empire. He is bound to listen to such a warning, coming from a man with gravitas.'

'I shall act in all conscience, Count of Pergen.'

52

'You look washed out, my dear Mozart,' observed Salieri.

'I'm just a bit tired.'

'You finished *La Clemenza di Tito* in record time. What a feat! With all my heart, I hope the opera will please the emperor. It is a big day for him. And I am proud to be directing the programme of religious music for the coronation ceremony. To prove to His Majesty that his court musicians are all on excellent terms, I have selected two of your pieces, a Mass and a Motet*.'

'That was most thoughtful of you, thank you.'

The Motet was an arrangement of the first chorus from *Thamos, King of Egypt*. Salieri must want to show that

---

* K317, *Coronation Mass*, and K345.

he was fully aware of his colleague's Masonic allegiance and that he did not disapprove.

Prague, 6 September 1791

The Archbishop of Prague bared the emperor's left shoulder and anointed it with holy oils. Then he rubbed it with bread and salt, before handing Leopold St Wenceslas's crown, sceptre and the golden apple as a symbol of the universe over which he was called to reign. Around his waist, he fastened the ritual sword.

The solemn vows were spoken and the sound of trumpets and timpani filled St Guy's Cathedral. Outside, cannon fire proclaimed the happy coronation of the new King of Bohemia.

Prague, 6 September 1791

At half-past seven, at the Prague National Theatre, the court attended the premiere of *La Clemenza di Tito**, an *opera seria* in two acts by Mozart.

For those lucky enough to have a seat, entry was free.

Dark and serious, the work brought out the Emperor Titus' noblemindedness for pardoning his enemies instead of subjecting them to cruel punishment.

* K621.

Maria Louisa of Spain hated the austere opera, calling it *porcheria tedescha*, or 'German dross'. All she liked was Anton Stadler's brilliant playing of the basset horn and clarinet.

Unenthusiastic himself, the emperor received Count Rottenham in his royal box. The count was clearly vexed.

'I have been enquiring into the Prague Masonic lodges, Your Majesty, and I suspect Love and truth of being a refuge for Illuminati. I realise their Order has been officially disbanded but they are continuing to propagate their pernicious ideas through the Freemasons. And Mozart is their secret leader.'

'Do you have proof of that?'

'Mozart is a disciple of Ignaz von Born, an Illuminatus and dissident Freemason, and he is following exactly the same path. On 9 September, a lodge is going to pay Masonic tribute to him to thank him for his services and for his ideas which will be conveyed in his next opera, *The Magic Flute*. We should not underestimate this musician, Your Majesty. I believe him capable of conquering both Vienna and Prague and using his renown to seduce a wide audience. His *Clemenza di Tito* was just to butter you up.'

'You mean,' concluded the emperor, 'I have been duped.'

'Indeed, Your Majesty. We must stop Mozart from causing further damage at all costs.'

'Your feelings corroborate those of one of my counsellors, the Count of Pergen, the best specialist on the Freemasons. We shall act accordingly.'

Prague, 7 September 1791

From the window of his room, Mozart looked out over the countryside. The villa of his friends, the Duscheks, was a peaceful haven where he should have been able to forget his troubles. But Wolfgang's were too heavy.

'A total flop,' he told Constance.

'Don't exaggerate. Your work was played to the imperial couple: what an honour!'

'That is an illusion, my dear little wife. The empress had harsh words to say about it and the emperor has not paid it a single compliment. As for the people of Prague, I don't think they understood such austere music and the significance of a Roman theme. It's so different from *The Marriage of Figaro*!'

'Praising Titus's generosity didn't convince Leopold II?'

'On the contrary, he saw it as a provocation. Me, a Freemason, trying to whitewash my name!'

Prague, 9 September 1791

'Some admirers are asking to see you,' Thamos told Wolfgang.

The Egyptian led him to the Jewish cemetery of Beth-Khayim, 'the house of life', where a dozen Cabbalists were waiting for him.

Together, they walked through the cemetery where

the thoughts of men who had devoted their lives to the search for one of the forms of Wisdom still lingered.

Their elder grasped Mozart's hands.

'Death will have no hold over you. Your creation transcends time and space. Initiates must continue the work of the Creator and you have accomplished that duty with your whole being.'

The Cabbalists vanished and Mozart remained alone in the strange silence, half-way between heaven and earth, and he heard within him the first melodies of a Clarinet Concerto to be dedicated to the lodges of the Grotto.

Prague, 9 September 1791

As soon as Mozart crossed the threshold of Truth and Union Lodge, Count Canal stepped forward and gave him the ritual greeting.

The Brothers sang Mozart's Cantata to the joy of initiation[*] written in 1785, to the glory of his master, Ignaz von Born.

That evening, it was Mozart they were honouring, with his own music.

Thamos led the Great Magician to the Orient.

'It is your mission, Brother Wolfgang, to pass on Wisdom, the aim and secret of our Order.'

---

* *Die Maurerfreude,* or *The Joy of the Mason*, K471.

Swallowing his emotion, the musician praised von Born, then described the central theme of *The Magic Flute*: the alchemical marriage of the king and queen.

Thamos could sense the enthusiasm of some and the scepticism of others. Nevertheless, initiation was reborn.

53

Prague, 12 September 1791

Leopold Kozeluch, a dull composer who hated Mozart, 'that little man and little composer', bowed low before the Empress Maria Louisa.

'What we had to put up with, Your Majesty, with that abominable *Clemenza di Tito*! What forebearance you showed, sitting through such a despicable opera right to the end! You may be sure I shall do my utmost to ruin the unjustified reputation Mozart enjoys in Prague.'

'Would you like to work in Vienna?'

Kozeluch bowed even lower.

'It would be a very great honour, Your Majesty!'

'Mozart's post may soon fall vacant. It would be worth your while to replace him*.'

* Leopold Kozeluch had his wish granted in 1792 and was employed on double the salary Mozart had received.

Thrilled at the opportunity to spread his venom, Kozeluch gleefully related his interview to Salieri and received the composer's hearty congratulations.

Prague, 12 September 1791

'I must go back to Vienna to work on *The Magic Flute*,' Mozart told Thamos. 'Parts of it are incomplete and I want to finish off the orchestration.'

'Our Prague Brothers would like to see you before you go.'

'I have composed an aria for bass, "I am leaving you, dearest, farewell*!". They will realise that it is addressed to the lodge.'

The meeting ended with the occultation of the Three Great Pillars and the erasing of the lodge tablet showing the implements used by the Master of Work when he created the temple. Then the Brothers all gave Wolfgang the fraternal embrace and assured him of their support for his work and their eagerness to see *The Magic Flute*.

With tears in his eyes, the composer swore he would never cease to fight for initiation, no matter what the obstacles and difficulties.

'You need to take some rest,' suggested Count Canal. 'You look worn out.'

'I want to finish my opera. And then there's the voice

* K621a.

of that wonderful bass clarinet that I want to show off! Then, we'll see.'

Then, thought Count Canal, Mozart will go on working, because that is what the gods want.

Wolfgang was slow to leave, as though he thought he would never return to this lodge where he had enjoyed genuine brotherly friendship. They had shared privileged moments and he knew how much that was worth.

Would he experience so fervent a human chain ever again in Prague?

Vienna, 15 September 1791

Looking pale and drawn and joking far less than usual, Mozart was so hard at work that he seemed to forget the external world. He wanted to recreate the ritual of Isis and Osiris in a vast Clarinet Concerto dedicated to his future community of initiation.

Suddenly, he slumped forward unconscious and had to be helped to his bed by his servant and Constance, watched anxiously by Gaukerl.

Then he came to and his energy returned.

'Funny,' he told Constance. 'In the old days, I used to work harder and I was in better health.'

Wolfgang had not lost his appetite and enjoyed the beer and wine that were now being delivered by a new, less expensive supplier.

'But forget about my health, dear little wife; we must

think about yours. The last confinement wore you out and your leg is still painful. Shouldn't we think about another cure in Baden?'

'Later, darling. Let's enjoy watching our baby grow up; he is such a bouncy, sunny little boy!'

'It's a pity Karl Thomas is so naughty. We have not been strict enough.'

'He is just a child!'

'Exactly! If he gets into bad habits now, he will end up like a twisted branch. I'm sorry . . . I have to get on with my work.'

Vienna, 15 September 1791

Countess Thun invited Mozart to a private dinner at which there were just the two of them.

'Have you told your Sisters about our project?'

'Most of them are too afraid or are reticent. For them, initiation is just a hobby and not a spiritual commitment. They like worldly evenings where they can flirt with the Brothers or be seduced by them. Some just want to ape the men and become Venerable Mistresses, Overseers or Experts. They don't realize that they are selling their souls by turning into men. I've only found seven who want to experience true initiation.'

'But that's an enormous number!' exclaimed Wolfgang. 'I doubt there are that many Brothers.'

'Is the situation that bad?'

'Yes and no. According to Thamos, even in Egypt there was only a small circle of initiates, and there is probably some eternal law about that. But the number doesn't matter so long as they can build the temple.'

Mozart's optimism reassured the countess.

'One of my sons-in-law, Razoumovsky, is an admirer of yours. He wants to get Prince Potemkin to invite you to Russia and organize a spectacular tour. Vienna is becoming stifling, my Brother. This city and its government don't deserve you. When the Grotto has been officially founded, you must leave the narrow bounds of Viennese lodges.'

'You are right, my Sister. But first we need to see the reactions to *The Magic Flute*.'

54

Vienna, 20 September 1791

Quite satisfactory, thought Joseph Anton.

La Clemenza di Tito was a disaster, Salieri's intervention was proving effective and Mozart's star was waning. At last, the emperor had fully appreciated the danger represented by a composer who was acting as a cipher for revolutionary ideas and who was a threat to the security of the empire.

It was no longer taboo to talk about getting rid of Mozart.

The authorities would certainly never be held responsible and the musician's death would look like a natural end due to overwork and material worries.

'Mozart is declining,' Geytrand declared, cheerfully. 'He has already collapsed several times and the doctors can't find a cause.'

Why didn't that genius stick to music? wondered

Joseph Anton, gripped by a strange sense of remorse. He could have had an ordinary career, like Gluck, Salieri or even Haydn, a Freemason who only attended his lodge once.

'You look troubled,' commented Geytrand. 'Don't worry, everything is going to plan.'

'Alas, the French situation is still deteriorating. On 14 September, King Louis XVI was forced to take an oath of loyalty to the constitutional laws passed by the Constituent Assembly. So, now he thinks he has saved his and his family's lives. It is terribly naïve!'

'Austria and Prussia have been put on their guard,' Geytrand said, 'and the revolutionaries would never dare assassinate the king!'

'There's nothing to stop them.'

'Then it is urgent we silence Mozart!'

'Yes, my good friend. We have become the last bastion against the forces of darkness that are threatening to invade Europe.'

Vienna, 28 September 1791

Feeling slightly better, Wolfgang finished *The March of the Priests* that opened Act II of *The Magic Flute*, then he finished the Overture. Thamos marvelled as he read it through. Serious but radiant, it was a fitting prelude to the vast initiation ceremony that would lead to the consecration of the royal couple.

'Tomorrow is the dress rehearsal of *The Magic Flute*,' Mozart told him. 'I have never felt more nervous. If I fail, it will be an irreversible catastrophe.'

'You are laying the foundations for the new temple and you will not fail.'

'I suddenly don't believe in anything any more! My music, the singers, the orchestra, the possibility of conquering the monster that wants to deprive us of freedom and initiation . . . I am just a man, too small to take on so onerous a burden.'

'You are the beloved of Isis. Your whole life has been oriented towards the Great Work. Doubt is an essential element in creation, provided it is constructive.'

Vienna, 29 September 1791

Kneeling on his prayer stool, the Archbishop of Vienna suddenly felt a stabbing pain in his calf and had to interrupt his dialogue with the holy Father. Annoyed, he struggled to his feet and limped back to his office where his secretary was waiting for him.

'News of Mozart?'

'Tonight is the dress rehearsal of *The Magic Flute*, your Grace, a demonic work said to be intended to propagate the subversive messages of Masonic teaching!'

'So Mozart is in perfect health!'

'He is exhausted and has collapsed a few times, but he still has the energy to put about his perverted doctrine.'

'Hasn't someone done the necessary?'

'The resilience of the little man beggars belief, your Grace. But our patience will be rewarded. Mozart is a mere mortal, after all!'

The secretary cleared his throat.

'Antonio Salieri would like to be confessed.'

'Tell him I am not well. You take care of him.'

'Should God forgive him his sins, your Grace?'

'God always forgives true believers.'

Vienna, 29 September 1791

The dress rehearsal did nothing to reassure Mozart. The orchestra and singers played their parts to perfection, but the *grand opera*, as it was called in the composer's private catalogue, seemed suddenly too severe to please a wide audience.

At least there was the libretto which clearly set out his intentions and which was sold for thirty pfennigs in the theatre foyer.

Ignaz Alberti, Wolfgang's lodge Brother, had kept his promise and printed the text on time, with a cover illustration of Egyptian and Masonic symbols. The hieroglyphs referred to Thoth, God of Knowledge and Sacred Sciences, and decorated the base of a pyramid. Suspended from the ceiling of a vaulted ceiling was a five-point star containing the secret of the two alchemical ways, the short way of illumination and the long way of the rites. Stones, statues and broken columns evoked the sanctuary that had to be rebuilt after its destruction by the forces of darkness. A great funerary urn recalled the death of the assassinated Master and his return to life during initiation to the third degree. An hourglass, one of the elements in the Chamber of Reflection, symbolized the passage from profane time to sacred time, from the ephemeral to eternity. A few tools, especially the compass, were those used by the Brothers to bring the plans to fruition.

'Isn't it rather rash to reveal so much?' Schikaneder asked, in alarm.

'Our convictions are honourable,' Mozart replied. 'So far, I have been careful to hide the path of initiation under the veil of the libretto. *The Magic Flute* is far more explicit.'

'Well, you can count on me and my troop, my Brother Wolfgang! It will be a triumph!'

55

The local district where Schikaneder's theatre stood comprised the church of St Rosalie, several workshops, houses, six large squares, an apothecary, a mill, an oil press, a pleasure garden criss-crossed by little paths with flowerbeds either side, and an inn beside a well in the shade of some old trees. Throughout the summer, it was here that the singers had come to slake their thirst between rehearsals.

The theatre itself was a wooden building with a tiled roof, measuring thirty metres by fifteen. It could seat a thousand and stood in the vast courtyard of a mansion belonging to the Stahremberg princes. Its generous stage, twelve metres deep, allowed for lavish sets and fantastic effects.

Before conducting the opening night of *The Magic Flute*, which coincided with the last night of *La Clemenza di Tito* in Prague, Mozart put in some work on his Clarinet Concerto. For a few hours, he withdrew and detached himself from the world.

The poster, where Mozart's name was hardly visible, proclaimed that the actors at the theatre Auf der Wieden had the honour to present *The Magic Flute*, a grand opera in two acts . . . by Emanuel Schikaneder!

Mr Mozart, out of deference to the benevolent and honourable public and friendship for the work's author, it stated, *will today conduct the performance in person.*

Thereafter, provided the whole thing was not a fiasco, Henneber, who played the bells on the evening of the premiere, would take over as conductor. As for Süssmayr, he would turn the pages.

Wolfgang hugged Constance.

'I have never been so frightened! This work is the accomplishment of my life as an initiate and a musician. If it fails, I shall never get over it.'

He could not hide his anxiety when Thamos came to fetch him.

'What if the singers forget their lines? Pamina, Miss Gottlieb, is only seventeen, and Gerl, Sarastro, seems too young to me! Winter, the Orator, is still only an Entered Apprentice, and the Queen of the Night, Mrs Hofer, sometimes sings off-key. So, I . . .'

'You must accept the imperfections of the premiere and focus on the overall coherence.'

At seven o'clock, the hall was filling up with a genial local audience who had come to be entertained by Schikaneder's fairy tales. Few of them were really interested in Mozart. What they wanted was a good show to cheer them up!

Extremely tense, Wolfgang conducted the majestic overture to *The Magic Flute* with as much dignity as if it had been a meeting dedicated to the Great Mysteries.

He had hardly put down his baton, when one of the musicians, Johann Schenk*, stole up to Mozart and with tears of admiration in his eyes kissed the master's hand for being the source of such immense artistic joy.

Still just as nervous, Wolfgang directed Act I from the harpsichord. To Thamos's supreme delight, he saw unfold before him the ritual they had worked on with Ignaz von Born, during so many unforgettable evenings. The death of the malevolent serpent, Tamino's awakening to this initiatory duty, Pamina's Quest, the different aspects of Papageno ensnared by his profane aspirations, the wrath of the Queen of the Night intent on destroying the initiates' sanctuary, the betrayal of black Monostatos as he tried to seduce Pamina, the intervention of the three celestial boys guiding Tamino to the truth, the first meeting between Pamina and Tamino in the presence of Venerable Sarastro as he led them to the temple of ordeals, the final choir praising the noble way of initiation that could turn the earth into the kingdom of heaven . . . Thamos felt the full intensity of that first act, but the audience, accustomed to less demanding shows, was unsettled.

* 1753–1836.

There was not much applause.

Mozart took refuge in the wings and put his head in his hands. His dream was crumbling; he had failed to give form to the work he had carried within him for so many years. His career as an opera composer was ending in disaster.

This failure was the failure of his whole life.

'All is not lost,' Schikaneder declared. 'They'll like Act II much more.'

'Pointless,' retorted Wolfgang. 'Henneber can take over.'

'You must persevere,' Thamos told him, 'and bring the ritual to its conclusion.'

Mozart shook off his discouragement and returned to the harpsichord to direct Act II, like a Venerable conducting a meeting.

With *The March of the Priests*, followed by Sarastro's consultation with the initiates about Tamino and Pamina's initiation, the audience's attitude changed.

The performers fell under the spell of the music and a profound bond was established between players and audience. Mozart charmed them all and drew them into Tamino and Pamina's fearful ordeals.

Thrilled by the emotion, the auditorium applauded every aria. This was no ordinary show but a communion between very different beings who were being elevated by the opera's power.

After the consecration of the royal couple and the triumph of initiation, the audience sat in stunned silence, as if those lucky enough to attend, on that 30 September 1791, understood the magnificence of the miracle they had just witnessed.

Then there was rapturous applause, which grew and grew until it seemed that it would never come to an end. They cheered for Mozart, they demanded he take a bow.

But the composer had left his harpsichord and was nowhere to be found. Schikaneder went to look for him in the wings and found him, at last, hiding in a corner, refusing to come out on stage. It took Süssmayr and Schikaneder together to drag Wolfgang back in front of the audience.

He would so much have preferred thoughtful silence! Awkward, not knowing what attitude to adopt, he thought of the opening bars of *Thamos, King of Egypt*. What a long way and how many ordeals he had traversed from there to his Great Work, *The Magic Flute*!

Weariness left him and he forgot his day-to-day troubles. When Thamos gave him the fraternal embrace, the two Brothers dedicated this success to Venerable Ignaz von Born. From high up in the Eternal Orient, he had given this birth his protection.

56

Vienna, 1 October 1791

Brother Karl Ludwig Giesecke, who both stage-managed *The Magic Flute* and took the role of the first slave, was amazed at the opera's success. At the second performance, which Mozart consented to conduct, the hall was full and just as enthusiastic as at the premiere.

'I knew it!' trumpeted Schikaneder, who was enjoying his personal triumph for his part as Papageno and his fabulous mimics. 'I never had a moment's doubt about its success. Good work, my Brother Giesecke.'

The stage manager puffed out his chest.

'On the other hand,' Schikaneder went on, 'I am far less happy about your recent declarations.'

'I . . . I don't understand.'

'Come, come, don't play the fool! You are a cultivated intellectual, a passionate mineralogist like von Born, and you won't always be in the theatre. But that's no reason

to claim that you wrote the libretto of *The Magic Flute*!
Our Brother Mozart is the only author, even if he let me
sign it. So, let's have no more untruths. I can't have you
getting above yourself.'

Schikaneder is right, thought Giesecke, *I'm not spending the rest of my life in this set-up!*

Vienna, 2 October 1791

Antonio Salieri was livid.

Of course, there was no comparison between audiences
at Auf der Wieden and the society people who frequented
the Burgtheater, and the nobility and critics had not
exactly showered Mozart with praise. But *The Magic
Flute* had still been a resounding success, the proof being
that it would be played throughout October! Some music-
lovers were even talking about a masterpiece.

Mozart . . . the name had become insufferable! If
the secret substance didn't take effect before long, the
fame of that confounded genius would go on growing
and put all his colleagues to shame, for none of them
could rival him.

Vienna, 2 October 1791

'A great success, did you say?' stuttered the Archbishop
of Vienna.

'I am afraid so, your Grace,' answered his secretary. 'Ordinary people are raving about *The Magic Flute*.'

'The populace . . . what do they matter?

'Mozart will make considerable money from his triumph and enjoy total independence as a result. Even some Freemasons are starting to feel wary of him.'

'Why?'

'The themes of this opera are revolutionary! Firstly, it makes a claim for paganism by defending the mysteries of Isis and Osiris, and secondly, it involves the initiation of women and therefore champions their equality with men.'

'Mozart is indeed going too far,' agreed the Archbishop, 'much too far.'

'That's not all, your Grace. Careless tongues have let slip that he wants to found a new Order based on the revelations of *The Magic Flute*.'

'Where women will be admitted!'

'More than that: they would be given an essential role. The Brothers would follow the traditional path – Entered Apprentice, Fellow Craft and Master Mason – and the Sisters would follow specific rituals passed down from Ancient Egypt and the Middle Ages. Then the initiates would come together at the top to celebrate the alchemical marriage.'

'He is throwing down the gauntlet before the Church! Preaching the existence of women's spirituality will lead to terrible disorder because no woman should ever be ordained and replace a priest. They must all remain subservient to men. Anyone who opposes that untouchable law will be severely punished.'

'Those are the words of the Evangelist, your Grace.'

'Mozart is insulting the Lord above and deserves supreme punishment. Stop beating about the bush and get cracking!'

Vienna, 2 October 1791

'*The Magic Flute* is a triumph, my lord,' Geytrand announced, in consternation. 'The critics disapprove but audiences are flocking to the theatre night after night and word is spreading like wildfire.'

Joseph Anton helped himself to a drop of plum brandy.

'So, he is touching people's hearts with his most overtly Masonic opera, and many will see only the victory of good over evil. After all, that's the main thing. These days, Mozart is wrong. Good equates with revolution, violence, corruption and injustice, while harmony, righteousness and respect for life are seen as evil. This musician comes from another planet and another time. No one will subscribe to his fantastical vision.'

'Mozart is becoming a popular composer,' Geytrand added. 'If he goes on pleasing and seducing the general public, his ideas will take root in a frightening fashion.'

'I always knew it would be so,' murmured Joseph Anton, 'from the moment I began keeping tabs on him.'

'Should we cut to the chase, my lord?'

Christian Jacq

'On no account, my good friend. Even if it takes a few more weeks, our strategy of attrition seems ideal to me. Also, I cannot imagine our various allies are resting on their laurels.'

Geytrand smiled wanly.

'Mozart really doesn't stand a chance.'

57

Vienna, 7 October 1791

After writing a contrapuntal study for two violins, viola
and cello on the melody 'Oh God! Look down on us
from Heaven*', Wolfgang composed almost the entire
final Rondo of his Clarinet Concerto†. In a few days, it
would be ready to send to Stadler, who had travelled to
Prague with Thamos to hold top-secret meetings with
Brothers interested in the creation of the Grotto.

'I am ready,' Constance announced.

Pretty, fashionable and tastefully dressed, Constance
looked even more alluring than usual.

Wolfgang embraced her.

'I really wish I didn't have to be on my own, but I
must stay here and work hard. And you, my love, must

---

* K620b, dated 3 October.
† K622.

get your health back in Baden. I shall miss you terribly! Now please be on your guard against any suitors!'

'I am taking our baby with me. He won't leave his mama. And Gaukerl will take good care of us.'

'Look after yourself, my darling.'

'Try not to over-work and enjoy the success of *The Magic Flute* to the full.'

'In Baden I wouldn't have the tools I need to hand, and I'd rather stay out of trouble. Well, there's nothing so pleasant as to live peacefully and produce a good piece of work.'

'I understand and I agree with you. I'll see you very soon, my love.'

As soon as Constance had left, accompanied by her sister Sophie, Wolfgang played two games of billiards with *Mr Mozart, the man who wrote the opera that is running at Schikaneder's theatre*, as he wrote to his wife.

Without too much regret, because these days he was too tired for his long morning rides, he sold his horse for fourteen ducats and ordered coffee to be brought up to him by his manservant and purveyor of fine foods, Joseph Primus, so named as a joke against the emperor of Austria, Josephus Primus, or Josef I! He drank his coffee, smoked a pipe of excellent tobacco, then settled down to work.

A letter from his friends the Duscheks informed him that, in Prague, they already knew about the splendid reception of *The Magic Flute* and that *La Clemenza di Tito* had been performed for the last time to tremendous applause, although the opera had been a financial disaster.

Perseverance, one of the major virtues of Masonic teaching and so hard to practise, was starting to make perfect sense.

At five o'clock, Wolfgang walked through the Stubentor out of the old town and took his favourite route through the Glacis to the theatre. Again that evening, the hall was full, and encores of several arias had to be played.

But what always gives me most pleasure, Wolfgang confirmed, in a letter written to Constance at half-past ten that night, *is silent approval*.

Vienna, 8 October 1791

At half-past five, Primus made up the fire and woke Wolfgang. At six on the dot, he had his hair dressed. Outside, it was raining hard, and the musician advised his wife to wrap up warm and not catch cold so as not to lose the benefit of her cure.

After devouring a delicious piece of sturgeon, he composed until one-thirty. As he hated to eat alone, he went to dine with his brother-in-law, Hofer. On the way, he bumped into his mother-in-law and promised to take her to hear the opera the next evening. When he got home, he worked all afternoon before yielding to the supplications of the horn player and cheesemonger, Leutgeb, who wanted to see *The Magic Flute*.

The evening was a torment for Wolfgang! The 'know-all' laughed and poked fun at everything, even the solemn scenes. In vain did the composer try to draw his attention to certain passages; Leutgeb was too stupid to understand.

'You're nothing but a Papageno!' Wolfgang exclaimed, and went to sit in a box on his own where he could listen to the rest of the opera in peace.

When Papageno sang to the chimes of the jingle bells, he decided to play a trick on Schikaneder, who struck him as a little too full of his own success. Mozart disappeared into the orchestra and took up the Glockenspiel.

At the point where Schikaneder paused, he played an arpeggio. Startled, the singer looked into the pit and caught sight of Mozart. When he refused to go on, there came another arpeggio. Annoyed, Schikaneder struck the bells himself and said 'Shut up!' eliciting a ripple of laughter from the audience. As a result, many of the spectators understood for the first time that Papageno was not playing the bells himself.

That evening, *The Magic Flute* was again received to rapturous applause.

Before he went to bed, Wolfgang wrote to Constance that the music sounded much better when heard from a box close to the orchestra than from the gallery, and he promised that when she returned, he would take her to try for herself. And because no letter could go off without a hearty joke, he bade his wife pinch Süssmayr's nose, black his eye and pull his pigtail, so that the fellow could never say that he had not got something from her.

The Beloved of Isis

Wolfgang rose at seven o'clock and enjoyed the half capon that Primus brought up to him. Then the two men looked high and low for his yellow winter trousers that went with his boots and decided that Constance must have sent them to the laundry.

Afterwards, he had to go to Mass at the Piarists' at ten o'clock and try to persuade the director of the school to take Karl Thomas. The little boy was disobedient and needed a strict education.

Wolfgang lunched with the Piarists before returning home. Primus brought him two tiresome pieces of news, firstly, that the postal coach had left before seven and there would not be another until late afternoon so Constance would not receive his letter until Sunday evening; and secondly that rumour had it that a great many people were ill in Baden! Was it true? Wolfgang asked her. His little wife must be careful and not trust the weather. He promised to join her in a week's time.

In the evening, he took his mother-in-law to see *The Magic Flute*. Although Maria Cecilia Weber had read the libretto, her son-in-law concluded summarily: *Of course, she saw the opera but did not hear it.*

58

Prague, 10 October 1791

Thamos was not very happy with the first secret meetings with the few Prague Freemasons interested in contributing to the creation of the Grotto. They liked the idea but were afraid of incurring administrative sanctions, and above all, they thought it would involve too much work. Mozart had superhuman energy! Also, a genuine female initiation was likely to pose awkward problems. Most of the Sisters were against the idea because one should not confuse the sublime idea of *The Magic Flute* with the reality of the lodges.

The Egyptian would not give up.

Calmly and patiently, he explained again and again why they needed to create a spiritual centre where the full power of initiation would be revived.

Anton Stadler supported Thamos's arguments and confirmed that in Vienna a small number of Brothers and

Sisters were sick of the way Freemasonry had become tainted by profane ideas and were fully committed to the new Order.

The Egyptian's teaching, he said, would provide them with an invaluable resource and *The Magic Flute* was a brilliant illustration. According to the founders of the Grotto, the opera opened the way to other ritual structures, for both Sisters and Brothers.

After heated debates, Thamos and Stadler left the building where the secret meetings were held.

An icy rain was falling on old Prague.

The Egyptian grasped his Brother's arm.

'We are being watched,' he whispered.

'We can't be, no one knows this address!'

'Except the men who attended the meeting.'

'Has one of them given us away?'

'Very likely.'

'We all swore to keep silent!'

'How many men are can keep their oath? The worst traitors are the initiates who betray their word. And as the ritual of the degree of Master Mason tells us, there are plenty of them.'

Stadler froze.

'Go out through the back courtyard,' Thamos advised. 'There may be no one in the lane. Shout out loud "Stop thief", if anyone stops you, and I'll come to your rescue.'

'How will you . . .'

'I shall find a way.'

The Egyptian waited for a good quarter of an hour.

No cry came. Stadler must have got away.

The freezing rain continued to fall steadily and mercilessly.

Thamos thought of the autumn sunshine in Upper Egypt; autumn had been his favourite season. Then, the heat was less intense, the sand dunes stretching away into the distance turned golden in the setting sun, the summer's fire was past, the nights were cooler and everyone breathed more easily and found restorative sleep at last. At the end of an evening, Abbot Hermes would take him into the desert to discuss his research. And a single sentence would suddenly make everything clear. The disparate elements came together and the shadows dispersed.

Drawing up the collar of his heavy coat closer about his face, the Egyptian walked briskly away. His pace would make him harder to follow.

There must be at least two of them, he decided. Would they just follow him or were they going to arrest him?

He had studied the city's topography in readiness for this sort of incident and knew every street in the old town, and he soon threw off his spooks who ended up bumping into each other and nearly came to blows.

Cursing, they headed off in different directions.

They were replaced, shortly afterwards, by three other men. More henchmen joined them.

This deployment of forces implied serious intent to put a stop to the secret meetings in Prague. The former

Minister of Police, the Count of Pergen, was relaunching his service.

It was not easy to escape the trap. But the police officers were slaves to their orders and took no initiatives. Once he had figured out how many there were and where they were positioned, the Egyptian gave them the slip and returned to the hotel where Stadler was already sleeping the sleep of the just.

Vienna, 10 October 1791

In Paris, the revolutionaries were radically opposed to the monarchists. This time, there would be no more concessions. One or other camp would take over and dictate its law. With his hands tied, Louis XVI would probably not have the courage or opportunity to enter into a decisive battle. The country was still unstable and resembled a sinking ship.

'Prague is under control,' Geytrand confirmed.

'Mozart?' asked Joseph Anton.

'He didn't leave Vienna, and his wife is taking the waters in Baden.'

'How is he doing?'

'He seems to have picked up but it is just a remission. I'm afraid it's been difficult getting him to swallow the potion recently, because his man-servant keeps getting in the way. But we shall soon be back to normal. And I am hoping to use an interesting fellow: Franz Hofdemel, a former Mason, who left his lodge in February. He is a wealthy lawyer, and his wife, Maria Magdalena, is a pupil of Mozart. She is pregnant so we can accuse the musician of being the father. Hofdemel will be mad with rage and want to murder his rival without being caught, so he'll be ready to use the poison we shall give him. He will be an extra suspect, my lord.'

'Brilliant, my good Geytrand.'

59

Vienna, 10 October 1791

As he left his house, Mozart came face to face with the old man in the dark cloak whose existence he had nearly forgotten about.

'How is the *Requiem* coming along, Mr Mozart?'

'I have too much work.'

'I shall give you an extra thirty ducats.'

'What is the name of the commissioner?'

'I am not allowed to say.'

'Is he an honourable man?'

'You should have no doubt about that, Mr Mozart. The sooner you finish it, the happier my employer will be.'

'Well, give me a month. No . . . more! Please tell me your name!'

'I am just an unimportant messenger. Goodbye, Mr Mozart.'

Wolfgang was keen to write this *Requiem*. As he

committed the first notes to paper, he felt himself pass through the doors of death, like a Master Mason putting knowledge above belief. And the immensely powerful *Kyrie* was the perfect link between his craft and Bach's. Mozart was writing his own liturgy, harnessing the words to the music to evoke the terrible confrontation with the forces of destruction. Every death involved rupture and pain. But an enlightened mind was able to repel it and uncover the hidden face of life.

Tomorrow, Wolfgang would go back and see his *Magic Flute* with Stoll, the Baden Kapellmeister, and Süssmayr, who could give him Constance's latest news; he was missing his wife more and more as the days went by.

Thamos, meanwhile, was accomplishing a difficult mission in Prague, and he did not know when he would return.

Prague, 12 October 1791

'In the circumstances,' Count Canal said to Thamos, 'I think we should put off founding this Grotto.'

'That would be a grave mistake,' returned the Egyptian. 'I have gathered together a few brave Brothers determined to attempt this enterprise.'

'Not brave, reckless. This time, the empire's police officers are not just observing the Freemasons of Prague, they are hassling them. The future is darkening, my

Brother. And this is surely not the moment to challenge the regime. Everyone must think first of his own safety. We will do everything to rein in our activities, take care not to worry the authorities and be sure to praise their leniency. Believe me, there is no other solution.'

'Mozart, however, will never give up.'

'Don't you think he went a bit far writing *The Magic Flute*? His celebrity doesn't make him untouchable.'

'Do you have precise information?' Thamos asked, anxiously.

'I am just worried. And I do think our dear Brother Mozart should abandon his project.'

For a fleeting instant, the Egyptian wondered if Count Canal was collaborating with the police to protect his position and his interests.

'I can no longer guarantee the safety of the Brothers who attend the secret meetings,' declared the Count. 'That is why I am asking you to drop all illicit activity.'

'Illicit activity . . . Is that how you see initiation?'

Canal avoided the Egyptian's gaze.

'You are asking too many questions, my Brother. Freemasonry cannot possibly fight all the injustices and imperfections on its own.'

'Mozart and I are not utopians, and we are fully aware of the danger. But if we show resilience, we shall strengthen our position. If we bow to circumstances, we shall be crushed.'

'Each to his own method, Thamos. Mine is to let the storm blow over.'

'This storm will not pass over so quickly. If we don't build a robust spiritual centre, there will be nothing but ruins left behind.'

'When are you expecting to leave Prague?'

'Once Stadler has given the first performance of Mozart's Clarinet Concerto. It should mark the birth of the Grotto here, in this city, which he loved so much and which has brought him fame.'

'Farewell, my Brother. But don't wait too long.'

Was this advice, or a threat? Now, he would have to forget about Prague and turn his attention to other towns and other countries.

As he left Count Canal's palace, Thamos scanned the environs. The emperor's police could well be waiting for him.

A man with a moustache came up to him.

'Do you have the time?'

The Egyptian consulted his pocket watch.

'Nearly midday.'

'Thank you, my Brother. You are most kind. You must leave Prague without delay.'

The pedestrian disappeared, and no one set on Thamos.

He still appeared to be free to move about.

60

Vienna, 13 October 1791

Wolfgang could scarcely believe his eyes. Salieri, none other than Antonio Salieri had written to ask him for two seats to *The Magic Flute*! Was it the height of hypocrisy or an attempt at reconciliation? He sent him a reply in the affirmative and agreed to take him to the theatre that evening at six o'clock.

The composer was going to take another lucky person, his son Karl Thomas, who was boarding at the school in Perchtoldsdorf.

'You're looking very well,' his father commented.

'I like it here. I run about in the garden in the morning and eat a nice lunch and then I play in the afternoon.'

'And what about your lessons?'

The little boy pouted.

'I don't care for them very much.'

Karl Thomas was not one whit better! He had the same

329

bad habits and no taste for work. The Perchtoldsdorf school was teaching its children nothing at all. It was time to send the little rascal to the Piarists where they would give him a proper education.

'Are you staying to lunch, Papa?'

'Yes, and I've got a surprise for you.'

Karl Thomas's eyes lit up.

'Tell me, quickly!'

'I'm taking you to the opera tonight.'

The little boy jumped for joy.

'I wish we were already there!'

At the appointed hour, Mozart went to fetch Salieri and his mistress, the singer Madame Cavalieri.

'You are doing us an immense favour, dear friend, dear great friend! Without you, we would have had to arrive at four o'clock and endure the stress of not knowing whether we were going to get a decent seat. The opera is such a success that it is attracting huge numbers of spectators!'

'You can have my box so you can enjoy the show in peace.'

The couple were all kindness and rapt attention, with Salieri calling out *bravo* and *bello* after every number.

At the end of the opera, he and his mistress fell over themselves to compliment him on such a magnificent piece, declaring it worthy of gracing the grandest festivals attended by the greatest monarchs!

As they climbed into the carriage Mozart had reserved for them, Salieri continued to pour out his admiration and promised to see this marvellous work very often.

'You're really keen on it,' his mistress observed.

'Not enough, you mean!'

'I've never seen you so enthusiastic.'

'I have never heard such a great work before!'

'Are you serious?'

'Totally! This opera is unique.'

Salieri was gripped by remorse. He should not have targeted a creator of this stature so basely. But no one could stop the march of fate.

Vienna, 13 October 1791

Still puzzling over Salieri's sincerity, Mozart took the joyful Karl Thomas to dine at Hofer's. He had only spent one night there, finding that the lazy mornings at his brother-in-law's house disrupted his timetable and habits and put him out of humour.

So, father and son drove back home.

Before going to bed for a sound sleep, Wolfgang thought of Thamos. Was he managing to gather a few Brothers and Sisters from Prague to form the first lodges of the Grotto?

Vienna, 14 October 1791

'I have received a disturbing document,' Leopold II told Joseph Anton, and he showed him an unsigned letter denouncing a Masonic plot against the empire and declaring revolution imminent.

Like France, Austria would be the victim of blood-thirsty fanatics for whom a ruler who simply enjoys life does not deserve to occupy the throne.

Most astonishing, however, was the fact that the author of this abominable statement was von Schloissnigg, Cabinet Secretary and now the head of the last Illuminati. And the person responsible for appointing him to his official position was Baron Gottfried Van Swieten!

'These accusations are extremely grave,' said Leopold II. 'Do you think they are credible?'

'No, Your Majesty. In my opinion it is just an ambitious courtier settling accounts. As for Baron van Swieten, although he has sometimes been suspected of sympathizing with the Freemasons, I have nothing on him. All the same, I shall start a full investigation into his activities. On the other hand, we should take threats of revolution and the plot fomented by the Illuminati very seriously because they are now hidden behind the mask of Freemasonry.'

'Is my court nothing but a hotbed of hypocrites and revolutionaries?'

'There is no shortage of them, Your Majesty, and first among them is Mozart, the real leader behind the plot to overthrow your throne. The ordinary lodges are no longer enough for him and he is planning to set up a new Order. The blazing triumph of *The Magic Flute* is giving him a considerable following.'

The emperor's face froze.

'I thought that problem had been dealt with, Count of Pergen.'

'It will be, Your Majesty. Let me have some time. In the circumstances, Mozart's death must on no account cause a scandal. Otherwise people will be clamouring for an investigation and blame the police, or worse still, accuse you of despotism. Contrary to my expectations, the death of Ignaz von Born, Mozart's spiritual master, did nothing to weaken him. Rather, his soul seems to have been passed on to his disciple and made him more powerful.'

'I hope you're not falling under the spell of Masonic mysticism?'

'Heaven forefend! But I don't underestimate the powers of the initiates.'

'Do you think this *Magic Flute* is as dangerous as all that?'

'It is the most formidable war machine ever designed by a Freemason.'

61

Vienna, 16 October 1791

Mozart and Karl Thomas finally set off to visit Constance in Baden. Temperatures had plummeted, and snowfalls complicated a journey that should have been short. Winter had come surprisingly early, and the peasants were predicting that it would be long and hard.

Warm clothes, boots and a comfortable carriage: Wolfgang had not stinted on precautions. The coachman negotiated roads that had turned treacherous suddenly, and it was with intense relief that husband and wife fell into each other's arms.

Gaukerl leapt up to lick his master's face and everyone rejoiced at the baby's excellent health. There was no denying how well Franz Xaver was doing.

'Has your cure done you good, my darling?'

'My leg and foot have both stopped hurting.'

'*The Magic Flute* is a huge success, so all our material problems will soon be over. Schikaneder is expecting to keep the opera running for several months. Every evening, the audience is enthusiastic. Some of them want to come back and see it several times over so they can savour every detail!'

'You look terribly pale . . . Have you been eating properly in the past few days?'

'Sometimes I'm ravenously hungry and at other times I have no appetite at all. It's not easy combining the routine of daily life with the rigours of artistic creation! But everything will be better now.'

Prague, 16 October 1791

Anton Stadler was at last going to premiere Mozart's Clarinet Concerto* and make a new instrument sing as only he knew how!

Thamos would wait until after the concert to mention the failure of their mission. The Prague Freemasons had refused to get involved in the new initiation Order Mozart had designed, but the Egyptian had not given up hope of convincing a few Brothers to take part in the venture, in defiance of the prohibitions.

If the empire turned out to be too inhospitable, they would have to go into exile. And England, the land of

* K622, in A major.

freedom, out of reach of the excesses of the French Revolution, would be the ideal destination.

With total assurance, Anton Stadler gave his audience a moment's grace with this music from another world intended for the Grotto.

Serenity, detachment and a striving for the light characterized the masterpiece. Thamos thought back to words spoken by Abbot Hermes and which seemed so perfectly to encapsulate it: 'Imagine you are everywhere at the same time, in the sea, on land and in the sky. Imagine you had never been born, that you are still an embryo, young and old and beyond death.'

The lawyer Franz Hofdemel crumpled the anonymous letter in his hand and stepped nervously into the inn where his mysterious correspondent had arranged to meet him.

A tall, heavy-jowled man came towards him.

'Let's go and sit near the back. I have serious revelations to make.'

Hofdemel demurred.

'Who are you?'

'You don't need to know,' retorted Geytrand. 'I have a high regard for moral values and I can't bear to see you being humiliated.'

'Your letter casts doubt on my wife, Maria Magdalena. What do you mean by it?'

'Are you ready to hear the truth?'

'I demand to hear it!'

'You are not the father of the child your wife brought into the world.'

'You're mad! This is disgraceful!'

'The real father is her lover and piano teacher, Wolfgang Mozart.'

Franz Hofdemel was tempted to lash out at his informer but he restrained himself: he might be telling the truth.

'A man of your standing must not let himself be treated like this,' Geytrand advised, in honeyed tones. 'Above all, don't react with violence, otherwise you could ruin your career. You used to belong to the Freemasons, didn't you?'

'Mozart was my Brother! And that makes his ignominy all the more despicable.'

'The Illuminati of Bavaria used to use *aqua toffana* to get rid of traitors. It is made from a mixture of arsenic, antimony and lead oxide and was once considered the best way to purge the earth of vile men. In the form of either powder or liquid, it can easily be added to a person's wine or beer. Here, take this phial – use it judiciously.'

In spite of himself, Hofdemel took the poison.

'Justice must be done,' Geytrand added, before vanishing.

Vienna, 17 October 1791

'Were you the one, Baron, who had von Schloissnigg appointed cabinet secretary?' Joseph Anton asked.

'I was indeed,' Gottfried van Swieten acknowledged,

immediately on his guard. 'He had the necessary competence. Though lately, I admit I have been severely disappointed in him.'

'Why is that?' asked the Count of Pergen, in surprise.

'I have it from one of my subordinates that this hypocrite once belonged to the defunct Order of the Illuminati of Bavaria and that he is still putting its pernicious doctrine about and criticizing the emperor's policies.'

'Have you put that down in a proper report?'

'Of course, and I sent it to His Majesty.'

'Well done,' Anton approved. 'You have lived up to your reputation again, Baron.'

'You know how much I distrust the Illuminati and Freemasons.'

'Even Mozart?'

'Because of his talents, I have often invited him to my house for my Sunday concerts, and I flatter myself that I brought the greatness of Johann Sebastian Bach to his attention.'

'You should distance yourself from Mozart,' Joseph Anton advised, abruptly.

62

Vienna, 19 October 1791

'"You should distance yourself from Mozart," was what the Count of Pergen ordered,' Baron van Swieten told Thamos, who had just returned from Prague.

'You have been suspected of collusion with the Freemasons again and acquitted. The count has always held you in esteem.'

'And Mozart?'

'The success of *The Magic Flute* and his Masonic projects are attracting the wrath of the regime.'

'He should leave Vienna and go to London,' considered van Swieten.

'That is what I think, but he has just had a second son and his wife is in delicate health. The main thing is, he wants to found a new initiation Order.'

'Isn't that rather utopian?'

'Utopias don't lead anywhere. Initiation, on the other

hand, is the way to enlightenment. Why are so few people interested in it when it could open their eyes to the invisible and bring them serenity? I suppose, because humankind prefers war, hatred and destruction. And religions are so comfortable! Believers think they hold the absolute truth and they force it on other people, killing them when they have to. What is Mozart in this morass of stupidity and intolerance? In my opinion, he represents the essential: a breath of freedom and hope.'

Vienna, 19 October 1791

These were extraordinary times and an extraordinary meeting was arranged. When he got home with his family on the 17th, Mozart consulted Thamos, before going to Crowned Hope Lodge in the evening for a gathering of a small group of Brothers in the degree of Master Mason.

The Egyptian told the composer everything. Firstly, Prague Freemasons did not have the courage to take part in founding the Grotto, and secondly, the Masonic message of *The Magic Flute* was frowned on by the Church, the emperor, the police and even the Freemasons.

'I see no reason to give up,' concluded Wolfgang.

'The only one who wants to continue is Anton Stadler.'

'Don't forget Countess Thun. She knows some women who want to experience initiation. Our job is to win over Brothers who are undecided.'

Thamos did not try to dampen Mozart's ardour. Faith, after all, could move mountains.

The meeting took place in a tense atmosphere. As Wolfgang's arguments did not sound very convincing, Thamos took the floor. He recalled the origins of the Tradition, the permanent war initiates should wage against the darkness and the need to drag Viennese Freemasonry out of the mire and restore to it a true ideal.

During the banquet, many questions were raised, and it was agreed to discuss the subject again at the next meeting and consider the project in more detail.

Vienna, 20 October 1791

'The Archbishop of Vienna asked me to talk to you,' the Freemason from Crowned Hope Lodge told the Count of Pergen. 'I agreed, on condition that my name is never mentioned.'

'I do not know it, anyway,' Joseph Anton lied, 'and I undertake never to find it out. What do you have to tell me?'

The Church spy, who had infiltrated the lodge to inform on it, related Mozart's disturbing project.

'Our Freemasonry is no longer enough. *The Magic Flute* is a kind of initiation programme that he wants to bring to fruition.'

'Does he have serious support?'

'To be honest, only two Brothers are interested. The

341

first is the clarinettist, Anton Stadler, an old friend with limited powers of action, so far as I can see. He has eight children and is constantly scrounging off Mozart.'

'And the other one?'

'An odd fellow who goes by the name of Count of Thebes. He is not officially registered in a lodge, but he attends all of them and travels about Europe. Some weakminded Masons believe him to be an Unknown Superior charged with guiding the chosen to the supreme Light.'

'Do you know his address?'

'Unfortunately not. The Count of Thebes has accumulated a vast fortune from his alchemical work.'

'In that case,' remarked Anton, 'he could be helping Mozart to realize his dreams.'

'That is what I fear.'

'Do you have any other information about this Brother?'

'He is also known as Thamos, and the mystics claim he is using magic powers to protect Mozart from harm.'

'You have been extremely useful to me. Please pass on my greetings to his Grace.'

As soon as the false Freemason had left, Geytrand stepped out from behind a curtain.

'What a fascinating interview,' Joseph Anton said, thoughtfully.

'I am starting to understand some obscure points, especially the harassment of our officers who were observing Mozart. I'd had my suspicions about a mysterious protector for some time, but I had never managed to find out who he was.'

'Not so fast, my good friend. This may all just be idle gossip on the part of the archbishop's spy.'

'I am keen to discover whether what he says was true.'

63

Vienna, 20 October 1791

The wind veered abruptly and the southerly Föhn pushed temperatures up to a balmy eighteen degrees. Happy to emerge from the harsh early winter, the Viennese flocked to the public gardens.

In the pleasant autumn sunshine, Wolfgang and Constance were taking a walk along the alleys of the Prater.

But the musician was looking pale and drawn and had to sit down on a bench.

'Composing the *Requiem* is wearing you out,' his wife considered. 'Shouldn't you take a rest from it?'

'I am relaxing by writing a new Masonic Cantata. I think it is going to be very important, but you're right: the *Requiem* is taking its toll on my energies, and I'm finding it difficult to keep up the pace.'

'This isn't like you.'

'I think I know the reason, but I can hardly bring myself to tell you.'

'Please tell me!'

'I am composing my own *Requiem*.'

Constance clasped her husband's hands in her own.

'I wish you would stop having such horrible thoughts: they are destroying you.'

'I am sure I have been poisoned,' Wolfgang told her[*].

'Poisoned! By whom and what are they using on you?'

'I don't know who, but I believe they are using *aqua toffana*, a substance invented by a woman called Teofania di Adamo, in around 1500. When it is administered in small doses over time, it acts insidiously and leads to certain death. The Bavarian Illuminati promised to wipe out their enemies with it. Some people think I overstepped the limits with *The Magic Flute*.'

'I am going to take two decisions,' Constance decreed. 'One: I am going to take this confounded *Requiem* away from you, and two: I am going to consult a doctor.'

Vienna, 21 October 1791

Mozart protected by the mysterious Count of Thebes . . . So that was it! As a former Freemason, Geytrand did not deny the existence of Unknown Superiors. They were

---

[*] This statement was confirmed by Constance in a letter to the Novellos, an English couple, in 1829.

neither supermen nor spectres but initiates into the Great Mysteries. They travelled from country to country without ever settling in one place. If Thamos was really an Egyptian, he came from the motherland of esotericism and had profoundly influenced Ignaz von Born and Mozart by providing them with the subject of *The Magic Flute*.

As long as the Unknown Superior stayed close to Mozart, no harm would come to the musician and he would extricate himself from the most critical situations. It was like an invisible cloak and while he wore it, he would not notice the darts of destiny.

The first thing was to track the Egyptian down, arrest and imprison him and then get rid of him. Once deprived of his defence, the composer would become easy prey.

Thamos was bound to have several homes in Vienna and an alchemy laboratory.

Geytrand went to the house of von Born. The mineralogist's widow and daughters answered his questions politely. Yes, in the weeks leading up to his death, a man with an imposing bearing had come with Mozart to work on the libretto to *The Magic Flute*. They used to shut themselves up in von Born's office where, in spite of the latter's pain and failing health, he had been glad to welcome them.

What was the enigmatic visitor called? The women did not know.

Disappointed, Geytrand asked around a number of administrative services.

He could find no trace of the Count of Thebes.

The Egyptian had been using pseudonyms and had slipped through the net. He probably had connections at court. There again, he must have kept every detail of his private life and activities entirely secret.

Geytrand was facing a doughty adversary, one who could be a coachman in the morning and an aristocrat at night! Like all Unknown Superiors, he was protean because he had no attachments.

There was one person, however, who might give him away: Mozart.

For Thamos the Egyptian had spent years nurturing the musician's spiritual growth so that he would one day be capable of writing *The Magic Flute*. Month after month, he had trained him up to make him a Master Mason who could give Freemasonry the boost it required. That was why Mozart was so dangerous. Far from being an ordinary artist, he had acquired the spiritual stature that befitted a founder of an Order.

But the new temple would not be built in a day. If Geytrand got rid of Thamos the Egyptian, after winkling his secrets out of him, he could stop it being built.

There was one problem: no police officer had ever managed to lay hands on an Unknown Superior. Of course, the Church had got hold of Cagliostro, but the magus was not in the same category, even while he had certain powers at his disposal.

Who else but the Freemasons Thamos had rubbed shoulders with at lodge meetings could provide the start of a trail?

The obvious candidate was Prince Karl von Lichnowsky. He had no sense of loyalty and was always looking for ways to make money. And he was Mozart's enemy and would not be able to resist the pleasure of harming him one more time. Armed with the Count of Pergen's file, Geytrand knew that he could make the prince cooperate.

64

Vienna, 23 October 1791

After a lull, winter struck again, with icy winds and flurries of snow. Wolfgang and Thamos shivered and sipped a spicy punch that put the colour back in their cheeks. Vienna talked of bronchitis and already people were grieving for the dead.

'Have your enquiries not got anywhere?' the musician asked, anxiously.

'The mystery is revealed. Our Brother Puchberg met an eccentric, Count Walsegg-Stuppach. He buys compositions from musicians, signs them in his name and manages to pass them off as his own. He is looking for a *Requiem* to honour his wife's memory. If you want, you can go on composing it in exchange for an advance of ducats and a proper contract drawn up before a notary*.

* *Johann Nepomuk Sortschan.*

349

You don't have to worry, no one will take your work away from you. The only limiting clause is that you must give your manuscript to the commissioner.'

'Am I allowed to take a copy?'

'In theory, no, and the count says he will do that himself. As a precaution, ask Süssmayr to help you.'

'Süssmayr is pretty dull, but he is a good technician and will do an excellent copy. This *Requiem* means a lot to me, Thamos, and the commission has awoken in me the desire to confront the worst forms of death and annihilation. I shall need at least six months to complete it. That is why, on page one of the manuscript, I have written 1792.'

Vienna, 24 October 1791

In view of Prince Karl von Lichnowsky's high standing and his countless connections, only the Count of Pergen had the authority to interview him.

Hidden behind his favourite curtain with two peep-holes cut in it, Geytrand was nevertheless present.

'I agreed to see you,' Lichnowsky said to Anton, 'because, like you, I am very attached to law and order.'

'We are not here to exchange pleasantries, Your Highness.'

'My lord, I . . .'

'I have nothing against you, Lichnowsky. You may answer me without fear. This interview will never have taken place.'

'What is it you want to know?'

'At Crowned Hope, and perhaps in other lodges, you will have come across the Count of Thebes, Thamos the Egyptian.'

Lichnowksy scratched his chin.

'Precisely.'

'Tell me about this man.'

'He's a funny chap with a strong personality. He seems to have most of the Brothers under his spell.'

'A kind of magician?'

'Something like that.'

'Is this Count of Thebes a friend of Mozart?'

'His best supporter, so far as I can tell.'

'Is he rich?'

'Rumour has it he is very rich.'

'What about his professional activities?'

'No idea.'

'And his address?'

'I don't know. One of the Servant Brothers we had to dismiss may know.'

Lichnowsky gave Anton the name and address of this man.

'What's happened to my legal proceedings against Mozart?'

'On the right track,' replied Anton. 'I have done what was needed.'

Vienna, 25 October 1791

The former Servant Brother at Crowned Hope Lodge was a *bon viveur* and proud of his wine cellars. Now that he was not permitted to attend meetings, he looked after the gardens, maintenance and cleaning at the lodge, and he kept it supplied with wine for its festivities.

'Imperial police,' Geytrand announced. 'I want to ask you some questions.'

The old man leant on his spade.

'What about?'

'When you were employed by Crowned Hope Lodge, you came across a tall, sumptuously dressed character called the Count of Thebes.'

'I have a vague recollection of him . . .'

'Did you talk to him?'

'Only "hello" and "goodbye".'

'What did people say about him?'

'Oh, you know, I'm not the type to listen to gossip. I did my work as best I could and was happy with that.'

'Do you know where the Count of Thebes lives?'

'No.'

'Be careful how you answer! You used to deliver wine to the lodge grandees. I have it on good authority that one of them made the Count of Thebes a present of a few decent bottles, and it was you who took them to him. If you don't cooperate, I promise you, you will be in for serious trouble.'

'Ah, yes, I remember!'

'Where does the Count of Thebes live?'

'A private house in the old city at the end of a blind alley. The building is a bit run-down and looks abandoned. Do you have a map?'

'You can draw one on my notebook.'

The old Servant Brother drew a shaky plan. He was eager to be shot of this evil-looking, jowly police officer.

Geytrand was jubilant.

He would arrest Thamos the Egyptian that evening and deprive Mozart of all protection.

65

Vienna, 25 October 1791

Again, it was cold and snow was falling. Fortunately, the Mozart family was keeping well and the doctor had not found anything seriously wrong with Wolfgang. Constance agreed to give him back the *Requiem* so that he could go on with his work.

'I see it as a tragic opera,' he told his wife. 'Everything comes from and aspires to the hereafter, eternal rest and the transcendence of death which every soul strives for. It demands the terrible struggle of the *Kyrie,* a double fugue and the encounter between the visible and invisible. Wrath* is the outcome, reducing the world to ash through mankind's inadequacy. The celestial trumpet† calls all creatures to judgment, because nothing must

---

* *Dies irae.*
† *Tuba mirum.*

go unpunished. A trombone solo summons the just and delivers them from their chains, without fear of the King whose majesty will make evil-doers tremble[*]. After the last judgment, the Almighty spreads His benevolence and grants hope[†]. But the wicked are condemned to the horror of darkness, the cruelty of the flames and the abyss[‡]. Those who rise again leave behind the extreme pain of death and ask for serenity, a peaceful force that allows them to leave the abyss and rise up to the Light[§]. The souls delivered from the torments of hell are led to the Light by the Archangel Michael[¶]. But will the promise of supernatural enlightenment be fulfilled? The soul must embark on another struggle[**] to dispel all doubt and achieve genuine certainty[††]. After the divine blessing and the granting of true peace[‡‡] comes the communion with the eternal Light[§§].'

The gravity of the enterprise troubled Constance.

'I wish you would give up on this!'

'I have received the money and composed the first parts, and I have already put in a lot of work. It would be cowardly not to keep this appointment with death. When

---

[*] *Rex tremendae.*
[†] *Recordare.*
[‡] *Confutatis.*
[§] *Lacrimosa.*
[¶] *Domine Jesu Christe.*
[**] *Quam olim Abrahae.*
[††] *Hostias et preces.*
[‡‡] *Sanctus et Benedictus, Agnus Dei.*
[§§] *Lux aeterna.*

I have finished my *Requiem*, we will found the Grotto, and a new life will begin.'

Vienna, 25 October 1791

'Is everything ready?' Geytrand asked the plain clothes police officer in charge of the operation.

'My men are all in place.'

'He can't escape?'

'No chance!'

'Are you quite sure?'

'Absolutely.'

One of the spies came to report.

'A light on the first floor!'

'So,' exclaimed Geytrand, 'the bird is in its nest! Let's go.'

Their boots crunched into the fresh snow.

The squad leader hammered on the door of the Count of Thebe's house.

'Police: open up!'

When the door stayed shut, they heaved several times on the lock then used a battering ram.

The moment they burst in, two will-o'-the-wisps struck the tapestries and the fire was instantly out of control.

Boiling with anger, Geytrand kept his eyes on the house roof as the only escape route open to the Egyptian.

But the sky behind the flames and smoke was inky and Geytrand could make out nothing, not even a shadow.

Perhaps the Count of Thebes had perished in the fire he himself had ignited?

Vienna, 30 October 1791

'Can I see Wolfgang?' Schikaneder asked Constance.

'He sat up working very late last night, I am letting him sleep.'

'Wake him up! He'll thank me for it!'

Seeing the impresario's excitement, Constance yielded. Gaukerl jumped on to his master's bed and licked his face vigorously.

Schikaneder paced up and down outside.

'Ah, Wolfgang. At last!'

'What's going on?'

'The month's statement, the great statement! We've done more than twenty performances and that's just the start. Full house every night, applause to bring the roof down, and the revenue: 8443 florins!'

Wolfgang and Constance could barely believe their ears.

'Of course,' Schikaneder added, 'I have all sorts of fees to settle, but we'll still make a tidy profit. And after only a month! Can you imagine what's to follow? I daren't even predict how many performances there'll be in Vienna before *The Magic Flute* goes on tour. It will be rapturously received in several countries, especially if you agree to conduct the premiere yourself each time.

Don't you think you should write a sequel to the opera? My singers would be delighted.'

Vienna, 1 November 1791

'We have made considerable progress, Your Majesty,' Joseph Anton told Leopold II, 'and we now know that an Egyptian nobleman, Thamos Count of Thebes, is poisoning Vienna's Lodges. He is seen as an Unknown Superior and makes frequent trips abroad to spread his pernicious ideas. We tried arresting him at his home, but he gave us the slip by setting fire to his own house. The police report put down that he perished in the fire. In my opinion, the Count of Thebes has laid a trap for us and wants us to think that he is dead to gain extra cover and go on with his activities.'

'Do you think he has occult powers?'

'We shouldn't underestimate such a character, Your Majesty.'

'Did you find a corpse?'

'Yes, we did.'

'So, why don't you think he is dead?'

'Because its condition made it impossible to identify and one of my informants charged with observing the house has gone missing. The essential point is that Thamos the Egyptian is the friend, Brother and protector of Mozart. When the Count of Thebes is imprisoned, the situation will develop in our favour, but I am afraid the task looks extremely arduous. Therefore, for the purposes of this case, I should like Your Majesty to grant me full powers.'

'I grant them, Count of Pergen.'

'Thamos has connections at court and I must find out who these people are. Furthermore, he must have been warned about our plans to storm his house. I mean, a senior police officer informed him. I am afraid my intervention will cause clashes.'

'You have full powers.'

66

Heedless of the foul weather, Schikaneder's theatre gave the twenty-fourth performance of *The Magic Flute*, with the usual success.

Mozart put the *Requiem* aside for a while to concentrate fully on writing his new Masonic Cantata. He was prepared to break the ban on writing music for the lodges, because he thought the piece necessary to the inauguration of a new temple where Brothers would gather together to pursue research into initiation.

It would be a decisive stage before founding the Grotto, and the Cantata would be its founding hymn.

Mozart's grand plan was taking shape at last.

But he had not recovered his health and still less his usual energy.

In answer to a cryptic note from Thamos, Wolfgang

made his way to an inn frequented by local craftsmen. He sat down at a table in the shadows and ordered a beer.

A moment later, Thamos appeared opposite him.

'You were not followed,' he noted.

'Why are you anxious?'

'The situation has deteriorated. There is a persistent rumour going about that you have debts of thirty thousand florins.'

'That's a complete lie!' cried Mozart. 'The success of *The Magic Flute* has resolved all my difficulties and 1792 could not look better.'

'Unfortunately, the emperor believes this slander and will not hear of having a court musician who manages his affairs so carelessly.'

'Is my job at risk?'

'I have done what I can to counteract the rumours but my position is becoming tenuous.'

'Have you been threatened?'

'The emperor's police officers are on my trail. Only days ago, I escaped by the skin of my teeth. You must leave Vienna!'

The musician's colour drained from his face.

'Are you all right, Wolfgang?'

'I think . . . I think I have been given *aqua toffana*.'

'The poison used by the Illuminati of Bavaria! Have you seen a doctor?'

'His diagnosis reassured Constance.'

'He was obviously wrong.'

'Who could hate me so much that he wants to poison me?'

'I shall find out. In the short-term, we must get you back to health. If you have been given small doses of the substance for a few weeks, I can cure you. I shall use the Abbot Hermes's invaluable teaching to concoct a reliable antidote based on liquid gold. I shall contact you using our Master Mason's code and have a phial of the elixir delivered to you the day after tomorrow.'

Vienna, 7 November 1791

Leopold II's private counsellor, a wealthy nobleman, had exercised the same duties for the emperor's predecessor. Refusing ministerial positions, he was content to act as the emperor's *éminence grise*.

Breakfast was his favourite time of day while he perused his secret files. Then he received the gossipy courtiers. Late in the evening, he would pass on to the emperor any information worthy of interest.

That morning, he held a private audience for the former Minister of Police, the Count of Pergen, a fearsome character charged with secret missions.

'Would you like something to eat or drink?'

'I am on the trail of a dangerous criminal, and you can help me.'

'Me! You surprise me!'

'Yes, but you know the Count of Thebes.'

'Is it him you suspect? In that case, you are making a serious mistake! There is no more honest man and no one with more respect for law and order. Orphanages and alms houses benefit from his very generous contributions.'

'The foreigner has abused you, sir. Behind his honourable courtier's mask is a revolutionary Freemason of the worst sort.'

'Surely you are deluded, my lord!'

'Perhaps you would care to look over this damning file of evidence.'

The counsellor's stomach contracted.

'Tell me everything you know about the Count of Thebes,' demanded Joseph Anton.

'Very little! He never talks about himself.'

'What did he hope from you?'

'We used to talk about many things, exchanging impressions, arguing about ideas. I valued his intelligence and lucidity.'

'Was he an unconditional supporter of Mozart?'

'He proved the emptiness of all sorts of gossip aimed at tarnishing that excellent musician's reputation and which sometimes came to the ear of His Majesty. I was therefore able to tell Leopold II the truth.'

'On the contrary, sir. You were an unwitting accomplice in a plot. Do you know where the Count of Thebes lives?'

'He has a private house in the old city, I believe.'

'Any other properties in Vienna?'

'Not to my knowledge.'

'I have told the emperor of this Egyptian's real activities,' declared Anton, threateningly. 'If, by any chance, he should happen to contact you again, keep hold of him and alert the police.'

Vienna, 8 November 1791

Geytrand interviewed the Freemasons in the Viennese lodges who had met Thamos the Egyptian, in the hope of gleaning decisive information that would help him pin him down. They all described him as a powerful personality, but no one could give details about his fortune or his properties.

One affluent burger, recently raised to the degree of Fellow Companion, was resentful.

'I'm a good Christian, I am, and I will always defend our Holy Church. I didn't like that foreigner.'

'Was he disrespectful of religion?' asked Geytrand.

'Insidiously and perversely! He used to go on about Isis and Osiris. According to him, the appearance of monotheism was a seriously regressive step and Catholicism does not represent absolute truth. Men like this Count of Thebes have given Freemasons a bad name. And also, he was accused of weird and prohibited practices.'

'Such as?'

The burger crossed himself.

'Alchemy, the devil's science! Thamos has a laboratory inherited from Ignaz von Born.'

Geytrand knew the whereabouts of this outfit.

67

Vienna, 9 November 1791

Since the previous evening, the building that housed von Born's alchemy laboratory on the outskirts of Vienna had been under strict surveillance. Hordes of plain clothes police officers had been ordered to seize the Count of Thebes alive.

Meanwhile, Geytrand prowled about the neighbourhood, a district populated by ordinary working folk.

No one could give him any information.

But there was one white-haired baker, the father of six children. His lips and hands shook.

'Did you see anyone go into the house with closed shutters?'

'Yes, yes!' answered the baker, and gave a description of Ignaz von Born.

'No one else?'

'I . . . I don't think so.'

Geytrand rolled his eyes menacingly.

'You don't think so, or you are sure you didn't?'

'I can't answer, because of the coachman.'

'What coachman?'

'He was driving a fine carriage, stationed outside my baker's shop and house. The old man came in to buy bread and wine.'

'Are you authorised to sell wine?'

'No, but he was ever so thirsty! And his boss wouldn't let him talk to anyone.'

'Did he come here often?'

'I only ever served the coachman once, and that was a week ago.'

'Did he tell you his name?'

'No, although . . . '

'Think hard.'

Geytrand drew a ducat from his pocket.

'Think hard and you will be rewarded.'

The baker ran a hand through his hair.

'When he had emptied the bottle, the coachman said: "As my name is Fine-Teeth, that was good! "'

Without much hope, Geytrand left a policeman on the site and went to look for a coachman nick-named Fine-Teeth.

Vienna, 10 November 1791

Joseph Anton's investigations were over. A bundle of lines of enquiry was turning into positive proof, thanks to enquiries and witness reports. He summoned the district chief in whose jurisdiction Crowned Hope Lodge was.

Anton had promoted him for informing so zealously on Masonic meetings.

'I have missed you, my lord. Under your leadership, I was able to achieve serious work.'

'Has the situation changed?'

'Your successor is not fully aware of the danger. You, however, knew the Freemasons inside out!'

'I was not always sufficiently on my guard. So I did not know you were a Freemason!'

'My lord!'

'Like Thamos the Egyptian, your name did not appear on the register of any of the lodges. Nevertheless, I have it on good authority that you are the only one who could have warned your Brother, the Count of Thebes, of the police operation being mounted against him. You had been telling him for a long time. To maintain your strategic position, you were careful to give me important details that were not the main ones.'

'My lord . . .'

'There is no point denying it. I demand to know the truth.'

The district head realized that he would not escape Joseph Anton's clutches.

'What is going to happen to me?'

'You will live out your days in a house in a small town in the provinces.'

A slow death, in other words. His punishment could have been worse.

'I acted out of conviction, my lord, not self-interest. The lodge that welcomed me is not plotting against the state but it works on the symbol of the mysteries of Isis and Osiris. Many Freemasons refuse to go down that route, seeing it as too esoteric. However, it offers the genuine spiritual guidance today's world needs so badly.'

'Cut out the pointless speeches. Where does the Count of Thebes live?'

The district head described the location of the house that had burnt down.

'Any other houses?'

'I don't know.'

'Don't try my patience!'

'I don't know any more, I swear!'

The functionary knew he was beaten and was not lying.

'Instead of trampling on the law, you should have obeyed it and denounced this Egyptian. He is guilty of multiple infringements.'

The police officer bowed his head.

'Here is your letter of resignation. Sign it now. Then make yourself scarce.'

68

Vienna, 12 November 1791

'What! I've got to pay up?' exclaimed Mozart, reading the official document sent by the court. 'It's not possible!'

'I'm sorry, the Court of Lower Austria has delivered its final verdict. You must pay Prince Karl von Lichnowsky the sum of 1435 florins and thirty-two kreutzers, plus twenty-four florins for legal fees. If you can't pay immediately, your musician's salary at court will be seized up to half your earnings. And if you pervert the course of justice, your property will be sequestered*. My respects, Mr Mozart.'

The musician sank into a chair. Constance and Gaukerl ran to comfort him.

'We were getting out of our difficulties,' he murmured

---

* See *Correspondence*, Vol. V, p. 349, footnote 14.

'and now this incredible ruling! Why is my Brother hounding me in this way?'

'Because you didn't fawn on him as he wanted,' Constance ventured. 'He is dissolute and pretentious, and Lichnowsky can't stand to be contradicted. But this fine won't condemn us to penury. *The Magic Flute* is an unmitigated success and you will compose more dances and soon have a position at the Cathedral. Next year, our debts will be written off. And you have so many unborn works in your heart. You mustn't give in to despair. At least, this interminable affair will be put to rest now.'

'I can't bear injustice!'

'Isn't it in man's nature?'

Wolfgang thought of Sarastro, who could thrust injustice outside the temple. Could he make the ideal of *The Magic Flute* a reality?

Vienna, 13 November 1791

As a matter of urgency, Thamos needed to talk to the police officer who had kept him informed of the authorities' intentions since his arrival in Vienna. As the district head, he was acquainted with Joseph Anton's plans and alerted the Egyptian. It was thanks to this Brother, who believed in the need to practise the mysteries of Isis and Osiris, that the Count of Thebes had so far slipped through the net.

At regular intervals, they would meet under the porch

of the old Church of St Michael, opposite the Burgtheater, before disappearing into the crowd of loiterers.

Snow had started to fall again and an icy wind forced pedestrians to hurry along. When the weather was bad, the police officer left their usual meeting point and went to wait in the church so as not to attract attention.

Today, however, the district head stayed where he was by the door of St Michael's, in full view.

Why would he violate a strict safety measure except because he had fallen into Joseph Anton's hands?

He was being used as a lure.

The Egyptian went on his way but tried to make out the predators who had mounted this trap.

He spotted three in doorways, two others at the windows of houses and still more who were better concealed.

Thamos turned tail.

Without an essential ally, he was now blind and deaf.

The only solution was to leave Vienna, but he could not leave his Brother Mozart unprotected and uncared for. So he went back to his laboratory to make up another phial of the elixir, the only means of beating the poison. Thamos would give it to the laundry man who could smuggle it into Wolfgang's apartment without attracting the attention of the police, even if the house was under observation.

He would not entertain the idea of seeking refuge before the musician's complete recovery.

Vienna, 14 November 1791

The failure of the St Michael trap did nothing to rattle Geytrand's determination. He was now obsessed with the search for a coachman nicknamed Fine-Teeth. The profession was astonishingly well represented and included many day-workers. Yet despite hundreds of fruitless enquiries, Geytrand was indefatigable and would not give up.

Vienna, 14 November 1791

Leopold II was horrified at the news from Paris.

The revolutionary law on emigrants stipulated that they must return to France before 1 January 1791 on pain of having all their property confiscated by the new regime, which was gradually assuming all rights before eliminating its opponents.

The Church formed a sound bastion. But it was being destroyed by forcing priests and monks to take a civil oath to the Republic and thereby deny Rome and the Pope. If they refused, they would be seen as recalcitrant and poor citizens, liable to heavy punishments.

King Louis XVI had vetoed these decisions, but it was a pathetic gesture. The legislative Assembly forced him to dismiss his ministers, and the revolutionaries' decision would be the cause of millions of deaths: France was going to declare war on monarchical Europe.

If they combined their military forces, Austria and Prussia might stem the insanity. But Joseph Anton was afraid of the fanaticism of French ideologists who could lead a whole people into war. More tyranny and monstrous conflict was the only foreseeable outcome of these bloody confrontations.

He thought of the unhappy Marie Antoinette, caught up in the turmoil on an unimaginable scale. When she had left the court in Vienna, the pretty young woman thought she was going to a life of luxury and entertainment in Versailles. Today, she was a prisoner on the threshold of a dreadful death. For the Count of Pergen was in no doubt: the revolutionaries would not spare the king and his queen, that loathsome Austrian woman in league with the people's enemy.

The sovereign people . . . What a black joke! With cruelty greater than most kings, the new despots were drunk on power and would have no qualms about sacrificing anyone who stood in their way, including the royal couple. They would make a show of setting up a sham trial whose verdict was already known. The citizens' law would assassinate everyone legally.

Geytrand's sickly smile reflected total satisfaction.

'Did you get anywhere?'

'Don't sell the ass's skin, my lord. I didn't find this Fine-Teeth fellow, only a colleague who came across him. Our man was day-worker for a few wealthy noblemen.'

'Well, did you get an address?'

'Only the district where he lives. I've asked a dozen policemen to interrogate residents there.'

69

Vienna, 15 November 1791

Since swallowing the elixir, Wolfgang had felt better. He was happy to be able to take Gaukerl for a walk and was soon joined by Thamos.

'The Count of Pergen is pursuing two aims: to arrest me and hasten your end.'

'I am starting to rally,' the musician told him, confidently.

'The treatment will take some time, but you will get better. I have brought you a second phial. Have you finished your Cantata?'

'This very day! I think it will be ideal for the inauguration of our new premises, and it may be my best work*. It starts with a choir, reflecting the brotherhood.

---

* K623, *Laut verkünde unsere Freude*, the last work Mozart finished and entered in his album. It is not known whether it was Mozart himself who wrote the words. 'Why,' asks J.-V. Hocquard (*La Pensée*

Then the joyful sound of the orchestra celebrates the golden human chain that helps us build the temple. This sanctuary is the seat of Wisdom and is where the Great Mysteries are preserved. For, the prime virtue is Charity, the act of doing good, and the power of our divine duty depends, not on noise and pomp, but on silence. To achieve the plenitude of initiation, a Mason must banish all envy, cupidity and calumny from his heart.'

'I pray that the walls of the temple shall forever bear witness to our work,' murmured Thamos. 'Then we shall receive the true light of the Orient with dignity.'

'I have composed a very simple song* for the final human chain of the meeting,' Wolfgang added. 'It will mark the start of a new era.'

'The voice of the gods speaks through you and they

---

de Mozart, p. 644–646), 'does no one seem to recognize the greatness of this piece, as it deserves? My feeling is that it reflects the last "state" of Mozart's thought . . . The Cantata is a sequel, or rather a conclusion, to *The Magic Flute*.'

* K623a, *Lass uns mit geschlungenen Händen*, for men's choir and organ but which may not be by Mozart. Some musicologists attribute it to Brother Paul Wranitzky. The words are as follows: 'Let us join hands, my Brothers, so that we may finish the work in a resounding burst of joy. As our chain surrounds this hallowed place, may it embrace the whole earthly world. With our joyful songs, let us thank the Creator fulsomely; we rejoice that he is Almighty. See, the consecration is fulfilled! May the work to which we have devoted our hearts be fulfilled, too. May humanity worship Virtue. May our first duty henceforth be to learn to love ourselves and to love our fellows. Then, not only at sunrise and sunset, but also in south and north, the light will pour forth.'

have allowed you to make the long journey to this Cantata. Step by step, piece by piece, you have built the temple by building yourself. And now, you will open the doors to a new lodge where the Great Mysteries shall be celebrated.'

Vienna, 15 November 1791

At times acting as a coachman for rich luminaries and at others as a merchant of fine wines, Fine-Teeth got by pretty well. Good-looking and silver-tongued, he had both money and women aplenty and Viennese frivolity suited him perfectly.

In this filthy weather, he felt a compelling urge to doze by the hearth, and he was just nodding off when the door to his apartment burst open.

Several police officers pinned him to the floor.

'Don't make a mess of him,' Geytrand warned. 'Is your nickname Fine-Teeth?'

'Yes, yes.'

'If you answer my questions properly, you can go on with your business untroubled, otherwise . . .'

'All right, all right! I'm not guilty of anything!'

'Do you know Thamos the Egyptian, Count of Thebes?'

'I drove his carriage several times.'

'I need a complete list of all the places you took him to.'

'If you let me get my notebook out of my pocket, I can tell you immediately.'

Fine-Teeth had noted down the destinations and the money taken alongside abbreviations of his clients' names.

Geytrand studied the document.

His first feeling was one of disappointment: the house that had burnt down, von Born's house in the suburbs, lodges, palaces . . . But then came a surprise that might be the address he was looking for, on the northern edge of Vienna.

There was only one reference to it, a recent one.

Could it be the one slip the Egyptian had made?

70

Vienna, 16 November 1791

Thamos had his alchemy laboratory in a disused iron-works on the northern edge of Vienna.

On his first visit, he had used the services of his favour-ite coachman, Fine-Teeth, a day-worker with a good knowledge of the locality who spoke in favour of the area's tranquility. Since that time, he had used a differ-ent carriage on every occasion and, when the weather permitted, he went there on foot.

That morning, the sky was brighter but the roads were still bad. The Egyptian wanted to prepare another bottle of the antidote Mozart needed to get better.

He paid the coachman handsomely, scanned the envi-rons then headed for the entrance.

The door opened before he reached it.

Geytrand stood on the threshold, a sickly smile on his lips.

'You made me run, Count of Thebes.'

Two police officers armed with pistols flanked the ugly man.

'Don't try to escape: your laboratory is surrounded.'

Thamos turned and saw twenty guards all brandishing firearms.

If they wanted him alive, they would not shoot, so he ran hell for leather to a copse of trees hard by.

Geytrand had anticipated his reaction: other policemen were waiting for him there.

Caught in the net, the Egyptian head-butted his first attacker, sent the second one flying with a blow to the jaw then joined his fists together, brought them down on the head of the third and knocked him out.

There were too many of them, and they soon overcame Thamos and tied him up.

Geytrand swaggered over him.

'You do us a great deal of wrong, Count of Thebes.'

Vienna, 17 November 1791

The previous evening, the Kärntnertor Theatre, which had been closed since February 1788 because of the Turkish war, had re-opened. Perhaps the concerts and operas would start up again.

When he got up, Wolfgang saw that the weather had deteriorated. Gaukerl was asleep on a rug and no one wanted to go out. But tonight was the inauguration of the new temple. The secretary had sent out invitations and many people were looking forward to hearing Mozart's new Cantata.

But the archbishop's spies were still keen to emphasize the danger of listening to the musician.

As he was getting dressed, Wolfgang was suddenly overcome by a violent headache and stomach ache.

Gaukerl woke up in a trice, sat up and eyed his master anxiously.

'I can't stand up,' Wolfgang groaned.

Constance helped him lie down, and he lay prostrate, clutching his burning stomach.

'I'll fetch a doctor.'

'There's no point, I'll wait for my medicine.'

He knew Thamos was mixing up the potion but wondered whether he would have finished in time to relieve his suffering so that he could attend tonight's meeting.

The hours passed, and Wolfgang began to write a letter of apology. He could not hold back a few tears. *No one will be missing out more than I*, he declared, in despair that he might not be able to conduct his Cantata.

Then a kind of miracle occurred: as darkness fell, his headache passed off and the burning in his stomach abated.

'I'm going to the meeting,' he said, decidedly.

'But you're so pale!'

'I feel much better.'

Vienna, 17 November 1791

Anton Stadler greeted Mozart.

'We'd given up hope of seeing you!'

'Has Thamos arrived?'

'I'm afraid not. Let's get started, the Brothers are impatient.'

The profound joy of the Cantata banished all thoughts of the rigours of winter and the flu epidemic.

Mozart conducted the choir of Brothers, but his mind was on Thamos whose absence was bothering him.

Then they formed the human chain linking them to the initiates of yesterday, today and tomorrow, and they worshipped the creative principle and saw the light flow out to the four cardinal points.

Vienna, 18 November 1791

Geytrand struck a second time.

His gloved hand smashed Thamos' cheekbone, and the blood glistened.

Josef II had banned the use of torture but this prison had no legal existence.

Joseph Anton's entrance interrupted the session.

'Clean the prisoner up and make his face look human again.'

Nettled, Geytrand did as he was told.

'I am the Count of Pergen under orders from the

emperor and I advise you to answer our questions.'

'So, you have crawled out of the shadows at last! You've been trying to destroy Freemasonry for a long time. What devil possesses you?'

'Why are you living in Vienna, Count of Thebes?'

'So that orphans and the dispossessed can benefit from my wealth in the asylums and schools I support.'

'A smoke screen! You are one of Freemasonry's nine Unknown Superiors and you are making alchemical gold. That is where your fortune comes from. But our lamented Empress Maria Theresa prohibited that satanic art. You are therefore charged with unlawful practices for which you will spend years in prison and undergo serious interrogations. But that is not your only crime.'

'What are you accusing me of?'

'Of plotting against the state. Unknown Superior, Illuminatus of Bavaria and Freemason, you approve the French Revolution and are planning to assassinate our Emperor Leopold II.'

'Lies, pathetic lies, and you know that perfectly well.'

'My convictions are quite otherwise and are based on a mountain of evidence. All I am waiting for are your confessions.'

'You will never have them from me.'

'I am sorry to resort to barbarous methods, but you leave me no option. However, I shall show some leniency if you answer one specific question: why are you sheltering Mozart?'

'What do you think?'

Joseph Anton gave a sigh of irritation. The Egyptian was still too resistant.

'Carry on roughing him up,' he ordered Geytrand.

71

Vienna, 19 November 1791

On this cold, gloomy day*, Mozart pushed open the door of the Golden Snake Tavern where Joseph Deiner, alias Primus, was landlord.

The composer sank heavily on to a bench in exhaustion and laid his head in the crook of his arm. Why was Thamos not sending him another bottle of the elixir? He had no means of contacting the Egyptian, so without much hope, he asked Stadler to go and ask around the Brothers, in case any of them knew where he was.

Without the antidote, the composer of *The Magic Flute* would not have long to live.

He came out of his torpor and called to a bar tender.

'Bring me some wine, please.'

---

* What follows is taken from Joseph Deiner's memoirs.

'No beer, as usual?'

'I would rather have wine, tonight.'

Wolfgang did not touch it.

Pale and dishevelled, he caught sight of Primus.

'How are you, Joseph?'

'Isn't it rather I who should be asking you how you are, Mr Music-Master? You look terrible. Are you ill?'

'I'm shivering and strangely cold. I don't think I shall be composing for long.'

'Come, now! This confounded flu is giving you black ideas. You go home, put some warm clothes on and let the Missus make a fuss of you. And don't forget to drink some punch! Nothing like it for keeping the chills at bay.'

Vienna, 20 November 1791

The beatings began again with the same vehemence.

Geytrand was enjoying torturing this foreigner, knowing that sooner or later, he would force him to reveal his alchemical and Masonic secrets.

Thamos's resistance irritated him. No amount of violence had made him change his statement that he wanted merely to practise charity according to the official Masonic ideal.

'I want the complete list of your accomplices,' Geytrand demanded.

'I only know Brothers.'

'I don't care what you call them! Well?'

'You will find their names in the lodge registers of Vienna, Prague and . . .'

'That will do! If you want to get out alive, tell me who your fellow conspirators are.'

'There aren't any. And you, ex-Freemason, perjurer and coward, you have no intention of letting me live.'

Geytrand lashed out at him, striking him again and again, until one of his assistants felt obliged to intervene.

'If he dies before he talks,' he reminded Geytrand, 'the Count of Pergen will be angry.'

Geytrand calmed down.

'Clean him up. The boss hates blood and filth.'

Vienna, 20 November 1791

Doubled up in pain, unable to stand or even sit, Mozart went to bed.

His forehead was burning and he could not stop vomiting. Constance saw that his hands and feet were swollen.

The poison was ravaging his body.

'Have we not received another phial of elixir?' he asked, between two spasms.

'I'm afraid not. The doctor has just arrived.'

Thirty-seven-year-old Thamos Franz Closset was an experienced practitioner and he suspected meningitis.

'Make sure Wolfgang's room is well aired and keep him in bed. You look worn out, Constance.'

'My mother and my sister Sophie will help me. My husband will get better, won't he?'

'We will do everything we can.'

'This poison . . .'

'Stop torturing yourself with that absurd idea! I shall come back soon.'

Vienna, 22 November 1791

'This really isn't sensible, Count of Thebes,' Joseph Anton admonished him, 'and your obstinacy is leading nowhere. I admire your courage, but no prisoner can resist well-conducted interrogations. As you can see for yourself, my friend Geytrand is a conscientious specialist. To prove my kind-heartedness, I have brought you a good meal. Smoked fish, cabbage, fresh bread and a glass of wine. Don't you miss your freedom and long journeys? Speak, and I shall allow you to leave Vienna.'

Thamos ate slowly. He needed to regain his strength and find a way of leaving his cell. His thoughts returned constantly to Wolfgang, now deprived of his essential antidote. How long would his body withstand the poison?

'On your advice,' Anton went on, 'Mozart wanted to found a new subversive Order. What were its aims?'

'To restore initiation to the mysteries of Isis and Osiris and make it accessible to the Brothers and Sisters who wanted to experience it.'

'I have read the libretto of *The Magic Flute* several

times, and I find your explanation inadequate. Tell me the real purpose of this occult brotherhood.'

'I have told you the truth.'

'Who wanted to join it?'

'I can give you two names: Mozart and myself.'

The Count of Pergen kept his sang-froid.

'We have plenty of time, Thamos. The same is not true for Mozart, I believe.'

72

Vienna, 23 November 1791

His illness was not improving and Dr Closset's treatment was having no effect. As Wolfgang could not turn over because of the swelling, his sister-in-law Sophie had made him a nightshirt that he could put on from the front.

'Here is a comfortable padded nightshirt for your convalescence,' she told him. 'I sewed it myself.'

The composer's ghastly smile broke her heart.

'Would you like to see Stadler?' Constance asked, her face gaunt.

'Of course!'

'Good news,' announced the clarinettist, cheerfully. 'Our Brother Artaria is going to publish the first extracts of *The Magic Flute*! And the public is still flocking to see it.'

'Every evening,' Wolfgang confided, 'I see the opera again, from the first to last scene. I can hear the singers, I go through their ordeals and I see the light of the temple of the sun!'

'Get better soon. We need you!'

'Thamos?'

'Vanished! Some people think he has left Vienna.'

'Without telling us? He wouldn't do that! No, the truth is far more sinister. Thamos has been arrested and imprisoned.'

Stadler's usual optimism could not counter this hypothesis.

'Try to find out more,' Wolfgang insisted.

'And you go on resting! With women like this around you, you're sure to make a speedy recovery!'

Gaukerl sat subdued and no longer left his master's room.

Vienna, 24 November 1791

Archbishop Migazzi had finally agreed to confess Antonio Salieri, who was relieved to receive absolution. God would now forgive him his sins and he could stop feeling remorse, forget about Mozart and get on with his brilliant career as a courtier and composer[*].

While he tucked into venison cooked in wine, the

[*] Antonio Salieri died in 1825 aged seventy-five. In 1823 when he was in hospital, he blamed himself for having assassinated Mozart, but his declarations were thought to be the ravings of a senile old man and were not taken seriously.

archbishop received his private secretary, who was wringing his hands nervously.

'The Lord has heard our prayers, your Grace, and his righteous anger has struck the wicked.'

'Mozart, you mean?'

'He is very ill and the physician's medicines are proving useless. There is talk of a fatal outcome.'

'We must take the necessary precautions: make sure no priest delivers the last rites. This Freemason must be damned, in accordance with the demands of the Almighty.'

'May His will be done, your Grace.'

Vienna, 25 November 1791

The lawyer Franz Hofdemel was in a foul temper.

Why had his wife, Maria Magdalena, humiliated him like this? She had fallen pregnant by Mozart and flouted the honour of a devoted husband. Day and night, he imagined her piano lessons! He, Franz Hofdemel, cuckolded and forced to bring up a child that was not his own!

Using poison was the coward's way out . . . Sometimes he reproached himself. But he would have been wrong not to react and let the wretched musician go unpunished. In any case, he had no way of knowing if his action had taken effect and whether the quantity had been adequate.

The lawyer pondered his revenge.

The Beloved of Isis

Thamos knew every square inch of his cell from floor to ceiling. Alas, there was not a single weak point. The stone walls offered no defects and despite the harsh weather, the place was not even damp.

Any attempt to escape looked impossible.

Yet, he had to get out and send Mozart the medicine he could not do without.

For two days, he had had no visits from his torturers. They brought him food and were allowing him a respite but only so they could break him down more effectively.

Outside, an armed policeman stood guard. Every six hours, the officers changed over.

Before Geytrand entered the cell, a guard chained up the Egyptian. The guard was forbidden to talk to the prisoner and meals were delivered through a hatch that was immediately slammed shut afterwards. He could have no knife, fork or spoon.

Refusing to give way to despair, Thamos prayed to Abbot Hermes to come to his aid.

Vienna, 28 November 1791

'Let me introduce my illustrious colleague, Dr Sallaba, head doctor at the General Hospital,' Closset said to Constance. 'He has agreed to examine Wolfgang.'

The physician stood for a moment at the sick man's bedside.

When he left the bedroom, closing the door carefully behind him, his jaw was clenched and his eyes downcast.

'What is your diagnosis?'

'Let us move away. I do not want your husband to hear any of this.'

Beside herself with worry, Constance led the practitioner to the vestibule.

'I am in no doubt, we must prepare for the worst.'

'You mean . . .'

'Yes, Madam, Mozart is beyond help.'

'Is there nothing we can do, can you not . . .'

'My excellent colleague, Dr Closset, will help you. Be brave.'

73

Vienna, 1 December 1791

On the day the highly respected Berlin journal, the *Musikalische Wochenblatt*, published its definitive judgment of *The Magic Flute* – 'not an unmitigated success, because the subject and libretto are really too bad' – Thamos saw Geytrand reappear.

'Have you still not resolved to talk?'

'I have said everything already.'

'You leave me no option but to change my methods. This time, you will give in. I shall start on your eyes.'

Thamos shrank back against the wall in horror.

'I confess, I know how to make alchemical gold!'

An evil gleam lit up Geytrand's face.

'At last, a move in the right direction. Can you prove it?'

'Take me to my laboratory.'

'No fear! You'll have laid a trap.'

'Then bring me the necessary material.'

'What form will the gold take?'

'One will be liquid, the other solid.'

'Will there be a lot of it?'

'It all depends on the quality of the primary matter.'

If Thamos was not boasting, Geytrand stood a chance of getting rich. After the first alchemical experiment, he would seize the booty and say nothing about it to Joseph Anton. Then, and only then, would he let him know.

'I shall get you something to write with, Egyptian. Tell me carefully what you need.'

Vienna, 3 December 1791

For want of better treatment, Dr Closset bled Mozart. Wolfgang recovered a little energy and asked to see his brother-in-law, Hofer, and his Brothers Gerl, who had sung Sarastro in *The Magic Flute*, and Schack, his Tamino, so that they could sing through the parts of the *Requiem** that were already composed.

Encouraged, the company took hope.

The work stopped at the beginning of the *Lacrimosa* with the emergence from the jaws of death when the souls of those who were resurrected rose to the Light.

Gaukerl's behaviour was exemplary and he sat quietly

* K626.

through the whole rehearsal. Then the singers went back to the theatre.

Wolfgang thought of Thamos. Had he fallen into the hands of the secret police? Would he manage to escape?

Constance was comforted by his appearance and brought him some broth. The composer looked at his watch.

'*The Magic Flute* is starting! Soon, the serpent will chase Tamino and the ritual ordeals will begin . . .'

Throughout the evening, he followed the development of the ceremony in his mind, right up to the consecration of the royal couple in the temple to the sons and daughters of the Light.

Vienna, 4 December 1791

'Is that what you need, Egyptian?' asked Geytrand, setting down before him the retorts and queer-shaped vessels with their colourful substances and labels in indecipherable hieroglyphs.

Thamos studied the equipment.

'I cannot work in so small a space. I need a big room.'

'Your cell will have to do!'

'I'm sorry, I need more room. You saw the size of my laboratory!'

'We'll go up to the first floor, but you must stay chained up.'

The Egyptian found himself in the drawing room of a

private house where the secret police acted with impunity. There, the files on the Freemasons, accumulated over decades, were kept.

Two policemen occupied the premises day and night. Geytrand ordered them not to take their eyes off the prisoner.

'I shall have to have my hands free,' Thamos said.

'Out of the question!'

'If I make a false move, there'll be an explosion. If you keep your distance, you will be unharmed, but I shall be killed and you will not get your gold.'

As the police reports proved, accidents of the sort had indeed happened.

'You must keep the chains on your ankles on,' Geytrand decreed.

Thamos did not protest.

'How long do you need?'

'At least twenty-four hours before the first liquid is obtained. Bring me a big candle and another already lit. Then stand back.'

The Egyptian made the flame from the big candle spring up by muttering incomprehensible formulae from a ritual for the divine awakening in Egyptian temples.

Then he poured a little brown powder from a vessel bearing the inscription kemet*, the 'black earth', and held the light over it. By celebrating the marriage of the

---

* From which we get the word 'alchemy'.

elements, he recreated the primary matter at the basis of the Great Work.

Under the circumstances, Thamos had no option but to take the short way, although it was the more dangerous. Despite his experience, he could not be sure of success. The slightest error would be fatal.

But he had to act fast, produce the antidote and escape to save Mozart.

74

Vienna, 4 December 1791

'I have such a terrible headache,' groaned Wolfgang.

Sophie Weber placed a hand on the sick man's forehead. It was burning.

She called Constance.

'I'm going to send for Dr Closset,' Constance decided, before going to her husband's bedside, under Gaukerl's anxious gaze.

'I have the taste of death in my mouth,' the composer said. 'I am leaving you just as we were about to enjoy a more peaceful existence. With no more debts and constraints to musical fashion, I should have been free to compose as I liked, found the Grotto and make my wife and children happy.'

'You will get better, my darling!'

Mozart looked at his watch.

'Papageno is about to sing: "I am a merry birdcatcher, I . . ."'

The author of *The Magic Flute* lost consciousness.

Constance clung to Mozart's hands in dismay.

'I want to contract your illness and die with you!'

Sophie stopped her sister lying down beside the musician.

'Don't give in to folly, I implore you! Your sons need you.'

Dr Closset left the theatre and examined the patient.

'Place moist towels on his forehead,' he ordered Sophie.

The young woman recoiled.

'Won't the cold hurt him? Look, his arms and legs are still swollen!'

'Do as I say.'

The compresses set off a violent shivering, and the sick man vomited.

'A priest, hurry!' ordered the doctor.

Sophie ran to St Peter's.

'A dying man needs the last rites,' she told a clergyman there.

He smiled sympathetically.

'What is his name?'

'Wolfgang Mozart.'

The smile died on his lips.

'A heretic defies the Lord until his dying breath, and no priest could grant him the last sacrament. Do not insist, my child. Wherever you go, you will be refused.'

Sophie ran back to the Mozarts' house.

The composer had not recovered consciousness.

Constance was trying to comfort Karl Thomas, who understood that tragedy was afoot.

Suddenly, Gaukerl gave a series of pitiful little yaps.

It was five to one, on the morning of 5 December 1791.

Mozart had just died.

Vienna, 5 December 1791

Geytrand watched uncomprehending, never taking his eyes off the alchemist. He was attending the realization of the Great Work and witnessing the mystery come to pass, but he remained completely outside events.

Fearing sorcery, his two henchmen stood trembling at his side. Perhaps the devil would appear from a retort and carry off their souls.

A dish glowed red.

One of the policemen panicked and ran out of the hall. It was five minutes to one.

'Go and get your friend,' Geytrand ordered the other guard. 'Otherwise, you will both be punished.'

'The liquid gold is ready,' Thamos declared.

'Let me see!'

The alchemist held up the phial of elixir.

'It is a powerful remedy for most illnesses. It boosts

402

the system and strengthens the body against external assaults. Would you like to try it?'

'After you!'

Thamos drank from the phial.

'Solid gold is what I want!'

'I need more time.'

'Then get on with it!'

The two policemen had returned but stood stupidly outside in the antechamber, praying for protection to every saint they could think of.

An intense golden flash suddenly blinded Geytrand.

From the furnace, Thamos drew a small ingot.

'Give me that!' demanded the torturer, already seeing himself the possessor of vast wealth.

'No, no, you mustn't touch it!'

Geytrand thrust the prisoner aside and seized hold of the ingot.

Immediately, his hands stuck to the metal and were burned. Then infernal flames licked up his legs, engulfed his waist and torso and finally his head.

With howl after howl of pain, Geytrand's damned soul was slowly consumed by fire.

Driven mad by the visions Thamos had called up, the two policemen had shot each other.

The Egyptian took nothing but the primary matter of the elixir, freed himself from his chains and set fire to the building.

Could he still save Mozart?

75

Grief-stricken, Constance wrote a few lines in Wolfgang's album: *Darling husband! Immortal Mozart for me and for the whole of Europe, you will now rest forever! Too soon, oh far too soon, he left this world, which though certainly good was ungrateful, in his thirty-sixth year. Oh God! We were united for eight years by a tender and unbreakable bond. Ah, may I soon be united with you forever!*

'The Count of Thebes is asking for you,' her sister told her.

Constance burst into tears.

'Wolfgang is dead, Thamos!'

The Egyptian contemplated the Great Magician, Son of Enlightenment, Brother of Fire, Beloved of Isis. He crossed his hands on his breast, like Osiris, dressed him in the Master Mason's apron and put on him a dark cloak with a hood.

'I am going to fetch Baron van Swieten,' he decided.

'You and your children should go and stay with our Brother Joseph Bauernfeld.'

'I don't want to leave Wolfgang!'

'Do not put yourself in danger, Constance. Listen to me, please.'

The musician's widow yielded.

Vienna, 5 December 1791

Van Swieten hastily pulled on his clothes.

When he stood by Mozart's body, he bowed his head.

'There is not a moment to lose,' Thamos told him. 'Anton will soon be informed of my escape.'

'My informants tell me that Leopold II is convinced Viennese Freemasonry is a hotbed of revolutionaries who support the French Jacobins. We must get rid of any dangerous documents.'

The two men emptied the library until nothing remained of books that might raise suspicion or the statutes of the Grotto and rituals in preparation.

Removal men took away most of the furniture and valuable objects so that the widow would not have to deal with them.

At Thamos' request, Count Joseph Deym made a death mask* just before the body was placed in its coffin.

'I shall see to the burial,' promised van Swieten.

* This relic has disappeared.

Vienna, 5 December 1791

'Mozart was struck down by divine wrath,' the secretary announced to the archbishop.

'Were my instructions observed?'

'To the letter, your Grace. The subversive Freemason did not receive the last rites and will not rest in the Lord's peace.'

'Are you quite sure he is really dead?'

'Quite sure!'

'It's odd . . . I feel as though he is still with us.'

'Your Grace was the instrument of the will of the Almighty and . . .'

'Leave me alone.'

Vienna, 5 December 1791

'Dead, are you sure?' asked Salieri, in amazement.

'Quite sure,' his valet confirmed. 'The laying-out took place this morning.'

'How did you discover?'

'My friend, Joseph Deiner the innkeeper told me. He had it from Sophie, one of Constance Mozart's sisters.'

'So, he is dead! That is well. If he had lived, we would all have been out on the street.'

Vienna, 5 December 1791

In the smoking ruins of the house, three corpses were found covered in verdigris. Among them lay Geytrand, his body burned to a cinder, apart from his eyes staring dully from the sockets. His hands still clutched a lump of lead.

Mozart was dead, but Thamos had escaped. Not everything had gone to plan.

The Count of Pergen drove to the palace to tell the emperor.

'I have read your reports,' Leopold told him, 'and I am convinced that Freemasonry is a noxious influence. Its real purpose is to destroy Europe's monarchies.'

'The main agitator, Mozart, has just died.'

'That is not enough, Count of Pergen. We must pull up the evil by its roots, and it is not just among the Brothers. I want a list of sympathizers and I shall strip them of all their official duties. The state has the right to shut down the Viennese lodges.'

Joseph Anton ought to have felt immense joy at the total triumph of his long crusade.

But arias from *The Marriage of Figaro*, *Don Giovanni*, *Così van Tutte* and *The Magic Flute*, the four ritual operas describing the road to initiation into the Great Mysteries, would not stop running through his head.

Why had he and his allies assassinated Mozart? Because he had been a threat to the regime, to law and order, the Church and saccharine belief and to Freemasonry itself.

But what if the way Mozart proposed had been the right one? What if his music had provided a solution to the agonizing problems of a world in crisis because it had no true spirituality?

The Count of Pergen was a faithful servant to the state and would not give up his mission. Before long, the empire would be shot of its secret societies.

He had to get even with Thamos the Egyptian.

76

Vienna, 6 December 1791

The weather had improved, becoming mild and misty. Baron Gottfried van Swieten had organized Mozart's funeral service for three o'clock that afternoon, in front of the Chapel of the Crucifix in St Stephen's Cathedral.

Van Swieten was also paying for the service: eight florins and fifty-six kreutzers for a second-class burial, three florins for a hearse drawn by two horses, and in addition, a private tomb with a headstone inscribed with the composer's name.

Constance was completely spent and kept to her room. In attendance were van Swieten, Anton Stadler, Süssmayr, Joseph Deiner alias Primus, Hofer Mozart's brother-in-law, Sophie Weber and a few members of Schikaneder's troop.

The little group stood in silence, overwhelmed with grief. No one wanted to think that Mozart was really dead.

Joseph Anton approached Gottfried van Swieten.

'Change of plan, Baron.'

'What does that mean?'

'The official cause of death written on the Cathedral register is acute "sweat fever"*. As there's a fear of a cholera epidemic, we must comply with strict police regulations in these kinds of circumstances, and the body will be buried in a communal grave.'

'I've reserved a private tomb, and . . .'

'You no longer exist, Baron: you have been officially stripped of all your offices. You should think yourself lucky. The emperor is showing no tolerance to participants in the Masonic plot. In view of your brilliant career, you have got off lightly. Now, make yourself scarce.'

Van Swieten said nothing.

'Mozart will be buried in St Mark's cemetery four kilometres outside Vienna,' Anton went on. 'Given the distance, the law forbids anyone to accompany the hearse. The gravediggers will come and take away the remains at nightfall.'

Vienna, 6 December 1791

From the first floor of No. 10 Grünangergasse came the screams of a woman. Probably a husband beating his wife. The tradesman beat a prudent retreat.

On the stairs, he bumped into a neighbour.

---

* A fever characterized by copious sweating and the appearance of a rash.

Another ear-splitting scream.

'What's going on at the Hofdemels'?'

'I'm already late and I don't want to get involved in other people's affairs.'

The tradesman fled, leaving the visitor standing in vain outside the door. Alarmed, he went to fetch a locksmith.

A dreadful spectacle awaited them: Hofdemel, the razor still in his hand, had slit his throat after attacking his wife, Maria Magdalena, who was five-months pregnant. Her face, shoulders and arms had been slashed and she lay in a pool of blood.

Mad with jealousy, and believing himself to be responsible for poisoning Mozart, his wife's lover and the father of her child, Hofdemel had sought vengeance on the traitors before turning the blade on himself.

Geytrand's plan had worked to perfection. There would soon be no shortage of rumours.

Vienna, 6 December 1791

No Brother, relation or friend dared infringe the police regulations. Accordingly, at nightfall, a hearse bearing Mozart's body, which no doctor had been allowed to examine, set off for St Mark's cemetery.

The dog, Gaukerl, trotted behind in the dusk. Not in this world or the next would he abandon his master.

When the ditch was filled in, the grave-diggers left the cemetery.

Then Thamos approached the grave and uttered the formulae for transmutation into light. Mozart's spirit would shine among the stars and his work would convey initiation to anyone who had ears to hear.

After this modest ritual, a voice broke the stillness.

'I knew you would come, Count of Thebes,' said Joseph Anton.

Slowly, Thamos turned round.

The Count of Pergen appeared to be alone.

'Where are your men hiding?'

'I wanted to pay a final tribute to a genius who died for his ideal. As a loyal servant of the state, I obeyed orders. Without Mozart, your power as an Unknown Superior is reduced to nothing. Therefore I see no reason to arrest you. You will spend the rest of your nomadic existence thinking about this irreplaceable man whom you could not save.'

'You are trying to convince yourself of a victory not even you believe in. Mozart's light will never die.'

Joseph Anton nodded in an odd way, then vanished into the night.

77

Vienna, 7 December 1791

As the witness, the iron merchant and money-lender Joseph Goldhann signed the official inventory of Mozart's belongings. His piano was estimated at eighty florins, the billiard table at sixty, and they did their best to value miscellaneous objects and clothes, including eight fine suits.

The musician's debts came to nine hundred and fourteen florins[*].

'Mozart owed me nothing at all,' declared Brother Puchberg, dismissing the past, 'and I am happy to become

---

[*] Two hundred and eighty-two florins owed to the master-tailor Dümmer; nine to Dr Igl; one hundred and thirty-nine to the court apothecary; seventy-four to Frau Hasel, another apothecary; two hundred and eight to the upholsterer Reiz; thirty-one to the master shoemaker, Anhammer, and one hundred and seventy-one to miscellaneous suppliers.

the guardian of his two sons. They and Constance shall never want for anything.'

Anton Stadler produced an acknowledgment of a debt to Mozart that came to five hundred florins, but many other people forgot the composer's generosity towards them*.

Vienna, 11 December 1791

On the previous day, a Requiem Mass was celebrated at the St Michael's Church. Two of his Brothers, Bauernfeld and Schikaneder, paid for it.

'The emperor granted me one last audience,' van Swieten told Constance. 'I pleaded my innocence but above all I pleaded yours, and I assured him that Wolfgang would never have got involved in a plot against him. His Majesty agrees to receive a petition from you. Perhaps he will grant you a pension to prove his broad-mindedness.'

With van Swieten's help, Constance wrote to the emperor, asking him for a 'charitable salary', although her husband had not been ten years in his service. She stressed that, instead of moving abroad, he had stayed in Vienna and fulfilled his duties to the letter. The applicant trusted to Leopold II's supreme grace and paternal goodness.

---

* Franz Anton Gilowsky, a nephew of a surgeon at the court of Salzburg, submitted an acknowledgment of a debt for three hundred florins. Not only was Mozart not in dire straits, but on 29 March 1792, Constance had paid off all the debts.

'Of course,' added the Baron, 'we shall have to destroy all Mozart's Masonic correspondence. If any compromising letters fall into the wrong hands, you could have serious trouble.'

Constance agreed.

Vienna, early January 1792

On 14 December 1791, Prague had paid homage to Mozart with a Requiem Mass using one hundred and twenty musicians. Vienna was silent on the subject.

Crowned Hope Lodge merely held a funeral oration given by Brother Karl Friedrich Hensler[*]:

'It pleased the Eternal Architect of the World to take from our brotherly chain one of our best loved and most undeserving members,' Hensler lamented. 'Who did not know him, who did not esteem him, who did not love him, our worthy Brother Mozart? Only a few weeks ago, he was with us, glorifying with his enchanting music the consecration of our Masonic temple. Which of us could have guessed that his life was so near its end? Mozart's death is an irreplaceable loss for art. I was a zealous adept of our Order. His principal characteristics were love of his Brothers, sociability, permanent commitment to the good cause of charity and a true and profound

---

[*] Karl Friedrich Hensler, *Maurerrede auf Mozarts Tod*, printed in 1793. Excerpts are cited.

feeling of satisfaction whenever he could use his talents to help one of his Brothers. He was a good husband and a good father, a friend to his friends and a Brother to his Brothers. All he lacked were enough treasures to make hundreds of men like him happy, and that was his most heartfelt wish.'

Anton Stadler and the Jacquins asked the lodge to be generous to the musician's family, and they decided to publish in the press the advertisement of a splendid edition of Mozart's last Masonic Cantata[*], followed by a short song to accompany the human chain[†] that closed the meeting. It was hoped many copies would be sold[‡], and the profits would be paid to Constance.

Vienna, March 1792

'Who will Leopold II's successor be? I am sorry to hear he has died,' Stadler said to Van Swieten.

'Twenty-four-year-old Francis II. Freemasonry is condemned to death! He and his counsellors want to turn Austria into a police state. Before long, all the lodges will be forced to shut their doors[§].

[*] K623.

[†] K623a.

[‡] This was unfortunately not the case. The volume was not as lavish as had been hoped and did not appear until November 1792.

[§] In January 1795, the secret societies were all accused of high treason and banned by law.

EPILOGUE

When the world is crumbling around one, when the structures of a civilisation tremble, it is good to return to something in history that does not crumble but which, on the contrary, boosts man's courage, puts back together the pieces and spreads peace without causing pain. It is good to remember that creative genius is also at work in a history bent on destruction.

Albert Camus, *In Gratitude to Mozart*
L'Express, February 1956[*]

Figeac, 28 April 1793

There was one fact Joseph Anton did not know: the *ka* of a supreme being such as Mozart did not die. It would

[*] The author thanks Anne Gallimard for this quotation.

pass into another Great Magician whom Thamos must try to find so that he could give him The *Book of Thoth*. Yet he did not know where to begin his search.

As he left St Mark's Cemetery, the Egyptian saw that he was not alone: Gaukerl had adopted him.

Gaukerl . . . Wolfgang's dog would be his guide!

He would want to find Mozart and would track down the next carrier of his spirit.

Then began a long voyage, during which the alchemist stopped many times to make the gold he needed to support himself and to care for his companion. He let the dog choose his own pace and lead the way along roads that grew ever more hazardous because of the turmoil that was devastating Europe.

Several times, Thamos was alerted by Gaukerl and narrowly avoided an ambush. When his guide crossed the border into France where the revolutionary terror was raging, the Egyptian set his teeth.

Against all odds, he followed Gaukerl all the way to Figeac, a little town in the region of Quercy. A guillotine loomed up in the centre of the main square.

Suddenly the dog quickened his pace.

He stopped outside a modest dwelling and barked insistently.

A sturdy man in the prime of life slowly opened the door.

'Who are you and what do you want?'

'My name is Thamos and I need your help. My dog and I have travelled for a long time.'

'Where do you come from?'

'From the Orient.'

'As far as that! And who gave you my address?'

The man bent down and stroked the dog, and Gaukerl looked up at him with eyes full of gratitude.

'My name is Jacquou and I am a healer. Come in, I shall restore your energy.'

The carer filled two glasses with plum liqueur and gave Gaukerl some broth.

'Has your town suffered much in the Revolution?' asked the Egyptian.

'Some unfortunate wretches were executed, but the people don't like the fanatics. On 21 January, Louis XVI was guillotined and many people disapprove of such barbarous behaviour. Most likely, the revolutionaries won't hesitate to chop off the queen's head*. Anyway, what is the purpose of your journey?'

'I am looking for a special child with unique powers. I have a priceless gift that I should like to give him.'

'Indeed!' exclaimed Jacquou the healer. 'You're in luck!'

Gaukerl pricked up his ears.

'On 23 December 1790, I helped a woman give birth. When the baby came into the world, I had a vision of a land filled with sunshine and magnificent temples, and I cried out: "This boy will be a light for centuries to come!"'

'What is his name?'

---

* Marie-Antoinette was guillotined on 16 October.

'Jean-François Champollion*. His father owns a bookshop and the little lad revealed to me that he was learning to read and write by himself, in secret. I have no doubt he has a great future ahead of him.'

Thamos closed his eyes and saw a ship drawing into the port of Alexandria. On board, Champollion was coming to find his true homeland in the Egypt of the Pharoahs, whose sacred language he had deciphered.

Gaukerl had not been wrong. Mozart was reborn in Champollion. It was he who would read *The Book of Thoth* and pass down the complete Mysteries of Isis and Osiris. *The Magic Flute* continued; the tradition of initiation lived on.

'We shall meet Jean-François Champollion tomorrow,' Jacquou decided, 'and you can tell him about the Orient.'

---

* Jean-François Champollion (1790–1832) was an Egyptologist best known for deciphering the hieroglyphs on the Rosetta Stone.

BIBLIOGRAPHY

The following works were consulted in the writing of this third book on the life of Mozart:

ABERT, Hermann, *Mozart* (2 volumes), Leipzig, 1919.

ANGERMÜLLER, Rudolph, *Les Opéras de Mozart*, Milan, 1991.

ASSMANN, J., *Die Zauberflöte, Oper und Mysterium*, Munich-Vienne, 2005.

AUTEXIER, Philippe A., *Mozart et Liszt sub rosa*, Poitiers, 1984.

AUTEXIER, Philippe A., *Mozart*, Paris, 1987.

AUTEXIER, Philippe A., *La Lyre maçonne*, Paris, 1997.

BALTRUSAITIS, J., *Essai sur la légende d'un mythe. La Quête d'Isis*, Paris, 1967.

CARR, Francis, *Mais qui a tué Mozart?*, Drogenbos, s. d.

CHAILLEY, Jacques, *La Flute enchantée, opéra maçonnique*, Paris, 1968.

CLARY, Mildred, *Mozart. La Lumière de Dieu*, Paris, 2004.

Così fan tutte, L'Avant-Scène Opéra, 16/17, s. d.

DA PONTE, Lorenzo, *Memoires et Livrets*, Paris, 1954.

DEUTSCH, O. E., *Mozart und die Weiner Logen: zur Geschichte seiner Freimaurer-Kompositionen*, Vienna, 1932.

Dictionnaire Mozart, ed. B. DERMONCOURT, Paris, 2005.

Dictionnaire Mozart, ed. H. C. ROBBINS LANDON, Paris, 1990.

DUNAND, Françoise, *Isis, Mère des dieux,* Paris 2000.

EINSTEIN, Alfred, *Mozart, son caractère, son oeuvre*, Paris, 1954.

Encyclopédie de la Franc-Maçonnerie, Paris, 2000.

HENRY, Jacques, *Mozart, Frère Maçon*, Paris, 1997.

HOCQUARD, Jean-Victor, *Mozart*, Paris, 1994.

HOCQUARD, Jean-Victor, *Mozart, l'amour, la mort*, Paris, 1994.

HOCQUARD, Jean-Victor, *Cosi fan tutte*, Paris, 1978.

HOCQUARD, Jean-Victor, *Le Don Giovanni de Mozart,* Paris, 1978.

HOCQUARD, Jean-Victor, La Flûte enchantée, Paris, 1979.

HOCQUARD, Jean-Victor, *La Pensée de Mozart*, Paris, 1958.

HORNUNG, Erik, *L'Égypte ésotérique,* Paris, 2001.

IVERSEN, E., *The Myth of Egypt and its Hieroglyphs in European Tradition,* Princeton, 1993.

KOCH, H.-A., *Das Textbuch der Zauberflöte*, Jahrbuch des Freien Deutschen Hochstifts, 1969.

LE CORSU, F., *Isis, mythe et mystères,* Paris, 1977.

LE FORESTIER, René, *La Franc-Maçonnerie templière et occultiste aux* XVIIIe et XIXe siècles, Paris, 2000.

MASSIN, Jean and Brigitte, *Mozart*, Paris, 1970.

MORENZ, S., *Die Zauberflöte. Eine Studie zum Lebenszusammenhang Ägypten-Antike Abendland*, Münster-Cologne, 1952.

MOZART, *Correspondence*, vol. IV and V, Paris, 1991 and 1992.

NETTL, Paul, *Mozart und die königliche Kunst: die freimaurerische Grundlage der Zauberflöte*, Berlin, 1932.

NETTL, Paul, *Mozart und Masonry*, New York, 1957.

PAHLEN, Kurt, *Das Mozart Buch*, Zurich, 1985.

PAHROUTY, Michel, *Mozart, aimé des dieux*, Paris, 1988.

ROBBINS LANDON, H. C., *La dernière année de Mozart*, Paris, 1988.

ROBBINS LANDON, H. C., *Mozart, l'âge d'or de la musique à Vienne, 1781–1791*, Paris, 1989.

ROBBINS LANDON, H. C., *Mozart et les Francs-Maçons*, London and Paris, 1991.

Rosenberg, A., *Die Zauberflöte*, Munich, 1964.

SADIE, Stanley, *Mozart*, London, 1980.

STRICKER, Rémy, *Mozart et ses operas. Fictions et vérité*, Paris, 1980.

TERRASON, R., *Le Testament philosophique de Mozart*, Paris, 2005.

TUBEUF, André, Mozart: Chemins et chants, Paris, 2005.

WYZEWA, Théodore de, and SAINT-FOIX, Georges de, *W. A. Mozart. Sa vie musicale et son oeuvre*, Paris, 1986.

Concerning Freemasonry we consulted the following collection: *Les Symboles maçonniques* (Maison de Vie Éditeur), published volumes:

Christian Jacq
THE GREAT MAGICIAN

"*After 1500 years of waiting, Osiris has permitted the Great Magician to be reborn . . . Find the Great Magician, Thamos, protect him and enable him to create the work which will give the world hope.*"

Thamos, Count of Thebes, is one of the last members of a spiritual brotherhood, keeping alive the secrets of the pharaohs. Now he has been entrusted with a vital mission. He must leave Egypt for the cold lands of Europe to find and protect the 'Great Magician', a genius whose works will save humanity.

When he encounters a child prodigy, a six-year-old composer lauded throughout Prague, Vienna and Frankfurt, Thamos senses that he's found the one. Is this young musician really the 'Great Magician' foretold by Osiris, the one who can pass on the light of the East to mankind? And if he is, can Thamos succeed in saving the boy from the traps that lie in wait for him?

'An author who artfully combines story with truth' *Good Book Guide*

ISBN 978-1-41652-661-2

All these titles by Christian Jacq are available from your local bookshop or can be ordered direct from the publisher.

978-1-41652-661-2	The Great Magician	£6.99
978-1-41652-662-9	The Son of Enlightenment	£7.99
978-1-41652-663-6	The Brother of Fire	£6.99
978-1-84739-392-0	Tutankhamun: The Last Secret	£6.99
978-1-84739-367-8	The Queen of Freedom Trilogy (includes *The Empire of Darkness*, *The War of Crowns* and *The Flaming Sword)*	£9.99
978-1-84739-366-1	The Judge of Egypt (includes *Beneath the Pyramid*, *Secrets of the Desert* and *Shadow of the Sphinx*)	£9.99

Free post and packing within the UK
Overseas customers please add £2 per paperback
Telephone Simon & Schuster Cash Sales at Bookpost
on 01624 677237 with your credit or debit card number
or send a cheque payable to Simon & Schuster Cash Sales to
PO Box 29, Douglas Isle of Man, IM99 1BQ
Fax: 01624 670923
E-mail: bookshop@enterprise.net
www.bookpost.co.uk

Please allow 14 days for delivery. Prices and availability are subject to change without notice.